VAL McDERMID

DEAD BEAT

HarperCollins*Publishers*

This novel is entirely a work of fiction.
The names, characters and incidents portrayed
in it are the work of the author's imagination.
Any resemblance to actual persons, living or dead,
events or localities is entirely coincidental.

HarperCollins*Publishers*
77–85 Fulham Palace Road,
Hammersmith, London W6 8JB

www.**fire**and**water**.com

This paperback edition 2002
1

First published in Great Britain by
Victor Gollancz 1992
and Orion Books Ltd 1999

ISBN 978 0 00 783389 4

Set in Meridien by
Rowland Phototypesetting Ltd,
Bury St Edmunds, Suffolk

Printed and bound in Great Britain by
Clays Ltd, St Ives plc

Val McDermid

Val McDermid grew up in a Scottish mining community, then read English at Oxford. She was a journalist for sixteen years, spending the last three years as Northern Bureau Chief of a national Sunday tabloid. Now a full-time writer, she lives in Cheshire.

Dead Beat is the first of six novels featuring Kate Brannigan. The third, *Crack Down*, was shortlisted for the Crime Writers' Association Gold Dagger Award in 1994.

Val is also the author of three tense psychological thrillers featuring criminal profiler Tony Hill (the first of these, *The Mermaids Singing*, was awarded the 1995 Gold Dagger Award for Best Crime Novel of the Year), two stand-alone thrillers, *Killing the Shadows* and *A Place of Execution*; and five novels featuring journalist-sleuth Lindsay Gordon.

ACKNOWLEDGEMENTS

I picked a lot of people's brains and stole a few jokes during the writing of this book. I'd like to thank Diana Cooper, Lee D'Courcy, Brother Brian, everyone at Gregory & Radice ... Most of all, I owe an enormous debt to Linzi Day, who convinced me that I ought to believe in myself as much as she does.

Part One

1

I swear one day I'll kill him. Kill who? The man next door, Richard Barclay, rock journalist and overgrown schoolboy, is who. I had stumbled wearily across the threshold of my bungalow, craving nothing more exotic than a few hours' sleep when I found Richard's message. When I say found, I use the term loosely. I could hardly have missed it. He'd sellotaped it to the inside of my glass inner door so that it would be the first thing I saw when I entered the storm porch. It glared luridly at me, looking like a child's note to Santa, written in sprawling capitals with magic marker on the back of a record company press release. 'Don't forget Jett's gig and party afterwards tonight. Vital you're there. See you at eight.' Vital was underlined three times, but it was that 'Don't forget' that made my hands twitch into a stranglehold.

Richard and I have been lovers for only nine months, but I've already learned to speak his language. I could write the Berlitz phrasebook. The official translation of 'don't forget' is, 'I omitted to mention to you that I had committed us to going somewhere/doing something (that you will almost certainly hate the idea of) and if you don't come it will cause me major social embarrassment.'

I pulled the note off the door, sighing deeply when I saw the sellotape marks on the glass. I'd weaned him off drawing pins, but unfortunately I hadn't yet got him on to Blu-Tack. I walked up the narrow hall to the telephone table. The house diary where Richard and I are both supposed to record details of anything mutually relevant lay open. In today's space, Richard had written, in black felt-tip pen, 'Jett: Apollo then Holiday Inn'. Even though he'd used a different pen from his note, it didn't fool the carefully cultivated memory skills of Kate Brannigan, Private Investigator. I knew that message hadn't been there when I'd staggered out an hour before dawn to continue my surveillance of a pair of counterfeiters.

I muttered childish curses under my breath as I made my way through to my bedroom and quickly peeled off my nondescript duvet jacket and jogging suit. 'I hope his rabbits die and all his matches get wet. And I hope he can't get the lid off the mayo *after* he's made the chicken sandwich,' I swore as I headed for the bathroom and stepped gratefully under a hot shower.

That's when the self-pitying tears slowly squeezed themselves under my defences and down my cheeks. In the shower no one can see you weep. I offer that up as one of the great twentieth-century aphorisms, right up there alongside 'Love means never having to say you're sorry'. Mostly, my tears were sheer exhaustion. For the last two weeks I'd been working on a case that had involved driving from one end of the country to the other on an almost daily basis, staking out houses and warehouses from the hours before dawn till past midnight, and living on snatched sandwiches from motorway service stations and greasy spoons my mother would have phoned the environmental health inspectors about.

If that sort of routine had been the normal stock in trade of Mortensen and Brannigan it might not have seemed so bloody awful. But our cases usually involve nothing more taxing than sitting in front of a computer screen drinking coffee and making phone calls. This time, though, my

4

senior partner Bill Mortensen and I had been hired by a consortium of prestigious watch manufacturers to track down the source of high-quality copies of their merchandise which had been flooding the market from somewhere in the Greater Manchester area. Surprise, surprise, I'd ended up with the sticky end while Bill sat in the office moodily staring into his computer screens.

Matters had come to a head when Garnetts, the city's biggest independent jewellers', had been broken into. The thieves had ignored the safe and the alarmed display cases, and had simply stolen the contents of a cupboard in the manager's office. What they had walked away with were the green leather wallets that are presented free to purchasers of genuine Rolex watches, the luxury market's equivalent of a free plastic daffodil with every packet of soap powder. They'd also taken the credit card wallets that Gucci give to their customers, as well as dozens of empty boxes for Cartier and Raymond Weil watches.

This theft told the manufacturers that the counterfeit business – known in the trade as schneids – was moving up a gear. Till now, the villains had been content to sell their wares as copies, via a complicated network of small traders. While that had infuriated the companies, it hadn't kept them awake at night because the sort of people who part with forty pounds in a pub or at a market stall for a fake Rolex aren't the sort who've got a few grand tucked away in their back pockets for the real thing. But now it looked as if the schneid merchants were planning to pass their clever copies off as the genuine article. Not only might that take business away from straight outlets, it could also affect the luxury watchmakers' reputation for quality. Suddenly it was worth spending money to knock the racket on the head.

Mortensen and Brannigan might not be up there in the top ten of Britain's major private investigation companies, but we'd landed this job for two good reasons. Although our main area of work is in computer fraud and security systems, we were the first people who sprang to Garnetts' minds, since Bill had designed their computerized security system and they had ignored his suggestion that the cupboard in question be linked in to the overall system. After all, they'd argued, there was nothing in there worth stealing ... The second reason was that we were one of the few firms of specialist private investigators operating out of Manchester. We knew the territory.

When we took the job on, we anticipated clearing it up in a matter of days. What we hadn't grasped was the scale of the operation. Getting to grips with it had worn me into the ground. However, in the last couple of days, I'd started to feel that warm glow of excitement in the pit of my stomach that always tells me I'm getting close. I had found the factory where the schneid watches were being produced, I knew the names of the two men who were wholesaling the merchandise, and who their main middle men were. All I had to do was establish the pattern of their movements and then we could hand over to our clients. I suspected that some time in the next couple of weeks, the men I had been following would be on the receiving end of a very unwelcome visit from the cops and Trading Standards officials. Which would ultimately mean a substantial reward for Mortensen and Brannigan, on top of our already substantial fee.

Because it was all going so well, I had promised myself a well-deserved and much-needed early night after I had followed Jack 'Billy' Smart, my number one suspect, back to his Gothic three-storey house in a quiet, tree-lined suburban street that evening at six. He'd walked in with a couple of bottles of Moët and an armful of videos from the shop round the corner, and I figured he was all set for a kiss and a cuddle in front of the television with his girl-

6

friend. Come to that, I could have kissed him myself. Now I could go home, have a quick shower, send a cab out for a takeaway from nearby Chinatown and watch the soaps. Then I'd have a face pack and luxuriate in a long, slow bath and beauty routine. It's not that I'm obsessive about personal hygiene, by the way, just that I've always felt that showers are for getting rid of the dirt, while baths are for serious pleasures like reading the adventure game reviews in computer magazines and fantasizing about the computer I'll upgrade to when Mortensen and Brannigan's ship comes in. With luck, Richard would be out on the town so I could perform my ablutions in total peace, accompanied only by a long cool drink.

Well, I'd been right about one thing at least. Richard was certainly going out on the town. What I hadn't bargained for was being there with him. So much for my plans. I knew I was no match for Richard tonight. I was just too tired to win the argument. Besides, deep down, I knew I didn't have a leg to stand on. He'd bitten the bullet and got suited up to escort me to an obligatory dinner party the week before. After subjecting him to an evening with a bunch of insurance executives and their wives, spinach pancakes and all, I owed him. And I suspected he knew it. But just because it was my turn to suffer didn't mean I had to cave in without a whinge.

As I vigorously rubbed shampoo into my unruly auburn hair, a blast of cold air hit my spine. I turned, knowing exactly what I'd see. Richard's face smiled nervously at me through the open door of the shower cubicle. 'Hi, Brannigan,' he greeted me. 'Getting ready for a big night out? I knew you wouldn't forget.' He must have registered the snarl on my face, for he quickly added, 'I'll see you in the living room when you're finished,' and hastily shut the door.

'Get back in here,' I yelled after him, but he sensibly

ignored me. It's at moments like this I just don't understand why I broke all the rules of a lifetime and allowed
this man to invade my personal space.

I should have known better. It had all started so inaus-
piciously. I'd been tailing a young systems engineer whose
employer suspected him of selling information to a rival.
I'd followed him to the Hacienda Club, breeding ground
for so many of the bands that have turned Manchester
into the creative centre of the nineties music industry. I'd
only been there a couple of times previously because being
jammed shoulder to shoulder with a sweating mass of
bodies in a room where conversation is impossible and the
simple act of breathing gets you stoned isn't my idea of
the perfect way to spend what little free time I get. I have
to confess I'm much happier playing interactive adventure
games with my computer.

Anyway, I was trying to look unobtrusive in the Hassy
– not an easy task when you're that crucial five years older
than most of the clientele – when this guy appeared at my
shoulder and tried to buy me a drink. I liked the look of
him. For a start, he was old enough to have started shaving.
He had twinkling hazel eyes behind a pair of large tor-
toiseshell-framed glasses and a very cute smile, but I was
working and I couldn't afford to take my eyes off my little
systems man in case he made his contact right before my
eyes. But The Cute Smile didn't want to take no for an
answer, so it was something of a relief when my target
headed for the exit.

I had no time for goodbyes. I shot off after him, squeez-
ing through the press of bodies like a sweaty eel. By the
time I made it on to the street, I could see his tail lights
glowing red as he started his car. I cursed aloud as I ran
round the corner to where I'd parked and leapt behind
the wheel. I slammed the car into gear and shot out of my
parking place. As I tore round the corner, a customized

Volkswagen Beetle convertible reversed out of a side alley. I had nowhere to go except into the nearside door. There was a crunching of metal as I wrestled my wheel round in a bid to save my Nova from complete disaster.

It was all over in seconds. I climbed out of the car, furious with this dickhead who hadn't bothered to check before he reversed out into a main street. Whoever he was, he'd not only lost me my surveillance target but had also wrecked my car. I strode round to the driver's door of the Beetle in a towering rage, ready to drag the pillock out on to the street and send him home with his nuts in a paper bag. I mean, driving like that, it had to be a man, didn't it?

Peering out at me like a very shaken little boy was The Cute Smile. Before I could find the words to tell him what I thought of his brainless driving, he smiled disarmingly up at me. 'If you wanted my name and phone number that badly, all you had to do was ask,' he said innocently.

For some strange reason, I didn't kill him. I laughed. That was my first mistake. Now, nine months later, Richard was my lover next door, a funny, gentle divorcé with a five-year-old son in London. I'd at least managed to hang on to enough of my common sense not to let him move in with me. By chance, the bungalow next to mine had come on the market, and I'd explained to Richard that that was as close as he was going to get to living with me, so he snapped it up.

He'd wanted to knock a connecting door between the two, but I'd informed him that it was a load-bearing wall and besides, we'd never manage to sell either house like that. Because I'm the practical one in this relationship, he believed me. Instead, I came up with the idea of linking the houses via a huge conservatory built on the back of our living rooms, with access to both houses through patio doors. Erecting a partition wall to separate the two halves

9

would be a simple matter if we ever move. And we both reserve the right to lock our doors. Well, I do. Apart from anything else, it gives me time to clear up after Richard has been reducing the neat order of my home to chaos. And it means he can sit carousing with his rock buddies till dawn without me stomping through to the living room in the small hours looking like a refugee from the Addams family, chuddering sourly about some of us having to go to work in the morning.

Right now, as I savagely towelled my hair and smoothed moisturizer into my tired skin, I cursed my susceptibility. Somehow he always manages to dig himself out of his latest pit with the same cute smile, a bunch of roses and a joke. It shouldn't work, not on a bright, streetwise hard case like me, but to my infinite shame, it does. At least I've managed to impress upon him that there are house rules in any relationship. To break the rules knowingly once is forgivable. Twice means me changing the locks at three in the morning and Richard finding his favourite records thrown out of my living room window on to the lawn once I've made sure it's raining. It usually is in Manchester.

At first, he reacted as if my behaviour were certifiable. Now, he's come to accept that life is much sweeter if he sticks to the rules. He's still a long way from perfect. For example, being colour-blind, he's got a tendency to bring home little gifts like a scarlet vase that clashes hideously with my sage green, peach and magnolia decor. Or black sweatshirts promoting bands I've never heard of because black's fashionable, in spite of the fact that I've told him a dozen times that black makes me look like a candidate for the terminal ward. Now, I simply banish them to his home and thank him sweetly for his thoughtfulness. But he's getting better, I swear he's getting better. Or so I told myself as the desire to strangle him rose at the thought of the evening ahead.

Reluctantly abandoning the idea of murder, I returned to my bedroom and thought about an outfit for the evening. I weighed up what would be expected of me. It didn't matter a damn what I wore to the concert. I'd be lost in the thousands of yelling fans desperate to welcome Jett back in triumph to his home town. The party afterwards was more of a problem. Much as I hated having to ask, I called through to Richard, 'What's the party going to be like, clothes-wise?'

He appeared in the doorway, looking like a puppy that's astonished to have been forgiven so easily for the mess on the kitchen floor. His own outfit was hardly a clue. He was wearing a wide-shouldered baggy electric blue double breasted suit, a black shirt and a silk tie with a swirled pattern of neon colours that looked like a sixties psychedelic album cover. He shrugged and gave that smile that still made my stomach turn over. 'You know Jett,' he said.

That was the problem. I didn't. I'd met the man once, about three months before. He'd turned up on our table for ten at a charity dinner and had sat very quiet, almost morose, except when discussing football with Richard. Manchester United, those two words that are recognized in any language from Santiago to Stockholm, had unlocked Jett as if with a magic key. He'd sprung to the defence of his beloved Manchester City with the ardour of an Italian whose mother's honour has been impugned. The only fashion hint I'd had from that encounter was that I should wear a City strip. 'No, Richard, I don't know Jett,' I explained patiently. 'What kind of party will it be?'

'Not many Traceys, lots of Fionas,' he announced in our own private code. Traceys are bimbos, the natural successors to groupies. Blonde, busty and fashion-obsessed, if they had a brain they'd be dangerous. Fionas share the same characteristics but they are the rich little upper-crust girls who would have been debutantes if coming out had

11

not become so hopelessly unfashionable with everyone except gays. They like rock stars because they enjoy being with men who lavish them with gifts and a good time, while at the same time shocking their families to the core. So Jett liked Fionas, did he? And Fionas meant designer outfits, an item singularly lacking in my wardrobe.

I flicked moodily through the hangers and ended up with a baggy long cotton shirt splashed with shades of olive, khaki, cream and terracotta that I'd bought on holiday in the Canaries the year before. I pulled on a pair of tight terracotta leggings. That was when I knew the motorway sandwiches had to go. Luckily, the shirt covered the worst of the bulges, so I cinched it in at the waist with a broad brown belt. I finished the outfit off with a pair of high-heeled brown sandals. When you're only 5'3", you need all the help you can get. I chose a pair of outrageous earrings and a couple of gold bangles, and eyed myself in the mirror. It wasn't wonderful, but it was better than Richard deserved. Right on cue, he said, 'You look great. You'll knock them dead, Brannigan.'

I hoped not. I hate mixing business with pleasure.

2

We didn't have to scramble for a parking place near the Apollo Theatre, since we live less than five minutes' walk away. I couldn't believe my luck when I discovered this development halfway through my first year as a law student at Manchester University. It's surrounded on three sides by council housing estates and on the fourth by Ardwick Common. It's five minutes by bike to the university, the central reference library, Chinatown, and the office. It's ten minutes by bike to the heart of the city centre. And by car, it's only moments away from the motorway network. When I discovered it, they were still building the little close of forty houses, and the prices were ridiculously low, probably because of the surrounding area's less than salubrious reputation. I worked out that if I pitched my father into standing guarantor for a hundred per cent mortgage and moved another student into the spare room as a lodger, I'd be paying almost the same as I was for my shitty little room in a student residence. So I went for it and moved in that Easter. I've never regretted it. It's a great place to live as long as you remember to switch on the burglar alarm.

We arrived at the Apollo just as the support band were finishing their first number. We'd have caught the opener if they hadn't left the guest list in the hands of an illiterate. One of the major drawbacks to having a relationship with a rock writer is that you can't put support bands to their traditional use of providing a background beat while you have a few drinks before the act you came to hear gets on stage. Rock writers actually listen to the support band, just so they can indulge in their professional one-upmanship with lines like, 'Oh yes, I remember Dire Straits when they were playing support at the Newcastle City Hall,' invariably to some band that everyone has now forgotten. After two numbers, I couldn't take any more and I abandoned Richard in his seat while I headed for the bar.

The bar at the Apollo reminds me of a vision of hell. It's decorated in a mosaic of bright red glitter, it's hot and it reeks of cigarette smoke and stale alcohol. I elbowed my way through the crowd and waved a fiver in the air till one of the nonchalant bar staff eventually deigned to notice me. At the Apollo, they specialize in a minuscule selection of drinks, all served at blood heat in plastic tumblers. It doesn't matter much what you order, it all seems to taste much the same. Only the colours vary. I asked for a lager, which arrived flat and looking like a urine sample. I sipped tentatively and decided that seeing is believing. As I pushed my way back towards the door, I saw someone who made me stop so suddenly that the man behind me cannoned into me, spilling half my drink down the trousers of the man next to me.

In the chaos of my apologies and my pathetic attempts to wipe up the spilled beer with a tissue from my handbag, I took my eyes off the source of my surprise. When I managed to make my embarrassed escape, I looked over to the corner where he'd been standing. But it was now occupied by a threesome I'd never seen before. Gary Smart, brother and partner of Billy, had vanished.

I stared round the crowded bar, but there was no trace of him. He'd been standing with a tall, skinny man who'd had his back to me. I didn't hear a word of their conver-

14

sation, but their body language suggested a business deal. Gary had been putting some kind of pressure on the other man. It certainly hadn't looked like a pleasant, concertgoers' chat about which of Jett's albums they liked best. I cursed silently. I'd missed a great chance to pick up some interesting info.

With a shrug, I drank the few remaining mouthfuls of my drink and went back down to the foyer. I checked out the tour merchandise just to see if there was anything among the t-shirts, sweatshirts, badges, programmes and albums that I fancied. Richard can always get freebies, so I usually have a quick look. But the sweatshirts were black, and the t-shirts hideous, so I walked back through the half-empty auditorium and slumped in my seat next to Richard while the support band ground out their last two numbers. They left the stage to muted applause, the lights went up and a tape of current chart hits filled the air. 'Bag of crap,' Richard remarked.

'That their name or a critical judgement?' I asked.

He laughed and said, 'Well, they ain't honest enough to call themselves that, but they might as well have done. Now, while we've got a minute to ourselves, tell me about your day.'

As he lit a joint, I did just that. I always find that talking things over with Richard helps. He has an instinctive understanding of people and how their minds work that I have come to rely on. It's the perfect foil to my more analytical approach.

Unfortunately, before he could deliver his considered verdict on the Smart brothers, the lights went down. The auditorium, now full to capacity, rang with cries of 'Jett, Jett, Jett . . .' After a few minutes of chanting, wavering torch beams lit up pathways on the stage as members of Jett's backing band took the stage. Then, a pale blue spot picked out the drummer, high on his platform at the rear of the stage, brushing a snare drum softly. The lighting man focused on the bass player in pale purple as he picked up the slow beat. Then came the keyboards player, adding a shimmering chord from the synthesizer. The sax player joined in, laying down a line as smooth as chocolate.

Then, suddenly, a stark white spotlight picked out Jett as he strode out of the wings, looking as frail and vulnerable as ever. His black skin gleamed under the lights. He wore his trademark brown leather trousers and cream silk shirt. An acoustic guitar was slung round his neck. The audience went wild, almost drowning out the musicians in their frenzy. But as soon as he opened his mouth to sing, they stilled.

His voice was better than ever. I've been a fan of Jett since his first single hit the charts when I was fifteen, but I find it as hard now to categorize his music as I did then. His first album had been a collection of twelve tracks, mainly acoustic but with some subtle backings ranging from a plangent sax to a string quartet. The songs had ranged from simple, plaintive love songs to the anthemlike 'To Be With You Tonight' which had been the surprise hit of the year, hitting the top of the charts the week after its release and staying there for eight weeks. He had one of those voices that has the quality of a musical instrument, blending perfectly with whatever arrangement flows beneath it. As a lovesick teenager, I could lose myself completely in his yearning songs with their poignant lyrics.

Eight other albums had followed, but I'd increasingly found less delight in them. I wasn't sure if it was the changes in me that were responsible for that. Maybe what strikes a teenager as profound and moving just doesn't work once you're halfway through your twenties. But it seemed to me that while the music was still strong, the lyrics had become trite and predictable. Maybe that was a reflection of his reported views about the role of women.

It's hard to write enlightened love songs about the half of the population you believe should be barefoot and pregnant. However, the packed crowd in the Apollo didn't seem to share my views. They roared out their appreciation for every number, whether from the last album or the first. After all, he was on home ground. He was their own native son. He'd made the northern dream a reality, moving up from a council flat in the Moss-side ghetto to a mansion in the Cheshire countryside.

With consummate showmanship, he closed the ninety-minute set with a third encore, that first, huge hit, the one we'd all been waiting for. A classic case of leaving them wanting more. Before the last chords had died away, Richard was on his feet and heading for the exit. I followed quickly before the crowds built up, and caught up with him on the pavement outside as he flagged down a cab.

As we settled back in our seats and the cabbie set off for the hotel, Richard said, 'Not bad. Not bad at all. He puts on a good show. But he'd better have some new ideas for the next album. Last three all sounded the same and they didn't sell nearly enough. You watch, there'll be a few twitchy faces around tonight, and I don't just mean the coke-heads.'

He paused to light a cigarette and I snatched the chance to ask him why it was so important that I be at the party. I was still nursing the forlorn hope of an early night.

'Now that would be telling,' he said mysteriously.

'So tell. It's only a five-minute cab ride. I haven't got time to pull your fingernails out one by one.'

'You're a hard woman, Brannigan,' he complained. 'Never off duty, are you? OK, I'll tell you. You know me and Jett go way back?' I nodded. I remembered Richard telling me the story of how he'd landed his first job on a music paper with an exclusive interview of the normally

17

reclusive Jett. Richard had been working for a local paper in Watford and he'd been covering their cup tie with Manchester City. At the time, Elton John had owned Watford, and Jett had been his personal guest for the afternoon. After City won, Richard had sneaked in to the boardroom and had persuaded an elated Jett to give him an interview. That interview had been Richard's escape ticket. As a bonus, Jett had liked what Richard wrote, and they'd stayed friends ever since.

'Well,' Richard continued, interrupting my reference to my mental card index of his past, 'he's decided that he wants his autobiography written.'

'Don't you mean biography?' Always the nitpicker, that's me.

'No, I mean *auto*. He wants it ghosted, written in the first person. When we saw him at that dinner, he mentioned it to me. Sort of sounded me out. Of course, I said I'd be interested. It wouldn't be a mega-seller like Jagger or Bowie, but it could be a nice little earner. So, when he rang me up to invite us tonight and he was so insistent that you come along too, I thought I could read between the lines.'

Although he was trying to sound nonchalant, I could tell that Richard was bursting with pride and excitement at the idea. I pulled his head down to mine and planted a kiss on his warm mouth. 'That's great news,' I said, meaning it. 'Will it mean a lot of work?'

He shrugged. 'I shouldn't think so. It's just a case of getting him talking into the old tape recorder then knocking it into shape afterwards. And he's going to be at home for the next three months or so working on the new album, so he'll be around and about.'

Before we could discuss the matter further, the taxi pulled up outside the ornate façade of the grandiosely named Holiday Inn Midland Crowne Plaza. It's one of those extraordinary Manchester monuments to the city's first era of prosperity. One of the more palatable by-products of the cotton mills of the industrial revolution. I can remember when it used to be simply the Midland, one of those huge railway hotels that moulder on as relics of an age when the rich felt no guilt and the poor were kept well away from the doors. Then Holiday Inn bought the dinosaur and turned it into a fun palace for the city's new rich – the sportsmen, businessmen and musicians who gave Manchester a new lease of life in the late eighties.

Suddenly, in the nineties, London was no longer the place to be. If you wanted a decent lifestyle with lots of buzz and excitement packed into compact city centres, you had to be in one of the so-called provincial cities. Manchester for rock, Glasgow for culture, Newcastle for shopping. It was this shift that had brought Richard to Manchester two years before. He'd come up to try to get an interview with cult hero Morrissey and two days in the city had convinced him that it was going to be to the nineties what Liverpool was to the sixties. He had nothing to keep him in London; his divorce had just come through, and a freelance makes his best living if he's where the most interesting stories are. So he stayed, like a lot of others.

I followed him out of the taxi, feeling like partying for the first time since I'd come home. Richard's news had given me a real adrenalin rush, and I couldn't wait for the official confirmation of what he already suspected. We headed straight to the bar for a drink to give Jett and his entourage time to get over to the hotel.

I sipped my vodka and grapefruit juice gratefully. When I became a private eye, I tried to match the image and drink whisky. After two glasses, I had to revert to my usual to take the taste away. I guess I'm not cut out for the 'bottle of whisky and a new set of lies' Mark Knopfler image. As I drank, I listened with half an ear while Richard told me how he saw Jett's autobiography taking shape. 'It's a great rags to riches story, a classic. A poor childhood in the Manchester slums, the struggle to make the music he knew he had in him. First discovering music when his strict Baptist mother pushed him into the gospel choir. How he got his first break. And at last, the inside story on why his songwriting partnership with Moira broke up. It's got all the makings,' he rambled on. 'I could probably sell the serial rights to one of the Sunday tabloids. Oh, Kate, it's a great night for us!'

After twenty minutes of bubbling enthusiasm, I managed to cut in and suggest that we made our way to the party. As soon as we emerged from the lift, it was clear which suite Jett had hired for the night. Already a loud babble of conversation spilled into the hall, overlaying the mellow sounds of Jett's last album. I squeezed Richard's hand and said, 'I'm really proud of you,' as we entered the main room and the party engulfed us.

Jett himself was holding court at the far end of the room, looking as fresh as if he'd just got out of the shower. His arm was draped casually round the shoulders of a classic Fiona. Her blonde hair hung over her shoulders in a loosely permed mane, her blue eyes, like the rest of her face, were perfectly made up, and the shiny violet sheath that encased her curves looked to me like a Bill Blass.

'Come on, let's go and talk to Jett,' Richard said eagerly, steering me towards the far side of the room. As we passed the table where the drinks were laid out, a shirtsleeved arm sneaked out from a group of women and grabbed Richard's shoulder.

'Barclay!' a deep voice bellowed. 'What the hell are you doing here?' The group parted to reveal the speaker, a man of medium height and build, running slightly to paunch round the middle.

Richard looked astonished. 'Neil Webster!' he exclaimed with less than his usual warmth. 'I could ask you the same thing. At least I'm a bloody rock writer, not an ambulance chaser. What are you doing back in Manchester? I thought you were in Spain.'

'A bit too hot for me down there, if you catch my drift,' Neil Webster replied. 'Besides, all the news these days seems to happen in this city. I thought I was about due to revisit my old haunts.'

Their exchange gave me a few minutes to study this latest addition to my collection of Journalists Of The World. Neil Webster had that slightly disreputable air that a lot of women seem to find irresistible. I'm not one of them. He looked to be in his late thirties, though a journalist's life does seem to accelerate ageing in everyone except my own Peter Pan Barclay. Neil's brown hair, greying at the temples, looked slightly rumpled, as did the cream chinos and chambray shirt he was wearing. His brown eyes were hooded, with a nest of laughter lines etched white in his tanned skin. He had a hawk nose over a full pepper and salt moustache and his jaw line was starting to show signs of jowls.

My scrutiny was interrupted by his own matching appraisal. 'So who's the lovely lady? I'm sorry, my love, that oaf you came with seems to have forgotten his manners. I'm Neil Webster, real journalist. Not like Richard with his comic books. And you're . . . ?'

'Kate Brannigan.' I coolly shook his proffered hand.

'Well, Kate, let me get you a drink. What's it to be?'

I asked him for my usual vodka and grapefruit juice, and he turned to the bar to pour it. Richard leaned past him and helped himself to a can of Schlitz. 'You didn't say what exactly you were doing back here,' Richard pressed

Neil as he handed me my drink. I tasted it and nearly choked, both at the strength of the drink and the impact of Neil's reply.

'Didn't I? Oh, sorry. Fact of the matter is, I've been commissioned to write Jett's official biography.'

3

Richard's face turned bright scarlet and then chalky white as Neil's words hit him. I felt a cold stab of shock in my own stomach as I shared his moment of bitter disappointment. 'You've got to be joking,' Richard said in an icy voice.

Neil laughed. 'Quite a surprise, isn't it? I'd have thought he'd have gone for a specialist. Someone like you,' he added, twisting the knife. 'But Kevin wanted me. He insisted.' He shrugged disarmingly. 'So what could I say? After all, Kevin's an old friend. And he's the boss. I mean, nobody manages a top act like Jett a dozen years without knowing what's right for the boy, do they?'

Richard said nothing. He turned on his heel and pushed his way through the growing crowd round the bar. I tried to follow, but Neil stood in my way. 'I don't know what's rattled his cage, but why don't you just let him cool down,' he said smoothly. 'Stay and tell me all about yourself.'

Ignoring him, I moved away and headed towards Jett. I could no longer see Richard's dark head, but I guessed that's where he'd be. I reached Jett's couch in time to hear Richard's angry voice saying, 'You as good as promised me. The guy's a wasted space. What the hell were you thinking?'

The adulatory crowd that had been eagerly congratulating Jett and trying to touch the hem of his garment had fallen back under the force of Richard's onslaught. He was towering threateningly above Jett, whose Fiona looked thrilled to bits by the encounter.

Jett himself looked upset. His honey-sweet voice sounded strained. 'Richard, Richard. Listen to me. I wanted you to do the book. I said that all along. Then out of the blue, Kevin dumps this guy on me and tells me I have to play ball, that he knows who's the best man for the job. And it's too late for me to do anything about it. Kevin's already signed the man up on a contract. If I don't play, we still have to pay. So I have to play.'

Richard had listened in silence, his face a tight mask of anger. I'd never seen him so upset before, not even when his ex-wife was being difficult about his access to Davy. I reached his side and gripped his right arm. I know what he's like when he's angry. The holes in the plasterboard walls of his hall bear eloquent testimony to his frustrations. I didn't think he'd hit Jett, but I didn't want to risk it.

He stood and stared at Jett for what seemed like an eternity. Then he spoke slowly and bitterly. 'And I thought you were a man,' was all he said. He tore his arm out of my grip and plunged into the crowd towards the door. Only then was I aware that the room had fallen silent, every ear in the place tuned in to their conversation. I glared around, and slowly the buzz of conversation built again, even louder than before.

I desperately wanted to chase after Richard, to hold him and make useless offers of comfort. But more pressingly, I needed to know what my part in this whole charade was. I turned back to Jett and said, 'He feels very let down. He thought you asked me here tonight to celebrate a book deal with us.'

Jett had the grace to look sheepish. 'I'm sorry, Kate, I really am sorry. I feel like a piece of shit over this, believe

24

me. I wanted to tell Richard myself, not let him hear it from someone else. I know he'd have done a good job, but my hands are tied. People don't realize how little power guys like me actually have.'

'So why did you want me here tonight?' I demanded. 'To keep Richard under control?'

Jett shook his head. He half-turned his handsome head to the Fiona. 'Tamar,' he said, 'why don't you get yourself another drink?'

The blonde smiled cattily at me and poured herself off the couch. When we were reasonably private, Jett said, 'I've got a job for you. It's something that's very important to me, and I need to be able to trust the person I give it to. Richard's told me a lot about you, and I think you're the right one. I don't want to tell you about it tonight, but I want you to come and see me tomorrow so we can discuss it.'

'Are you kidding?' I flashed back. 'After the way you've just humiliated Richard?'

'I didn't think you were the kind of lady who let personal stuff get in the way of her work.' His voice was velvet. To an old fan, irresistible. 'I heard you were too good for that.'

Flattery. It never fails. I was intrigued, in spite of my anger. 'There's a lot of stuff Mortensen and Brannigan don't handle,' I hedged.

He looked around him, trying to appear casual. He seemed satisfied that no one was in earshot. 'I want you to find someone for me,' he said softly. 'But not a word to Richard, please.'

That reminded me how angry I was on Richard's behalf. 'Mortensen and Brannigan always respect client confidentiality,' I said, sounding stuffy even to my ears. God knows what the king of thirtysomething rock was making of it all.

He grinned, flashing a display of brilliant white teeth at me. 'Come to the manor tomorrow about three,' he said, not expecting any more problems.

I shook my head. 'I don't know, Jett. We don't usually touch missing persons.'

'For me? As a personal favour?'

'Like the one you've just done Richard?'

He winced. 'OK, OK. Point taken. Look, Kate, I'm truly sorry about that. I shouldn't have mentioned it to Richard and raised his hopes without clearing it with Kevin. When it comes to things like contracts, he's the man who makes the decisions. He keeps me right. In the business side of things, he's the boss. But this other thing, it's personal. This is really important to me, Kate. Listening to what I want won't cost you anything. Please,' he added. I had the feeling it was a word he'd lost familiarity with.

Wearily, I nodded. 'OK. Three o'clock. If I can't make it, I'll ring and rearrange it. But no promises.'

He looked as if I'd taken the weight of the world off his shoulders. 'I appreciate it, Kate. Look, tell Richard what I said. Tell him I'm really sorry, would you? I've not got so many friends among the press that I can afford to lose my best one.'

I nodded and pushed my way through the crowds. By the time I'd reached the door, Jett and his problems were at the back of my mind. What was important to me now was helping Richard through the night.

When the alarm went off the following morning, Richard didn't even stir. I slid out of bed, trying not to disturb him. If how I felt was any guide, he'd need at least another six hours' sleep before he returned from Planet Hangover. I headed for the kitchen and washed down my personal pick-me-up. Paracetamol, vitamins C and B complex and a couple of zinc tablets with a mixture of orange juice and protein supplement. With luck, I'd rejoin the human race somewhere around Billy Smart's house.

I had a quick shower, found a clean jogging suit and picked up a bottle of mineral water on the way out of the front door. Poor Richard, I thought as I slipped behind the wheel of the car and drove off. I'd caught up with him in the foyer, kicking his heels for want of a better target while he waited for a taxi. He'd been grimly silent all the way home, but as soon as he'd had half a pint of Southern Comfort and soda, he'd started ranting. I'd joined him in drink because I couldn't think of anything else to do or say that would make it better. He'd been shat on from a great height, and that was an end to it. It didn't make me feel any better about having agreed to Jett's request for a meeting, but luckily Richard was too wrapped up in his own disappointment to wonder why it had taken me so long to catch up with him.

I drove through the pre-dawn deserted streets and took up my familiar station a few doors down from Billy's house. It always amazes me that people don't pick up on it when I'm staking them out. I suppose it's partly that a Vauxhall Nova is the last car anyone would expect to be tailed by. The 1.4 SR model I drive looks completely innocuous – the sort of little hatchback men buy for their wives to go shopping in. But when I put my foot down, it goes like the proverbial shit off a shovel. I've followed Billy Smart to the garage where he swaps his hired cars every three days, I've tailed him in his Mercs and BMWs all over the country, and my confidence in my relative invisibility hasn't been dented yet. The only worry I have on stakeouts is a uniquely female one. Men can pee in a bottle. Women can't.

Luckily, I didn't have long to hang around before Billy appeared. I sat tight while he did his routine once-round-the-block drive to check he had no one on his tail, then I set off a reasonable distance behind him. To my intense satisfaction, he followed the same routine he'd used on the previous Wednesday. He picked up brother Gary from his flat in the high-rise block above the Arndale shopping centre, then they went together to the little back-street factory in the mean area dominated by the tall red-brick water tower of Strangeways Prison. They stayed in there for about half an hour. When they emerged they were carrying several bulky bundles wrapped in black velveteen, which I knew contained hundreds of schneid watches.

I had to stay close to their hired Mercedes as we wove through the increasing traffic, but by now I knew their routine and could afford to keep a few cars between us. True to the form of the last two weeks, they headed over the M62 towards Leeds and Bradford. I followed them as far as their first contact in a lock-up garage in Bradford, then I decided to call it a day. They were simply repeating themselves, and I already had photographs of the Wednesday routine from my previous surveillance. It was time for a chat with Bill. I also wanted to talk to him about Jett's proposition.

I got back to the office towards the end of the morning. We have three small rooms on the sixth floor of an old insurance company building just down the road from the BBC Oxford Road studios. The best thing I can find to say about the location is that it's handy for the local art cinema, the Cornerhouse, which has an excellent cafeteria. Our secretary Shelley looked up from her word processor and greeted me with 'Wish I could start work at lunchtime.'

I was halfway through a self-righteous account of my morning's work when I realized, too late as usual, that she was winding me up. I stuck my tongue out at her and dropped a micro-cassette on her desk. It contained my verbal report of the last couple of days. 'Here's a little something to keep you from getting too bored,' I said. 'Anything I should know about?'

Shelley shook her head, and the beads she has plaited into her hair rattled. I wondered, not for the first time, how she could bear the noise first thing in the morning. But then, since Shelley's mission in life is keeping her two teenage kids out of trouble, I don't think there are too many mornings when she wakes with a hangover. There are times when I could hate Shelley.

Mostly I find myself in her debt. She is the most efficient secretary I have ever encountered. She's a 35-year-old divorcée who somehow manages to look like a fashion plate in spite of the pittance we pay her. She's just under five feet tall, and so slim and fragile-looking that she makes even me feel like the Incredible Hulk. I've been to her cramped little two-up, two-down and in spite of living with a pair of teenagers, the house is spotlessly clean and almost unnaturally tidy. However, Richard has pointed out to me more than once that I am a subscriber to the irregular verb theory of language – 'I have high standards, you are fussy, she is obsessive.'

She picked up the cassette and slotted it into her own player. 'I'll have it for you later this afternoon,' she said.

'Thanks. Copy in Bill's system as well as mine, please. Is he free?'

She glanced at the lights on her PBX. 'Looks like it.'

I crossed the office in four strides and knocked on Bill's door. His deep voice growled, 'Come in.' As I shut the door behind me, he looked up from the screen of his turbocharged IBM compatible and grunted, 'Give me a minute, Kate.' Bill likes things turbo-charged. Everything from his Saab 9000 convertible to his sex life.

There was a fierce frown of concentration on his face as he scanned the screen, tapping the occasional key. No matter how often I watch Bill at his computers, I still feel a sense of incongruity. He really doesn't look like a computer boffin or a private investigator. He's six foot three inches tall and resembles a shaggy blond bear. His hair and beard are shaggy, his eyebrows are shaggy over his ice blue eyes, and when he smiles his white teeth look alarmingly like the ones that are all the better to eat you with. He's a one-man EC. I still haven't got the hang of his ancestry, except that I know his grandparents were, severally, Danish, Dutch, German and Belgian. His parents settled over here after the war and have a substantial cattle farm in Cheshire. Bill shook them to the core when he announced he was more interested in megabytes than megaburgers.

He went on to take a first in computer sciences at UMIST. While he was working on his Ph.D., he was head-hunted by a computer software house as a troubleshooter. After a couple of years, he went freelance and became increasingly interested in the crooked side of computers. Soon, his business grew to include surveillance and security systems and all aspects of computer fraud and hacking. I met him towards the end of the first year of my law degree. He had a brief fling with my lodger, and we stayed friends long after the romance was over. He asked me to do a couple of legal jobs for him – process serving, researching particular Acts of Parliament, that sort of thing. I ended up working for him in my vacations. My role quickly grew, for Bill soon discovered it was easier for me to go under-cover in a firm with problems than it was for him. After all, no one ever looks twice at the temporary secretary or data processor, do they? I found it all infinitely more interesting than my law degree. So when he offered me a full-time job after I'd passed my second year exams, I jumped at the chance. My father nearly had a coronary, but I appeased him by saying I could always go back to university and complete my degree if it didn't work out.

Two years later, Bill offered me a junior partnership in the firm, and so Mortensen and Brannigan was born. I'd never regretted my decision, and once my father realized that I was earning a helluva lot more than any junior solicitor, or even a car worker like him, neither did he.

Bill looked up from his screen with a satisfied smile and leaned back in his chair. 'Sorry about that, Kate. And how is Billy Smart's circus today?'

'Sticking to the pattern,' I replied. I brought him quickly up to date and his look of happiness increased.

'How long till we wrap it up?' he asked. 'And do you need anything more from me?'

'I'll be ready to hand over to the clients in a week or so. And no, I don't need anything right now, unless you want to get a numb bum watching Billy for a day or two. What I did want to discuss with you is an approach I had last night.' I filled him in.

Bill got up from his chair and stretched. 'It's not our usual field,' he said eventually. 'I don't like missing persons. It's time-consuming, and not everyone wants to be found. Still, it might be straightforward enough, and it could lead us into a whole new range of potential clients. Plenty of schneid merchants around in the record business. Go and see what he wants, Kate, but make him no promises. We'll talk about it tomorrow when you've had a chance to sleep on it. You look as if you could do with a good night's sleep. These all-night rock parties are obviously too much for you these days.'

I scowled. 'It's nothing to do with partying. It's more to do with mounting surveillance on a hyperactive insomniac.' I left Bill booting up his AppleMac and headed for my own office. It's really only a glorified cupboard containing a desk with my PC, a second desk for writing at, a row of filing cabinets and three chairs. Off it is an even smaller cupboard that doubles as my darkroom and the ladies' toilet. For decoration, I've got a shelf of legal textbooks and a plant that has to be replaced every six weeks. Currently, it's a three-week-old lemon geranium that's already showing signs of unhappiness. I have the opposite of green fingers. Every growing thing I touch turns to brown. If I ever visit the Amazonian rainforests, there'll be an ecological disaster on a scale that even Sting couldn't prevent.

I sat down at my computer and logged on to one of several databases that we subscribe to. I chose the one that keeps extensive newspaper cuttings files on current celebrities, and I downloaded everything they had on Jett into my own computer. I saved the material to disc, then printed it out. Even if we decided not to go ahead with Jett's assignment, I was determined to be fully briefed when we met. And since Jett himself had deprived me of my best source, I would have to do the best I could without Richard's help.

It didn't take me long to go through the printout, which ironically included a couple of Richard's own articles. I now knew more than I had ever wanted to about any pop star, including Bjorn from Abba, focus of my own pre-teen crush. I knew all about Jett's poverty-ridden childhood, about his discovery of the power of music when his deeply religious mother enrolled him in the local church's gospel choir. I knew about his views on racial integration (a good thing), drugs (a very bad thing), abortion (a crime against humanity), the meaning of life (fundamentalist Christianity heavily revised by a liberal dollop of New Age codswallop), music (the very best thing of all as long as it had a good tune and a lyric that made sense – just like my dad) and women (the object of his respect, ho, ho). But among all the gossipy pieces of froth were a couple of nuggets of pure gold. If I were a gambling woman, I'd have felt very confident about putting money on the identity of the person Jett wanted found.

4

Jett's new home couldn't have been more of a contrast to the area where he'd grown up, I reflected as I pulled up before a pair of tall wrought-iron gates. To get to this part of Cheshire from the centre of Manchester, you have to drive through the twitching heart of Moss-side, its pavements piled with the wares of the secondhand furniture dealers. Not the only kind of dealer you spot as you drive through the Moss. I'd been glad to get on to the motorway and even more glad to turn off into the maze of country lanes with their dazzling patches of spring bulbs.

I wound down the window and pressed the entryphone buzzer that controlled the security system on the gates. At the far end of the drive, I could just make out the honey-coloured stone of Colcutt Manor. It looked impressive enough from here. The entryphone quacked an inquiry at me. 'Kate Brannigan,' I announced. 'Of Mortensen and Brannigan. I have an appointment with Jett.'

There was a pause. Then a distorted voice squawked, 'Sorry. I have no record of that.'

'Could you check with Jett, please. I do have an appointment.'

'Sorry. That won't be possible.'

I wasn't exactly surprised. Rock stars are not widely renowned for their efficiency. I sighed and tried again. This time the voice said, 'I will have to ask you to leave now.'

I tried for a third time. This time there was no response at all. I shouted a very rude word at the entryphone. I could always turn round and go home. But that would have hurt my professional pride. 'Call yourself a private eye, and you can't even keep an appointment?' I snarled.

I reversed away from the gates and slowly drove along the perimeter wall. It was over seven feet high, but I wasn't going to let a little thing like that put me off. About half a mile down the lane, I found what I was looking for. Some kind of sturdy looking tree grew beside the wall with a branch that crossed it about a foot above. With a sigh, I parked the car on the verge and slipped off my high-heeled shoes, swapping them for the Reeboks I always keep in the boot. I stuffed the heels in my capacious handbag. I'd need them at the other end, since I was trying to impress a new client with my professionalism, not my ability to run the London marathon. Incidentally, it's one of life's great mysteries to me how men survive without handbags. Mine's like a survival kit, with everything from eye pencil to Swiss Army knife via pocket camera and tape recorder.

I slung my bag across my body and slowly made my way up the tree and along the branch. I dropped on to the top of the wall then let myself down by my arms. I only had about a foot to drop, and I managed it without any major injury. I dusted myself down and headed across the tussocky grass towards the house, avoiding too close an encounter with the browsing cattle. Thank God there wasn't a bull about. When I got to the drive, I swapped shoes again, wrapping my Reeboks in the plastic bag I always keep in the handbag.

I marched up to the front door and toyed with the idea of ringing. To hell with that. Whoever had refused me entry previously wouldn't be any better disposed now. On the off chance, I tried the handle of the massive double doors. To my surprise, it turned under my hand and the

34

door swung open. I didn't hang about thanking whoever is the patron saint of gumshoes, I just walked straight in. It was an awesome sight. The floor was paved with Italian terrazzo tiles, and ahead of me was an enormous staircase that split halfway up and headed in two different directions. Just like a Fred Astaire movie.

As I started to cross the hall, an outraged voice called from an open doorway near the entrance, 'What do you think you're playing at?' The voice was followed in short order by a blonde woman in her mid-twenties. She was strictly average in looks and figure, but she'd made the most of what she'd got. I took in the eyelash tint, the make-up so subtle you had to look twice to make sure it was there, and the tan leather jumpsuit.

'I'm here to see Jett,' I said.

'How did you get in? You've no right to be here. Are you the woman at the gate a few minutes ago?' she demanded crossly.

'That's me. You really should get someone to look at your security. We'd be happy to oblige.'

'If you're trying to drum up business, you've come to the wrong place. I'm sorry, Jett can't see anyone without an appointment,' she insisted with an air of finality. The smile she laced her reply with had enough malice to keep a gossip columnist going for a year.

For the third time, I said, 'I *have* an appointment. Kate Brannigan of Mortensen and Brannigan.'

She tossed her long plait over her shoulder and her cornflower blue eyes narrowed. 'You could be the Princess of Wales and you still wouldn't get past me without an appointment. Look for yourself,' she added, thrusting an open desk diary at me.

She couldn't have been more than twenty-three or -four, but she had all the steely intransigence of the Brigade of Guards. I glanced at the page she was showing me. As

35

she'd said, there was no appointment marked down for me. Either Jett had forgotten to mention it to her, or she was deliberately trying to keep me away from him. I sighed and tried again. 'Look, Miss . . .'

'Seward. Gloria Seward. I'm Jett's personal assistant. I'm here to protect him from being troubled by people he doesn't want to see. All his appointments go through me.'

'Well, I can only assume he forgot to mention this to you. The arrangement was only made last night after the concert. Perhaps it slipped his mind. Now, can I suggest that you pop off and find Jett and confirm our arrangement with him?' I was still managing to be sweet reason personified, but the veneer was beginning to wear thin.

'I'm afraid that won't be possible. Jett's working and can't be disturbed,' she smirked.

It was the smirk that did it. Beyond her, I could see the cool marble hall beckoning me. I pushed past her and I was halfway to the nearest door before she'd even realized what was going on. As I strode down the hall, not pausing to admire the paintings or the sculptures dotted around, I could hear her shrieking, 'Come back here. You've got no right . . .'

I opened the first door I came to. It was a square drawing room done out in watered blue silk and gilt. Very country house and garden. A stereo system heavily disguised as a Queen Anne cabinet was blasting out Chris Rea's *Road To Hell* album. The only sign of life was reclining on a blue silk sofa that looked too delicate for anything heftier than Elizabeth Barrett Browning in her last days. There was nothing tubercular about Tamar, however. She looked like she'd had more than the three hours' sleep I'd managed, that was for sure. She glanced up at me from the magazine she was reading and said, 'Oh, it's you again.'

She was wearing a cobalt blue shell suit that clashed so

violently with the furnishings it hurt my head to look at her. 'Hi,' I said. 'Where's Jett?'

'The rehearsal room. Straight down the hall, down the passage at the back and first right.' Before she'd even finished talking, she'd returned to her magazine, her foot tapping in time to the music.

I emerged in the hall to find a furious Gloria standing guard outside the door. 'How dare you!' she exploded.

I ignored her and set off to follow Tamar's directions. Gloria chased after me, plucking ineffectually at my jacket sleeve. When I got to the door of the rehearsal room, I shook off her arm and said, 'Now you'll see whether or not I've got an appointment.'

5

I opened the door and walked in to hear a man shouting, 'How many times do I have to tell you? You just don't need anyone else to . . .'

At the sound of the door, he whirled round and fell silent. There were two other men in the room. Neil Webster was sitting in a canvas director's chair with an air of fascinated satisfaction. Jett was leaning against a white grand piano with a sulky expression on his face. The third man, the shouter, I recognized at once. I'd seen him talking to Jett at the dinner where we'd met. Richard had told me he was Kevin Kleinman, Jett's manager.

Before any of us could say anything, Gloria erupted into the room and shoved past me. I couldn't believe the transformation in her. She'd altered from the dragon at the gates to a sweet little kitten. 'I'm so sorry, Jett,' she purred. 'But this woman just forced her way in. I tried to stop her, but she just pushed past me.'

Jett shrugged away from the piano with an exasperated sigh. 'Gloria, I told you I was expecting Kate. Christ, how could you have forgotten?'

The effect of Jett's words on Gloria was out of all proportion to their sting. She blushed scarlet and almost seemed to cringe out of the room, muttering apologies. To Jett, not to me. Her exit did nothing to diminish the air of awkwardness in the room. With an almost palpable effort,

38

Jett turned the full force of his charm on me and smiled. 'Kate,' he said. 'I'm really glad you could make it.'

My reply was drowned by Neil, who called across, 'You're really going to be doing all of us a big favour, Kate. I can't tell you how pleased I am for Jett that you're going to sort this business out.'

I caught Kevin's scowl at Neil before he too turned to me and gave a forced smile. 'Kate hasn't made any decision yet, if I understand it correctly,' he said. 'Maybe we should wait and see what she decides before we start dishing out the congratulations.'

I hadn't been too impressed by Kevin when I'd first seen him, and the second meeting wasn't improving my opinion. His average height and build were diminished by his lousy posture and rounded shoulders, and when he walked his feet seemed to slide over the floor. His thin brown hair was receding fast, emphasizing the sharpness of his features. Richard had told me he'd had a nose job, but looking at the finished product I found that hard to believe. Judging by his outfit – a soft brown leather blouson over a toffee-coloured cashmere crew neck and a pair of Levi 501s, he was doing his damnedest to ignore the fast approaching fortieth birthday. Aware of my scrutiny, he moved over to me and extended his hand. 'You must be the lovely Kate. I've heard so much about you from Richard. I'm Kevin, I take care of business for Jett.'

'Pleased to meet you,' I lied.

'I want to make it perfectly clear that whether or not you take on this job for Jett, it's vital that you do not mention outside this room what we discuss today. In the wrong hands, that information could do Jett a great deal of damage,' Kevin smarmed, holding on to my hand for fractionally too long. I had to fight the impulse to wipe it on my trouser leg.

'I've already told Jett that our confidentiality is guaranteed. We wouldn't have so many corporate clients if we had loose mouths.' My reply came out sharper than I intended and I noticed Neil smiling wryly.

'Fine, fine, I just wanted to be sure we understood each other,' Kevin oozed.

I deliberately walked away from him and crossed the room to Jett. 'Do you want to tell me why you've asked me here?'

He nodded and, taking my arm, he steered me across the room to a group of chairs round a low table. I took the chance to look around the large room. It was the size of a tennis court and was obviously a recent addition to the beautiful eighteenth-century mansion Jett had bought five years before. In one corner was a built-in bar, the only thing in the place that looked tacky. The long windows that looked out over the house's adjoining parkland had heavy shutters that could be drawn across to improve the room's acoustics. As well as the piano, there were banks of synthesizers, a few guitars, both acoustic and electric, a drum kit and an array of other percussion instruments. It was an impressive sight and I said so.

Jett smiled. 'It's not bad, is it? I've turned part of the cellars into a recording studio. I mean, for a man who can't tell Château Margaux from Country Manor, it was a hell of a lot of wasted space.'

Kevin walked across to join us. Jett ignored him and leaned on the bar, staring intently into my eyes. 'I want you to find someone for me. I knew as soon as we met that I could trust you, Kate. I had the feeling that we'd met before. In a previous life.'

My heart sank. I really wasn't in the mood for some rehashed New Age philosophy. The last thing I needed right now was a loop for a client.

'It's the flux. When I really needed someone to do this job for me, our paths crossed. I realize this isn't the kind

40

of thing you usually take on, but you have to do this one.' Jett patted my hand.

'So tell me about it,' I stalled, sipping my drink.

'When I started out, I had a partner. I suppose you know about that, huh? Moira was my soul mate, the one person I was meant to be with. We wrote all the songs on the first two albums together, we were magic. But we blew it. I didn't look after her needs, and she couldn't take the pressures without my support. So she went. I was too full of my success to realize what a fool I was to let her go. And she left enough of her energy with me for me to keep going a long time without noticing how much I'd needed her.' His eyes were shining with tears, but Jett showed no embarrassment at baring his soul in front of so motley a crew.

'I don't need to tell you that I've run out of that energy. My last two albums have been shit.' He looked up defiantly at Kevin, who shrugged. 'You know it's true. I just can't cut it any more. It's not just my music. It's my whole life. That's why I need you to find Moira for me.'

I congratulated myself silently on having guessed correctly. 'I don't know, Jett,' I hedged. 'Missing persons takes a lot of time. And if Moira doesn't want to be found, no amount of work will bring her back to you.'

Kevin, who had been bursting to interrupt, could contain himself no longer. 'That's exactly what I said, Jett,' he said triumphantly. 'I told you it would be nothing but grief. You don't know that she'd want to see you. You sure as hell don't know if she can still write lyrics the way she used to. Kate's right. It's a waste of time.'

'Don't tell me that shit,' Jett roared. I nearly fell off my stool with the shock of the sound wave. 'You're all the goddamn same,' he carried on shouting. 'You're all shit-scared of what will happen if she comes back. Neil's the only one of you who agrees with me. But just for once,

Kevin, I'm going to have what I want. And Kate's going to get it for me.'

The silence after his outburst was more deafening than the noise. I shook my head to clear it. I had to admit that Kevin's opposition had aroused the contrary side of me. I almost wanted to take it on just to spite him. I took a deep breath and said, 'I'd need a lot more information before I could decide if this is a case we can take on.'

'You got it,' Jett said.

'Just a minute,' Kevin said. 'Before we get into this, we should know what we're getting into. What's it going to cost?'

I named a price that was double our normal daily rate. If we were going to get embroiled in the search for Moira, they were going to have to pay for the privilege. Jett didn't bat an eyelid, but Kevin drew his breath in sharply. 'That's a bit heavy,' he complained.

'You pay peanuts, you get monkeys,' I replied.

'Getting Moira back would be cheap if it cost me everything I own,' Jett said softly. Kevin looked as if he was going to have a stroke.

Neil's smile had grown even broader during the last exchange. The prospect of me finding a major primary source for his book was obviously one that cheered him up. He got to his feet, slightly unsteady, and raised the glass of whisky he'd been nursing. 'I'd like to propose a toast,' he said. 'To Kate's success.'

I don't know if my smile looked as sick as Kevin's, but I hope I'm a better actress than that. I tucked my hand under Jett's elbow and steered him away from the others. 'Is there somewhere we can sit down quietly and you can fill me in on the details I'll need about Moira?' I asked softly.

He turned to face me and patted my shoulder paternally. 'OK, guys,' he said. 'Me and Kate have got some business to do. Neil, I'll catch up with you later, OK? You too, Kevin.'

'But Jett,' Kevin protested. 'I should be here if it's business.'

Jett was surprisingly adamant. Clearly, he had the boundaries between business and personal clearly defined in his own mind. In business matters, like who was going to ghost Jett's autobiography, Kevin's word was obviously law. But when it came to his own business, Jett could stand up for himself. It was an interesting split that I filed away for future reference.

Neil headed for the door, turning back on the threshold to wave his glass cheerily at us. 'Good hunting!' he called as he left.

Grumbling under his breath, Kevin picked up a filofax and a mobile phone from the bar and stomped down the room without a farewell. As I watched his departing back, fury written large across his slouched shoulders, I remarked, 'I'm surprised you chose a woman for a job like this, Jett. I thought you were a great believer in a woman's place being in the home.'

He looked a little suspiciously at me, as if he wasn't certain whether or not I was at the wind-up. 'I don't believe in working wives and mothers, if that's what you're getting at. But single women like you – well, you got to make a living, haven't you? And it's not like I'm asking you to do anything dangerous like catch a criminal, now, is it? And you women, you like talking, gossiping, swapping stories. If anyone can track down my Moira, it's another woman.'

'You want her back so you can work with her or so you can marry her?' I asked, out of genuine curiosity.

He shrugged. 'I always wanted to marry her. It was her didn't want to. My mother brought me up strict, to respect women. She taught me the way the Bible teaches. Now,

I've studied a lot of different philosophies and ideas since then, but I have never come across anything that makes sense to me like the idea of a family where the woman loves and nurtures her children and her husband. So, yes, I wanted Moira to be the mother of my children, wanted that more than anything. I don't know if that feeling's still there, so I can't answer you.'

I nearly got up and walked out right then. But I don't think it would have changed anything if I had. Certainly not Jett's neolithic view of women. I couldn't understand how a man of some intelligence and sensitivity, judging by his music, could still hold views like that in the last decade of the twentieth century. I swallowed the nasty taste in my mouth and got down to business. 'About Moira,' I began.

Two hours later, I was back in my own office. I'd just spent quarter of an hour persuading Bill that we should take on the case. I was far from convinced that we could get a result, but I thought the chances were better than evens. It would earn us a tasty fee, and if I did pull it off word would get around. Record companies have a lot of money to throw around, and they're notoriously litigious. Going to law and winning requires solid evidence, and private investigators are very good at amassing that evidence.

Now I'd pitched Bill into accepting the case, I had some work to do. Once I'd prised Jett away from Kevin and Neil I'd managed to get a substantial amount of background on Moira. The difficulty had been getting him to shut up. Now I needed to arrange my thoughts, so I booted up my database and started filling in all I knew about Moira.

Moira Xaviera Pollock was thirty-two years old, a Pisces with Cancer rising and a Sagittarius moon, according to Jett. I felt sure that piece of knowledge would help enormously in my task. They had been kids together in Moss Side, Manchester's black ghetto, where growing up without a drug habit or a criminal record is an achievement in itself. Moira's mother had three children by different fathers, none of them in wedlock. Moira was the youngest, and her father had been a Spanish Catholic called Xavier Perez, hence the unusual middle name that was such a godsend to an investigator. In the photographs Jett had given me, she looked both beautiful and vulnerable. Her skin was the colour of vanilla fudge and her huge brown eyes made her look like a nervous bambi peeping out from a halo of frizzy brown curls.

Jett and Moira had started dating in their early teens and they'd soon discovered that they both enjoyed writing songs. Moira wrote the poignant and enigmatic lyrics, Jett put them to music. She had never wanted to perform, seeing no need to compete with Jett's unique voice, but she'd done her best to organize gigs for him. He'd played a couple of local clubs, then she'd managed to get him a regular weekly spot in a new city centre wine bar. That had been the break they needed. Kevin, who'd bought the wine bar as a diversion from the family wholesale fashion business, immediately saw Jett's potential and informed the pair that he was going to manage them and to hell with the rag trade.

Seeing Jett now, it was hard to imagine what an enormous change it must have been for the two of them. Suddenly they were being wined and dined by Kevin Kleinman, a man who had a suit for every day of the week and then some left over.

Height, five foot, four inches, I typed in. She'd had a good figure too. The snapshots taken before Jett hit the top of the charts looked positively voluptuous. But later, she'd lost weight and her clothes had hung unbecomingly on her. Cutting through Jett's self-reproach, it seemed that

45

Moira had felt increasingly insignificant as Jett became the idol of millions.

So she had fallen for the scourge of the music industry. I could see how it had happened. Drugs are everywhere in rock, from the fans at the concerts to the recording studios. With Moira, it had all started when Kevin was piling on the pressure for more songs for the third album. She'd started taking speed to stay awake, working through the night with Jett on new songs. Soon she'd moved on to the more intense but shorter high of coke. Then she'd started freebasing coke and before too long she'd been chasing the dragon. Jett hadn't had a clue how to cope, so he'd just ignored it and tried to lose himself in his music.

Then one night, he'd come home and she hadn't been there. She'd just packed her bags and gone. He'd looked for her in a half-hearted way, asking around her family and friends, but I suspected that deep down he'd felt a kind of relief at not having to deal with her mood swings and erratic behaviour any longer. Now, his fear of falling into musical oblivion had spurred him into taking action. I could see why his entourage were nervous. The Return of the Junkie was not a feature eagerly awaited at Colcutt Manor.

I finished inputting all my notes, and checked my watch. Half-past six. If I was lucky, I might just be able to short circuit some of the tedium of tracing Moira. Her unusual middle name made the search through any computerized records a lot easier. I picked up the phone and rang Josh, a friend of mine who's a financial broker. In exchange for a slap-up meal every few months, he obligingly does credit checks on individuals for Mortensen and Brannigan.

His job gives him access to computerized credit records for almost everyone in the British Isles. These records tell him what credit cards they hold, whether they have ever defaulted on a loan, and whether there have ever been

County Court judgements against them for debt. Also, if you supply him with a person's full name and date of birth, he can usually come up with an address. Very handy. We could probably hack into the system and do it ourselves, but we do like to keep things semi-legal when we can. Besides, I like having dinner with Josh.

The next call I made was to ask for something strictly illegal. One of my neighbours on the estate is a detective constable with the vice squad. He's always happy to earn the twenty-five pounds I slip him for checking people out on the police national computer. If Moira had any kind of criminal record, I'd know by morning.

There was nothing more I could do that night to trace Moira Pollock. It had been a hell of a day. All I wanted was to go out and kick the shit out of someone. So I decided to do just that.

6

I shook my head to clear the sunburst of stars that filled my vision, trying to dodge the next blow. The woman who was bearing down on me was a good three inches taller and twenty pounds heavier than me and there was a mean look in her eyes. I tried to match her glare and circled her warily. She feinted a punch at me, but that opened up her defences and I swung my leg up and round in a short, fast arc. It caught her in the ribs. Even through her body protector, it winded her. She crashed at my feet, and I felt the last of the day's tensions flow out of me.

It was a burglar who got me into Thai boxing three years ago. Dennis O'Brien is what I like to think of as an honest villain. Although he feeds and clothes his wife and kids with the proceeds of other people's hard work, he's got his own rigid moral code that he adheres to more firmly than most of the supposedly honest citizens I know. Dennis would never rob an old lady, never use shooters, and he only steals from people he thinks can afford to be robbed. He never indulges in mindless vandalism, and always tries to leave houses as tidy as possible. He'd never grass a mate, and the one thing he hates more than anything else is a bent copper. After all, if you can't trust the police, who can you trust?

I'd been having a drink with Dennis one evening, asking his advice about an office I needed to have a quiet little

48

look round. In return, I was answering his questions about how I work. He'd been outraged when I'd revealed I had no self-defence skills.

'You want your head mending,' he exploded. 'There's a lot of very naughty people out there. They're not all like me, you know. Plenty of villains don't think twice about hitting a woman.'

I'd laughed and said, 'Dennis, I deal in white-collar crime. The sort of people I'm chasing don't think their fists have the answers.'

He'd interrupted, saying, 'Bollocks, Kate. Never mind work, living where you live, you need martial arts. I wouldn't bring the milk off the doorstep in your street without a black belt. Tell you what, you meet me tomorrow night and I'll have you sorted in no time.'

'Sorted' meant taking me to the club where his own teenage daughter was junior Thai boxing champion. I'd had a good look around, decided that the showers and the changing rooms were places where I'd be prepared to take my clothes off, and signed up there and then. I've never regretted it. It keeps me fit and gives me confidence when I'm up against the wall. And time has shown that just because a man has a fifty grand salary and a company Scorpio it doesn't mean he won't resort to violence when he's cornered. As long as the British government never takes us down the criminally insane road of the USA, where every two-bit mugger totes a gun, I guess it's all I'll need to keep me alive.

Tonight, I'd got what I came for. As I showered afterwards, my whole body felt loose and relaxed. I knew I could go home and listen sympathetically to Richard without biting his head off. And I knew that in the morning I'd be raring to go on the trail of Billy Smart and Moira Pollock.

I got home just after nine with a carrier bag bursting

with goodies from the Leen Hong in Chinatown. I let myself into Richard's house via the conservatory and found him sprawled on the sofa watching *A Fish Called Wanda* for what must have been the sixth time, a tall glass of Southern Comfort and soda beside him on the floor. Judging by the ashtray, he'd smoked a joint in tribute to each time he'd seen the movie. On the other hand, maybe he just hadn't emptied it for a week.

'Hi, Brannigan,' he greeted me without moving. 'Is the world still out there?'

'The important bits of it are in here,' I reported, waving the bag in the air. 'Fancy some salt and pepper ribs?'

That got a reaction. It's depressing to think that a Chinese takeaway provokes more excitement in my lover than my arrival. Richard jumped off the sofa and hugged me. 'What a woman,' he exclaimed. 'You really know what to give a man when he's down.'

He let me go and seized the bag from my hand. I went to his kitchen for some plates, but as soon as I looked in and saw the mound of dirty dishes in the sink, I gave up the idea. How Richard can live like this is beyond me, but I've learned the hard way that his priorities are different from mine. A dishwasher is never going to win a contest with an Armani suit. And I refuse to fall into the trap of washing his dishes for him. So I simply took a couple of pairs of chopsticks from a drawer, picked up the kitchen roll and headed back for the living room before Richard polished off all the food. I know from bitter experience just how fast he can go through Chinese food when the dope-induced raging munchies get him in their grip.

I was pissed off that I couldn't tell him about my assignment from Jett, because I really needed to pick his brains. However, Richard was still smarting from his humiliation the previous evening, and it didn't take much prompting from me to put some more flesh on the bare bones of my

50

information. The only hard part was getting him off the subject of Neil Webster.

'I just don't understand it,' he kept saying. 'Neil Webster, for God's sake. Nobody, I mean nobody, in the business has got a good word for the guy. He's ripped off more people than I've had hot spring rolls. He got fired from the *Daily Clarion* for fiddling expenses, you know. And when you think that every journalist in the history of newspapers has fiddled their expenses, you begin to realize just what a dickhead the guy must be.

'He's been in more barroom brawls than anybody else I know. And he treats people like shit. Rumour was, his first wife had a lot more black eyes than hot dinners from him. After he got the bullet from the *Clarion*, he set up as a freelance agency in Liverpool. He was bonking this really nice woman who worked for the local paper there. He persuaded her to bankroll him in his new venture. He even promised to marry her. On the day of the wedding, he left her standing like a pillock at the register office. That's when he took off to Spain. After he'd gone, she discovered he'd left her with a five grand phone bill, not to mention a load of other debts. Then her boss found out she'd been putting him down in the credits book for payments for jobs he hadn't actually done, so she got the boot. That's the kind of guy that Kevin thinks is right for the job.' He stopped speaking to attack another rib.

'Maybe Kevin's got something on Neil, something to keep him in line with,' I suggested.

'Dunno,' Richard mumbled through his Chinese. He swallowed. 'I guess it was just that Jett wasn't bothered enough about who did it to hold out for me.'

'Perhaps Kevin wants to make sure it's a whitewash job,' I tried.

Richard snorted with laughter. 'You mean he thinks he can keep Neil on a leash? He thinks he can tell Neil exactly what to do and Neil will do it? Shit, he's in for a rude awakening. Neil will feather his own nest, regardless of Kevin laying down the law.'

'Yes, but at the end of the day, Neil's not a rock journalist. You know exactly what stones to turn over, where to start looking if you wanted to dish some dirt, to get behind the headlines to the real story. But Neil doesn't even know where to start, so to some extent, he's going to have to go with whatever Kevin feeds him. And they've got him right where they want him, you know. According to Jett, Neil's got an office and everything right there at Colcutt. He's actually living there while he does the book.'

'That's exactly what I mean,' Richard pounced. 'Looking after number one. And he's the only one who will come out of this on the up, I'd put money on it. Kevin might think he can control Neil more than he could me, but I'd give you odds that Neil will end up biting the hand that feeds him, just you wait and see.'

'Sounds like a bad deal for Jett.'

'Wouldn't be the first time Kevin's done that. And it won't be the last.'

That sounded fascinating. And it was a good way to get off Neil and on to the other members of Jett's entourage. 'How do you mean?' I asked sweetly, helping myself to more vermicelli before it all disappeared into the human dustbin.

'Always seems to me that Jett has to work a lot harder than other people at his level in the business. I'd love to pin Kevin down as to why that is.'

'Maybe he just likes it,' I suggested.

Richard shook his head. 'Not the amount of stuff he does,' he said. 'He's always on the road for a couple of circuits a year. He should be able to get away with one tour, fewer venues, that sort of thing. On top of that, he's doing an album a year. And even though he hates it,

Kevin's always plugging him into chat shows. He even had him doing local radio slots earlier this year, can you believe it? Jett has hardly had any time off, I mean proper time off, for the last four years. He shouldn't have to do that. And the tour merchandise – they really push that stuff. There's nothing laid back about Kevin's operation, and somebody should be asking why. Maybe it is just bad deals, bad judgement. Or maybe they're making sure that when they retire they'll never have to lift a finger again. But if I was Jett, I'd be looking for a new manager.'

I put some of the lyrics down to sour grapes, but I filed the general melody away for future reference. As Richard tore into the spicy pork, I tried another strategy. 'Couldn't you go ahead anyway and write the unauthorized biography, warts and all?' I asked. 'You must know a lot about the things that Jett wouldn't necessarily want to make public. Like the split with . . . Moira, wasn't it?'

'Sure, I could spill any amount of beans,' Richard agreed. 'But I don't know if I want to do that. I mean, Jett's a mate.'

'He's got a funny way of showing it,' I mumbled through a mouthful of beef koon po.

'It would be the last exclusive I got from him.'

'There are plenty more people in the rock business who trust you,' I replied.

'But an awful lot of them wouldn't be happy about talking to me if I'd dropped Jett in it,' Richard reasoned.

'Surely they'd understand why you'd done it?' We were going down a side alley that wasn't taking me any further, but I couldn't help myself. Offering support to Richard was a lot more important to me than helping Jett.

Richard shrugged. 'I don't know. But anyway, there wouldn't be enough of a market for two books. Jett's not quite in the international megastar league.'

I got up and helped myself to a bottle of Perrier from the

executive drinks fridge Richard keeps in the living room. It had been a birthday present from a friendly roadie who'd stolen it from a Hilton room. 'What if . . .' I said slowly. 'What if you wrote a story for one of the Sunday tabloids. The things you won't be reading in Jett's autobiography, that kind of thing? You must have plenty up your sleeve like that.'

Wonders will never cease. Richard stopped eating. 'You know, Brannigan, you just might have something there . . . If I flogged it on the quiet, they could put a staff reporter's byline on it and that would protect my other contacts.'

That was enough to open the floodgates. I knew that when he was sober in the cold light of morning, Richard would have changed his mind about plastering Jett across the front pages of the gutter press. But by the time we made our amorous way to bed a couple of hours later, as far as Jett and his entourage were concerned, I had picked Richard's brains as clean as he'd picked the salt and pepper ribs.

7

The following morning, the sun was shining and I was full enough of the joys of spring to cycle into work. I was in the office even before Shelley, keying in all the information Richard had unwittingly given me the night before. I couldn't imagine how it could be relevant, but I'd rather have it neatly stored in my database just in case. It's a hell of a lot more reliable than my memory, especially when you consider how many brain cells shuffle off this mortal coil with every vodka and grapefruit juice. God help me if my computer ever gets the taste for Stolichnaya.

A few minutes after nine, Shelley put a call through to me. It was my friendly neighbourhood copper. Derek's a career constable. He doesn't like the hassle that his seniors have to live with, so he tries to keep his head down whenever promotion is suggested. He does, however, like the vice squad. It makes him feel virtuous and he likes the perks. I've yet to meet a thirsty vice cop.

'Hi, Kate,' Derek greeted me cheerfully. 'I popped round to the house, but I couldn't get a reply, so I thought I'd try a long shot and call you at the office.'

'Very funny,' I replied. 'Sorry I missed you, but some of us have to work long hours keeping the streets safe.'

He chuckled. 'With your respect for the police, Kate, you really should have stuck to being a lawyer. Any road, I've got what you wanted. Your young lady does indeed have a record. First was five years ago. Soliciting. Fifty pound fine. There are three others for soliciting, ending up with two years' probation just over a year ago. There's also Class A possession charge. A small amount of heroin, personal use. She got a three hundred pound fine for that, but the fine must have been paid because there's no record of a warrant for non-payment.'

I scribbled frantically to keep up with his sad recital of what had become of the talented writer of Jett's best lyrics. 'What address have you got?'

'I've got as many addresses as there are offences. All in the Chapeltown area of Leeds.'

Just what I needed. I didn't know Leeds well, but I knew enough to know that this was bedsitterland. The kind of area where junkies and prostitutes rub shoulders with the chronically poor and students who try to convince themselves there's something glamorous about such Bohemian surroundings. It isn't an easy belief to sustain, especially after the murderous depredations of the Yorkshire Ripper ten years ago. I copied down the three latest addresses as Derek read them out at dictation speed. I had no real hopes of them but at least I now knew that when Moira had fled from Jett she'd headed over the Pennines. It was a start.

I thanked Derek and promised to drop his money in that evening. It looked like I was going to have to go over to Leeds, which meant I wouldn't be looking after the Smart brothers for another day. That didn't worry me as much as it perhaps should have, because they'd followed an identical pattern on the two previous Thursdays. The days I still needed to keep watch were Mondays and Tuesdays when they did most of their irregular deliveries. I knew if Bill was worried about their surveillance he could bring in one of the freelances that we occasionally use for routine jobs when we're overstretched. The extra cash we were making on Jett would more than cover the outlay.

Before I left, I gave Josh a quick call to see if his computer searches had come up with anything. Like Derek, all he had for me was bad news. When she left Jett, Moira had had a five-star credit rating. Within two years of her departure, she'd run up a string of bad debts that made me wince. She owed everybody – credit cards, store accounts, hire purchase, two major bank loans. There were several County Court judgements against her, and a handful more still pending. The court hadn't been able to find her to serve the papers. That really filled me with confidence. But it also explained why she'd not been staying at any one address for too long.

I left the office by half-past nine and cycled home, where I changed into a pair of jogging pants that were past their best and a green Simply Red road crew sweatshirt, one of the few donations from Richard that hadn't been despatched straight back next door. If I was going down those mean streets, then I wanted to make damn sure I looked a bit mean myself. I pulled on a pair of hi-top Reeboks and a padded leather jacket that was a bit scuffed round the edges. I picked up the last bottle of mineral water from the fridge and threw a packet of fresh pasta with yesterday's sell-by date into the bin. I made a mental note to hit the supermarket on my way home.

I didn't want to risk getting snarled up in the crosstown traffic, so I took the longer but faster motorway route out to the western edge of the C-shaped almost-orbital motorway and picked up the M62 to cross the bleak moors. Within the hour, I was driving out of Leeds city centre north into Chapeltown, singing along with Pat Benatar's *Best Shots* to lift my spirits.

I cruised slowly around the dirty streets, attracting some equally dirty looks when the whores who were already out working moved forward to proposition me, only to discover a woman driver. I found the last address that Derek had given me without too much difficulty. Like so many of the Yorkshire stone houses in the area, it had obviously once been the home of a prosperous burgher. It was a big Victorian property, standing close to its neighbours. Behind the scabby paintwork of the window frames there was an assortment of grubby curtains, no two rooms matching. In front of the house, what had once been the garden had been badly asphalted over, with weeds sprouting through the cracks in the tarmac. I got out of the car and carefully set the alarm.

I climbed the four steps up to a front door that looked as if it had been kicked in a few times and examined an array of a dozen bells. Only a couple had names by them, and neither was Moira's. Sighing deeply, I rang the bottom bell. Nothing happened, and I started working my way systematically up the bells till I reached the fifth. I heard the sound of a window being opened and I stepped back and looked up. To my left, on the first floor, a black woman wearing a faded blue towelling dressing gown was leaning out. 'What d'you want?' she demanded aggressively.

I debated whether to apologize for troubling her, but decided that I didn't want to sound like the social services department. 'I'm looking for Moira Pollock. She still living here?'

The woman scowled suspiciously. 'Why d'you want Moira?'

'We used to be in the same line of business,' I lied, hoping I looked like a possible candidate for the meat rack.

'Well, she ain't here. She moved out, must be more'n a year ago.' The woman moved back and started to close the window.

'Hang on a minute. Where would I find her? Do you know?'

She paused. 'I ain't seen her around in a long while.

Your best bet's that pub down Chapeltown Road, the 'ambleton. She used to drink there.'

My thanks were drowned by the screech of the sash window as the woman slammed it back down. I walked back to the car, shifted a large black and white cat which had already taken up residence on the warm bonnet, and set off to find the pub.

The Hambleton Hotel was about a mile and a half away from Moira's last known address. It was roadhouse style, in grimy yellow and red brick with the mock-Tudor gables much beloved by 1930s pub architects. The inside looked as if it hadn't been cleaned since then. Even at half-past eleven in the morning, it was fairly lively. A couple of black men were playing the fruit machine, and a youth was dropping coins into a jukebox which was currently playing Jive Bunny. By the bar was a small knot of women who were already dressed for work in short skirts and low-cut sweaters. Their exposed flesh looked pale and unappetizing, but at least it lacked the bluish tinge that ten minutes' exposure to the cold spring air would lend it.

I walked up to the bar, aware of the eyes on me, and ordered a half of lager. Something told me that a Perrier wouldn't do much for my cover story. The blowsy barmaid looked me up and down as she poured my drink. As I paid, I told her to take one herself. She shook her head and muttered, 'Too early for me.' I was taken aback. Before I could ask her about Moira, I felt a hand on my shoulder.

I tensed and turned round slowly. One of the black men who'd been playing the fruit machine was standing behind me with a frown on his face. He was nearly six feet tall, slim and elegant in chinos and a shiny black satin shirt under a dove grey full length Italian lambskin coat that looked like it cost six months of my mortgage. His hair was cut in a perfect flat-top, accentuating his high cheek-

59

bones and strong jaw. His eyes were bloodshot and I could smell minty breath-spray as he leaned forward into my face and breathed, 'I hear you been looking for a friend of mine.'

'News travels fast,' I responded, trying to move away from his hot breath, but failing thanks to the bar behind me.

'What d'you want with Moira?' There was a note of menace in his voice that pissed me off. I controlled the urge to kick him across the bar and said nothing as he leaned even closer. 'Don't try telling me you're on the game. And don't try telling me you're a cop. Those fuckers only come down here mob-handed. So who are you, and what d'you want with Moira?'

I know when the time for games is past. I reached into my pocket and produced a business card. I handed it to the pimp who was giving me a severe case of claustrophobia. It worked. He backed off a good six inches. 'It's nothing heavy. It's an old friend of hers who wants to make contact. If it works out, there could be good money in it for her.'

He studied the card and glared at me. 'Private Investigator,' he sneered. 'Well, baby, you're not gonna find Moira here. She checked out a long time ago.'

My heart did that funny kind of flip it does when I get bad news. Two days ago, I couldn't have cared less if Moira were alive or dead. Now I was surprised to find that I cared a lot. 'You don't mean . . . ?'

His lip curled in a sneer again. I suspected he'd perfected it in front of a mirror at the age of twelve and hadn't progressed to anything more adult. 'She was still alive when she left here. But the way she was pumping heroin into her veins, you'll be lucky to find her like that now. I kicked her out a year ago. She was no use to anybody. All she cared about was getting another fix into her.'

'Any idea where she went?' I asked with sinking heart.

He shrugged. 'That depends on how much it's worth.'

'And that depends on how good the information is.'

He smiled crookedly. 'Well, you're not going to know that till you check it out, are you? And I don't give credit. A hundred to tell you where she went.'

'Do you seriously think I'd carry that kind of cash in a shit pit like this? Fifty.'

He shook his head. 'No way. Fancy bit of skirt like you, you'll have a hole-in-the-wall card. Come back here in half an hour with a oner and I'll tell you where she went. And don't think you'll get the word off somebody else. Nobody round here's going to cross George.'

I knew when I was beaten. Whoever George was, he clearly had his patch sewn up tight. Wearily, I nodded and headed back towards the car.

8

The short drive from Leeds to its neighbouring city of Bradford is like traversing a continent. Crossing the city boundary, I found myself driving through a traditional Muslim community. Little girls were covered from head to foot, the only flesh on display their pale brown faces and hands. All the women who walked down the pavements with a leisurely rolling gait had their heads covered, and several were veiled. In contrast, most of the men dressed in western clothes, though many of the older ones wore the traditional white cotton baggy trousers and loose tops with incongruously heavy winter coats over them, greying beards spilling down their fronts. I passed a newly erected mosque, its bright red brick and toytown minarets a sharp contrast to the grubby terraces that surrounded it. Most of the grocery shops had signs in Arabic, and the butchers announced Hal-al meat for sale. It almost came as a culture shock to see signs in English directing me to the city centre.

I stopped at a garage to buy a street directory. There were three Asian men standing around inside the shop, and another behind the counter. I felt like a piece of meat as they eyed me up and down and made comments to each other. I didn't need to speak the language to catch their drift.

Back in the car, I looked up my destination in the map's index and worked out the best way to get there. George's information represented the worst value for money I'd had in a long time, but I wasn't in any position to stick around and argue the toss. All he'd been able to tell me was that Moira had moved to Bradford and was working the streets of the red light district round Manningham Lane. He either didn't know or wouldn't tell the name of her pimp, though he claimed that she was working for a black guy rather than an Asian.

It was just after one when I parked in a quiet side street off Manningham Lane. As I got out of the car, the smell of curry spices hit me and I realized I was ravenous. It had been a long time since last night's Chinese, and I had to start my inquiries somewhere. I went into the first eating place I came to, a small café on the corner. Three of the half dozen formica-topped tables were occupied. The clientele was a mixture of Asian men, working girls and a couple of lads who looked like building labourers. I went up to the counter, where a teenager in a grubby chef's jacket was standing behind a cluster of pans on a hotplate. On the wall was a whiteboard, which offered Lamb Rogan Josh, Chicken Madras, Mattar Panir and Chicken Jalfrezi. I ordered the lamb, and the youth ladled a generous helping into a bowl, opened a hot cupboard and handed me three chapatis. A couple of weeks before, their hygiene standards would have driven me out the door a lot faster than I'd come in. However, on the Smart surveillance, I'd learned that hunger has an interesting effect on the eyesight. After the greasy spoons I'd been forced to feed in up and down the country, I couldn't claim the cleanliness standards of an Egon Ronay any longer. And this café was a long way from the bottom of my current list.

I sat down at the table next to the prostitutes and helped myself to one of the spoons rammed into a drinking tumbler on the table. The first mouthful made me realize just how hungry I'd been. The curry was rich and tasty, the meat tender and plentiful. And all for less than the price of a motorway sandwich. I'd heard before that the best places to eat in Bradford were the Asian cafés and restaurants, but I'd always written it off as the inverse snobbery of pretentious foodies. For once, I was glad to be proved wrong.

I wiped my bowl clean with the last of the chapatis, and pulled out the most recent photograph I had of Moira. I shifted in my chair till I was facing the prostitutes, who were enjoying a last cigarette before they went out to brave an afternoon's trade. The café was so small I was practically sitting among them. I flipped the photograph on to the table and cut through their desultory chatter. 'I'm looking for her,' I explained. 'I'm not Old Bill, and I'm not after her money either. I just want a chat. An old friend wants to get in touch. Nothing heavy. But if she wants to stay out of touch, that's up to her.' I dropped one of my business cards on the table by the picture.

The youngest of the three women, a tired-looking Eurasian, looked me up and down and said, 'Fuck off.'

I raised my eyebrows and remarked. 'Only asking. You're sure you don't know where I'll find her? It could be a nice little earner, helping me out.'

The other two looked uncertainly at each other, but the tough little Eurasian got to her feet and retorted angrily, 'Stuff your money up your arse. We don't like pigs round here, whether they're private pigs or ones in uniform. Why don't you just fuck off back to Manchester before you get hurt?' She turned to her companions and snarled, 'Come on, girls, I don't like the smell in here.'

The three departed, teetering on their high heels, and I picked up the photo and my card with a sigh. I hadn't really expected much co-operation, but I'd been a bit surprised by the vehemence of their reaction. Clearly the pimps in Bradford had drilled their employees in the perils of talking to strange women. I was going to have to do this the hard way, out on the streets and in the pubs till I found someone who was prepared to take the risk of talking to me.

I left the café and went back to move the car. I didn't feel happy about leaving it parked in such a quiet street for any length of time. I'd look for a nice big pub car park fronting on the main drag for a bit more security. As I started the engine, I was aware of a flash of movement at the edge of my peripheral vision and the passenger door was wrenched open. Bloody central locking, I cursed silently. My mouth dried with fear, and I thrust the car into gear, hoping to dislodge my assailant.

With a flurry of legs and curses, a woman threw herself into the passenger seat and slammed the door. I almost stalled in my surprise. 'Just keep fucking driving,' she yelled at me.

I obeyed, of course. It seemed the only sensible thing to do. If she was carrying a blade, I wasn't going to win a close encounter inside my Nova. I flashed a glance at her and recognized one of the women who'd been in the café. But she gave me no chance to ask questions. At the end of the street, she shouted at me to turn left, then right. About a mile from the café, she stopped shouting and muttered, 'OK, you can stop now.'

I pulled in to the kerb and demanded, 'What the hell is going on?'

She looked nervously behind us, then visibly relaxed. 'I didn't want anybody to see me talking to you. Kim would shop me soon as look at me.'

'OK,' I nodded. 'So why were you so keen to talk to me?'

'Is it true, what you said back there? You're not after Moira for anything?' There was a look in her pale blue eyes as if she desperately wanted to trust someone and wasn't sure if I was the right person. Her skin looked

65

muddy and dead, and there was a nest of pimples round her nose. She had the look of one of life's professional victims.

'I'm not bringing her trouble,' I promised. 'But I need to find her. If she tells me she doesn't want to make contact with her friend, that's fine by me.'

The woman, who in truth didn't look much older than nineteen, nervously chewed a hangnail. I was beginning to wish she'd light a cigarette so I'd have an excuse to open the window – the smell of her cheap perfume was making me gag. As if reading my thoughts, she lit up and exhaled luxuriously, asking, 'You're not working for her pimp, then?'

'Absolutely not. Do you know where I can find her?' I wound down the window and gulped in fresh air as unobtrusively as possible.

The girl shook her head and her bleached blonde hair crackled like a forest fire. 'Nobody's seen her for about six months. She just disappeared. She was doin' a lot of smack and she was out of it most of the time. She was workin' for this Jamaican guy called Stick, and he was really pissed off with her 'cos she wasn't workin' half the time 'cos she was out of her head. Then one day she just wasn't around no more. One of the girls asked Stick where she'd gone and he just smacked her and told her to keep her nose out.'

'Where would I find Stick?' I asked.

The girl shrugged. 'Be down the snooker hall most afternoons. There or the video shop down Lumb Lane. But you don't want to mess with Stick. He don't take shit from nobody.'

'Thanks for the advice,' I said sincerely. 'Why are you telling me all this?' I added, taking thirty pounds out of my wallet.

The notes vanished with a speed Paul Daniels would

have been proud of. 'I liked Moira. She was nice to me when I had my abortion. I think she maybe needs help. You find her, you tell her Gina said hello,' the girl said, opening the car door.

'Will do,' I said to the empty air as she slammed the door and clattered off down the pavement.

It took me ten minutes to find the snooker hall off Manningham Lane. It occupied the first floor above a row of small shops. Although it was just after two, most of the dozen or so tables were occupied. I barely merited a glance from most of the players as I walked in. I stood for a few minutes just watching. Curls of smoke spiralled upwards under the strong overhead table lights, and the atmosphere was one of masculine seriousness. This wasn't the place for a few frivolous frames with the boys after work.

As I looked on, a burly white man with tattoos snaking up both his bare arms came over to me. 'Hello, doll. You look like you're looking for a man. Will I do?' he asked jocularly.

'Not unless you've had your skin bleached,' I told him. He looked confused. 'I'm looking for Stick,' I explained.

He raised his eyebrows. 'A nice girl like you? I don't think you're his type, doll.'

'We'll let Stick be the judge of that, shall we? Can you point him out to me?' I demanded. It seemed like a waste of time to tell this ape that I was neither nice, nor a girl, nor a doll.

He pointed down the hall. 'He's on the last table on the left. If he's not interested, doll, I'll be waiting right here.'

I bit back my retort and headed down the aisle between the three-quarter-sized tables. At the end of the room, there were four competition-sized tables. A chunky black man was bending over the last table on the left. Behind him, in the shadows, was the man I took to be Stick. I could see how he'd earned the name. He was over six feet tall, but skinny as his cue. He looked like a stick insect, with long, thin arms protruding from a white t-shirt and twig-like legs encased in tight leather trousers. His head was hidden in the shadows, but as I approached, he emerged and I could see a gaunt face with hollow cheeks and sunken eyes surrounded by black curly hair grown in a thick halo to counteract the pinhead impression he'd otherwise have given.

At the edge of the light, I stopped and waited till the man at the table made his stroke. The red ball he'd been aiming for shuddered in the jaws of the pocket before coming to rest against one cushion. With an expression of disgust, he moved away, chalking his cue. The thin man walked up to line up his shot and I stepped forward into the light.

He frowned up at me, and I met his eyes. They were like bottomless pools, without any discernible expression. It was like looking into a can of treacle. I swallowed and said, 'George from Leeds said I should talk to you.'

Stick straightened up, but the frown stayed in place. 'I know a George from Leeds?'

'George from the Hambleton Hotel. He said you could help me.'

Stick made a great show of carefully chalking his cue, but I could tell he was sizing me up from under his heavy eyebrows. Eventually he put his cue on the table and said to his opponent, 'Be right back. Do not move a fucking ball. I have total recall.'

He strode across the hall and I followed him as he unlocked a side door and entered a stuffy, windowless office. He settled down in a scruffy armchair behind a scratched wooden desk and waved me to one of the three plastic chairs set against the wall.

He pulled a silver toothpick from his pocket and placed

it in his mouth. 'I'm not like George,' he said, the traces of a Caribbean accent still strong in his voice. 'I don't usually talk to strangers.'

'So what's this? A job interview?'

He smiled. Even his teeth were narrow and pointed, like a cat's. 'You too little for a cop,' he said. 'You wearing too much for a whore. You not twitchy enough for a pusher. Sweatshirt like that, maybe you a roadie's lady looking for some merchandise for the band. I don't think I've got anything to be afraid of, lady.'

I couldn't help smiling. In spite of myself, I felt a sneaking liking for Stick. 'I hear you might be able to help me. I'm looking for somebody I think you know.'

'What's your interest?' he demanded, caution suddenly closing his face like a slammed door.

I'd given the matter of what to say to Stick some thought on the way there. I took a deep breath and said, 'I'm a private inquiry agent. I'm trying to get in touch with this woman.' Again, I took out the photograph of Moira and handed it over.

He glanced at it without a flicker of recognition. 'Who she?'

'Her name is Moira Pollock. Until recently, she was working the streets round here. I'm told you might know where she went.'

Stick shrugged. 'I don't know where you get your information, but I don't think I can help you, lady. Matter of interest, what you want her for?'

In spite of his nonchalant appearance, I could see Stick had taken the bait. I reeled out my prepared speech. 'Some years back, she was in the rock business. Then she dropped out of sight. But all those years, her work's been earning her money. The record company held on to it and they won't hand it over to anyone. Now her family badly need that money. They want to sue the record company. But to do that, they either need to prove Moira's dead or get her to agree.'

'Sounds like a lot of bread to me, if it's worth paying you to find out. So you working for this Moira's family?'

'A family friend,' I hedged.

He nodded, as if satisfied. 'Seems to me I might have heard her name. This family friend . . . They pay your expenses?'

I sighed. This job was turning into a cash-flow nightmare. And none of my payees were the kind to hand out receipts. 'How much?' I groaned.

Stick flashed his smile again and took a joint out of the desk drawer. He lit it with a gold Dunhill and took a deep drag. 'A monkey,' he drawled.

'You what?' I spluttered with genuine surprise. He had to be kidding. He couldn't really think I would pay five hundred pounds for a lead on Moira's whereabouts.

'That's the price, take it or leave it. Lot of money involved, it's got to be worth it,' Stick said calmly.

I shook my head. 'Forget it,' I replied. 'You told me yourself, you don't even know the woman. So anything you can tell me has got to be pretty chancy.'

He scowled. He'd forgotten the pit his caution had dug for him. 'Maybe I was just being careful,' he argued.

'Yeah, and maybe you're blagging me now,' I retorted. 'Look, I've had an expensive day. I can give you a hundred now, without consulting my client. Anything more and I have to take advice, and I don't think I'll get the go-ahead to pay five hundred pounds to someone who didn't even know Moira. You can take it or leave it, Stick. A definite oner now, or a probable zero later.'

He leaned back in his chair and gave a low chuckle. 'You got a business card, lady?' he asked.

Puzzled, I nodded and handed one over. He studied it, then tucked it in his pocket. 'You one tough lady, Kate

Brannigan. A man never knows when he might need a private eye. OK, let me see the colour of your money.'

I counted out five twenties on the desk top, but kept my hand on the cash. 'Moira's address?' I demanded.

'She left the streets about six months ago. She checked in at the Seagull Project. It's a laundry.'

'A what?' I had a bizarre vision of Moira loading table-cloths into washing machines.

Stick grinned. 'A place where they clean you up. A drug project.'

That sounded more like it. 'Where is this Seagull Project?' I asked.

'It's on one of those side streets behind the photography museum. I can't remember the name of it, but it's the third or fourth on the left as you go up the hill. A couple of terraced houses knocked together.'

I got to my feet. 'Thanks, Stick.'

'No problem. You find Moira and she gets her bread, you tell her she owes Stick the other four hundred pounds for information received.'

9

I parked the car in a pay and display behind the National Film and Television Museum. I walked round to the museum foyer and found a telephone booth which miraculously contained a phone book. I looked up the Seagull Project, and copied its address and number into my notebook. I checked my watch and decided I deserved a coffee, so I walked upstairs to the coffee bar and settled myself down in a window seat looking out over the city centre.

The pale spring sun had broken through the grey clouds, and the old Victorian buildings looked positively romantic. Built on the sweatshops of the wool industry, the once prosperous city had fought its urban decay and depression by jumping on the tourism bandwagon that's turning England into one gigantic theme park. Now that the nearby Yorkshire countryside had been translated into The Brontë Country, Bradford had seized its opportunity with both hands. Even the biscuits in the tearooms and snack bars are called Brontë. But it was the Asian community who'd really revitalized the city's slum areas, producing oases of industrial and wholesaling prosperity. I'd been around a few of those in the past few weeks, hot on the trail of Billy Smart's personal mobile circus.

I tore my eyes away from the view and looked up the Seagull Project's address in my street directory. Stick's information was sound so far. The street was third on the left, off the hill that climbed up the side of the Alhambra Theatre. I finished my coffee and set out on foot.

Five minutes later, I was outside two three-storey stone-built terraced houses that had been knocked together with a board on the front proclaiming 'Seagull Project'. I stood around uncertainly for a few minutes, not at all sure what was the best way to play it. The one thing I was sure about was that introducing myself and explaining my mission was the certain route to failure. Bitter experience has taught me that voluntary organizations make the Trappists look like blabbermouths.

I eventually settled on my course of action. More lies. If my childhood Sunday School teacher ever finds out about me, she'll put me straight to the top of the list for the burning fire. I walked up the path and turned the door handle. I walked into a clean, airy hallway painted white with grey carpeting. A large sign pointing to the left read 'All visitors please report to reception.'

For once, I did as I was told and walked into a small, tidy office. Behind a wide desk, a mop of carrot red hair was bent over a pile of papers so high it almost hid its owner from view. I felt a pang of sympathy. I knew just how she felt. My own hatred of paperwork is so strong that I ignore it till Shelley practically locks me in my office with dire threats of what she'll do to me if I dare to emerge before it's finished. It's just the same at home; if I didn't force myself to sit down once a month and pay all the bills, the bailiffs would be a permanent fixture on the doorstep.

As the reception door closed behind me, a pale, freckled face looked up. 'Hi, can I help you?' she asked in a tired voice.

'I don't know, but I hope so,' I replied with my most ingratiating smile. 'I was wondering if you needed any volunteer workers here right now?'

The tiredness evaporated from her face and she grinned.

'Music to my ears!' she exclaimed. 'Those are the first good words I've heard today. Sit down, make yourself comfortable.' She gestured expansively at the two worn office chairs on my side of the desk. As I settled on the less dilapidated one, she introduced herself. 'I'm Jude. I'm one of the project's three full-time employees. We're always desperate for volunteers and fund-raisers.' She opened a drawer and took out a long form. 'Do you mind if I fill this out while we talk? I know I'm being quick off the mark, but it saves time in the long run if you do decide to help us.'

I shook my head. 'No problem. My name's Kate Barclay.' I knew Richard wouldn't mind me borrowing his name. After all, he knew I'd never be making the loan permanent.

'And where do you live, Kate?' Jude asked, scribbling furiously. I plucked a number out of the air and attached it to Leeds Road, which I knew was long enough to reduce the chances of her knowing a near neighbour.

We went through the formalities quickly. I told her I'd been working abroad as a teacher and that I'd just moved to Bradford with my boyfriend. I explained I'd heard about the project from the city council's voluntary services unit and had come along to offer my services. All the while, Jude nodded and wrote on her form. At the end of my recital, she looked up and said, 'Have you any experience with this kind of work?'

'Yes. That's why I came to you. We've been living in Antwerp for the last three years and I did some work with a drug rehabilitation charity there,' I lied fluently.

'Right,' said Jude. 'I'd no idea they ran something like that in Antwerp.'

I smiled sweetly and refrained from saying that that's why I'd chosen the Belgian city. No one in Britain has ever been to Antwerp, though I don't know why. It's more attractive, interesting and friendly than almost any other city I've ever been to. It's where Bill's parents came from originally and he still has a tribe of aunts, uncles and cousins there that he visits regularly. I've been over with him a couple of times, and fell in love with it at first sight. I always use Antwerp now for obscure cover stories. No one ever questions it. Jude was no exception. She swallowed my story, made a note on her form then got to her feet.

'What I'll do is show you round now, to let you see exactly what we've got going here. Then I suggest you come to our weekly collective meeting tomorrow evening and see if you feel you'll fit in with us, and we feel we'll fit in with you,' she added, moving towards the door.

My heart sank. The thought of enduring a meeting of the Seagull Project's collective filled me with gloom. I hate the endless circular debate of collectives. I like decisions to be made logically, with the pros and cons neatly laid out. I know all the theory about how consensus is supposed to make everyone feel they have a stake in the decision-making. But in my experience, it usually ends up with everyone feeling they've been hard done by. I couldn't imagine any reason why the Seagull Project would be any different.

I hid my despair behind a cheerful smile and followed Jude on her tour of the building. My target was clearly the second room we entered. There were filing cabinets the length of one wall and an IBM PC clone on one of the two desks. As well as its hard disc drive, I noted a slot for 5.25" floppies. A man in his early thirties was sitting at the computer keyboard, and Jude introduced him as Andy.

Andy looked up and grinned vaguely at me before returning to his keyboard.

'The filing cabinets hold details of all the clients we've

had through here, all the other agencies we work with, and all our workers. We're trying to transfer all our records to computer, most recent cases first, but it's going to take a while,' Jude explained as we left Andy to his task. I noticed that the only lock on the door was a simple Yale.

The other office on the ground floor was the fund-raising office. Jude explained that Seagull was kept on the wing by a mixture of local authority and national grants and charitable donations. The staff consisted of herself as administrator, a psychiatrist and a qualified nurse. They had an arrangement with a local inner-city group practice, and there were always a few biomedical sciences students from the university who were glad to help.

The first floor contained a couple of consulting rooms, two meeting rooms and a common room for the addicts who were living in. On the top floor, addicts in the early stages of kicking heroin sweated and moaned through the first weeks of their agony. If they made it through that, they moved on to a halfway house owned by the project, which tried to find them permanent jobs and homes well away from the temptations of their old stamping grounds. The whole place seemed clean and cheerful, if threadbare, and I thought that Moira could have done a lot worse for herself.

'We run an open door policy here,' Jude explained as we made our way back downstairs. 'We have to. As it is, we have to turn more away than we can treat. But they're free to go any time. That way, if they make it they know they've done it themselves and not had a cure imposed on them. We believe it makes them less likely to fall into the habit again.'

I knew better than to ask about their success rate. It would only depress Jude to talk about it, and she seemed so happy to have a new volunteer on her hands I didn't want to disappoint her any more than I was going to have to do anyway. As we reached the front door, I shook Jude's hand and asked when I should turn up the following evening.

'Come about half-past eight,' she said. 'The meeting starts at seven, but we have a lot of confidential stuff to get through first. You'll have to ring the bell when you get here because the front door's locked at six.'

'Open door policy?' I queried.

'To keep people out, not in,' Jude pointed out with a wry smile. 'See you then.'

'I can hardly wait,' I muttered under my breath as I walked down the path and headed back to the car. I felt a complete shit, having raised her hopes of finding another volunteer. Maybe I could pitch Jett into giving them a substantial donation once I'd reunited him with Moira. After all, he'd said he'd be happy to give everything he owned to get her back.

It was just after eight when I drew up at the foot of the carriage turning-circle outside Colcutt Manor. On the way back to Manchester, I'd dictated a report for Shelley to type up and fax to Jett so he'd know I wasn't just sitting around collecting my daily retainer. I pulled off the motor-way to hit the ASDA superstore. I wandered around the aisles trying to fill my trolley only with the essential items on my mental shopping list, but I fell by the wayside at the deli counter, as usual, and loaded up with a dozen little treats to cheer myself up. Then I called the manor to ask for the fax number. I asked to speak to Jett. That was my first mistake.

'I'm sorry, Jett's unavailable at present,' Gloria informed me, unable to keep the spark of pleasure from her voice.

'Gloria,' I warned, 'I haven't got the energy to play games right now. Let me speak to him, please.'

'He really is unavailable,' she protested, her voice going

from silky to sulky. 'They're in the recording studio. But he left a message for you,' she admitted grudgingly.

'And are you going to tell me or are we going to play twenty questions?'

'Jett said that he wants you to come round and give him a progress report.'

'I have a progress report right here. I'm about to drop it off in my secretary's in-tray. It'll be on your desk tomorrow morning,' I told her.

'He wants you here in person,' she retorted smugly.

I sighed. 'I'll be there in an hour.' I dropped the phone back in the cradle and stomped back to the car. Unfortunately, the trolley wouldn't go in a straight line, so the effect wasn't quite what I'd had in mind. Luckily there were no small children around to laugh. That saved me the aggravation of an assault charge.

I really wasn't in the mood for trekking over to Colcutt. Apart from anything else, my carton of double choc chip ice-cream would have melted by the time I got home. But I couldn't see any alternative. If I refused, it would give Gloria more ammunition than she'd need to see me off. Besides, we were charging Jett such astronomical fees I could hardly deny him a face-to-face. Maybe I could ask permission to put my ice-cream in their freezer.

At least Gloria had grown out of the silly childishness with the entryphone. This time she let me in right away. I was surprised to find the circle in front of the house crammed with the kind of motors the likes of me don't even know the price of. Top of the range Mercs, BMWs, even a couple of Porsches. It looked like a march past of Billy Smart's hire cars. For somebody who was working hard only an hour ago, Jett sure knew how to throw an impromptu party I thought as I opened the front door to a blast of Queen.

I looked uncertainly round the hall, not sure where to

78

start a search for Jett. The music seemed to be coming from everywhere rather than one specific room, though the noise of raised voices was definitely on the left somewhere. I'd just set off on the long walk to what was probably once the ballroom when Tamar practically flattened me as she bounced out of a loo tucked under the stairs.

She giggled tipsily as I grabbed at her to steady myself. 'Well, well, well,' she gurgled. 'If it isn't our very own Sherlock Holmes. Come to check your burglar alarms, have you? Well, you've picked the wrong night.'

I pasted a smile on my tired face. 'Why's that, Tamar?'

'Celebration. World and his dog all celebrating the fact that we've finally got one bastard track that everyone's happy with. Jett's actually managed to write something that hasn't put the entire household to sleep.' She hiccuped and pulled away from me to head unsteadily towards the din. 'Whoops,' she muttered. 'Not supposed to say that to the hired help. Anyway, what exactly are you doing here?' she added, pirouetting so that her sequinned jacket sparkled, and fixing me with a bleary stare.

'Jett wanted to see me,' I said. Well, it was more or less true.

'About burglar alarms? At this time of night? Today?' Then the incredulity vanished from her voice, replaced by suspicion. 'You're not really installing a new alarm, are you?'

I shrugged. It wasn't my job to tell her my business. Apart from the rules of confidentiality, if Jett hadn't told her what I was doing, I certainly wasn't about to bring her wrath down on my head. 'That fucking bitch,' she swore under her breath. She tossed her expensively tousled hair back from her forehead and stormed down the hall. Curious, I followed her back towards the front door and into the office, where Gloria sat at her word processor, apparently doing the housekeeping accounts, judging by the pile of bills beside her. She glanced up at Tamar, then coolly carried on typing.

'You told me she was here to sort out a burglar alarm,' Tamar accused Gloria, a mottled flush rising from her neck to her cheeks.

Gloria's fingers didn't even falter. 'And that's what I'll tell you now if you ask properly instead of barging in here like a spoilt child,' she said primly. She stopped typing and ran a hand over her blonde hair, pulled back so tightly that in the light from her desk lamp it looked like it had been painted on.

'She's looking for Moira, isn't she?' Tamar raged.

'Why don't you ask Jett? He'll tell you anything he wants you to know,' Gloria replied insultingly. I almost wished Tamar would flatten her. It would have made my day, and I wouldn't mind betting I wouldn't have been alone.

Instead, Tamar, who seemed to have sobered up under the influence of so much adrenalin, pushed past me and went back up the hall at a speed I wouldn't have believed possible on four-inch stilettos. I threw a vague smile in Gloria's direction and followed her. The cabaret was worth the trip.

I caught up with Tamar on the threshold of what looked like it had once been a Regency ballroom. The plaster swags were still in place. But everything had been painted gold and black. It would have given the National Trust an apoplexy, or a surfeit, or one of those other things they were always dying of way back then. There were no Regency bucks there tonight, however, just a couple of dozen ageing rockers with a fascinating array of bimbettes on their knees, arms or various other parts of their anatomy. It was hard to tell in the dim light.

Jett was leaning on the gilded mantelpiece, his arm round Kevin in a friendly sort of way. As we approached,

I could see the unfocused look of a man who is on his way to being seriously drunk. It was quite an achievement for someone who had been in the studio just over an hour before. It must have been some track he'd just laid down. Tamar landed like a cloudburst on his parade.

'Why didn't you tell me she was looking for Moira?' she hissed.

Jett turned away from us and stared bleakly at the wall. Tamar grabbed his arm and repeated her question. Kevin quickly moved behind her, gripped her tightly above both elbows and stepped back. She had no choice but to move with him. Using the same grip, he turned her round and frogmarched her out of the door. She was so astonished she didn't say a word till they were halfway across the room. But then her yells caused less of a stir than a mugging in Moss-side. As far as everyone else was concerned, it was just a bit of good clean fun.

I moved closer to Jett. 'You wanted a report,' I said. 'I'm making progress. I know where she was a few months ago. By tomorrow night, I should have a current address.'

He turned his head to face me. When I got a whiff of the alcohol on his breath, I wished he hadn't bothered. 'Is she all right?' he slurred.

There wasn't a way to soften the blow. I called it like I saw it. 'She might be. She was on the streets, Jett. She was doing smack as well. But she'd checked into a clinic to clean herself up. Like I say, I'll know more tomorrow. I'll fax you a full update in the morning.' He didn't look like he was in the mood for details now.

He nodded. 'Thanks,' he mumbled. I felt like the last of the great party poopers as I trudged across the room. I found Tamar halfway up the stairs, just where they split into two. Tears had done serious damage to her make-up. She looked like an aerial shot of a war zone. 'Don't bring her back,' she pleaded with me. 'You'll spoil everything.'

I sat down beside her. 'What makes you think that?'

'You wouldn't understand,' she said, pushing herself upright. She ran a hand through her hair like a tragedy queen. 'Your kind never do. You just create havoc and walk away. Well, I'm telling you nobody wants Moira back. Not even Jett, not deep down. He doesn't want her back out of love, or out of his desperation to make a good album. He wants her back so he can play the lead in the parable of the prodigal son,' she complained cynically. 'The thing he needs most of all right now is to feel good about himself, and she's the perfect vehicle. I mean, where's the kick in getting it on with me? I don't need saving, I don't need putting on track in my karmic journey. Moira's a fucking godsend, literally.'

She looked as if she was going to say more, but Kevin appeared at the head of the stairs. 'For God's sake, Tamar, pull yourself together. I don't bloody want it any more than you do. But at least if you keep him happy, maybe he won't fall for her shit again. OK?'

He glared at me as he came downstairs. 'Thanks for your contribution to the celebrations,' he said sarcastically. 'Have you found her yet?'

I shook my head.

'Good,' he commented bitterly. 'Take as long as you like. I'd rather pay your exorbitant fees for six months than have her back here.' That made me realize just how serious Kevin was about Moira.

Tamar sighed and headed upstairs. I followed Kevin down to the hall, in time to see Gloria lock her office behind her and head towards the ballroom. Good old Gloria. Nothing could make everyone's life a misery like her literal interpretation of the boss's instructions. Now she'd be able to toddle off and offer the hero a shoulder to cry on. He sure as hell wouldn't be getting any offers of comfort from Tamar tonight.

10

I dropped the tape off in Shelley's in-tray and headed home, determined to have some time to myself. I was in luck. Richard had gone to sit in on an Inspiral Carpets rehearsal session. The first time he'd come home talking about the band, I couldn't believe my ears. Thought he'd finally started taking an interest in interior design. Silly me.

After a languid bath, I booted up the computer. Until I met Bill, I'd always thought people who played computer games were intellectual pygmies. But Bill introduced me to role-playing adventures, so different from arcade shoot-em-ups that I can hardly bring myself to mention them in the same breath. The way the games work is that the player takes on the role of a character in the story, explores locations, achieves tasks, and solves complex puzzles. A really good game can take me up to a couple of months to complete. From there, I discovered strategy simulations, and that was the end of my relationship with the television set. Can't say it shows signs of missing me.

I loaded up Sierra's Leisure Suit Larry and spent a bawdy hour as the eponymous medallion man in the white polyester suit, looking for love in all the wrong places, from a whore's boudoir to a filthy toilet. I've played the game half a dozen times, but it's one of the old favourites I always go back to whenever I want to relax rather than stretch my mind on a fresh set of puzzles. By the time I went to bed, I was feeling more laid back than any carpet, inspiral or otherwise. I almost didn't mind when the alarm went off at six, catapulting me into another wonderful day of chasing the Smarts. We'd been to Glasgow and back by mid-afternoon, when I abandoned them to the delights of a late lunch in Chinatown and headed back to the office with a takeaway pizza, calabrese with onion and extra cheese. Shelley gave me a filthy look as the smell filled her office, so I skulked off to my own cubbyhole where I tried to type up my surveillance report without getting mozzarella on the keys.

The drive back to Bradford to the strains of Tina Turner almost seemed relaxing after the stresses of chasing Billy and Gary up the motorway. But I couldn't afford to let myself become too confident. The hardest part of the day still lay ahead. I sat in the car till half-past seven, then walked up the path to the Seagull Project. I rang the bell and waited.

After a few minutes, I heard feet thundering down the stairs and the door was opened by Andy. He looked surprised to see me. 'I've come for the meeting,' I told him. 'I know I'm early, but I was in the area, and I thought I could wait inside rather than go to the pub on my own.' I gave him the full hundred-watt smile.

He shrugged and said, 'I don't see a problem with that. Come on in. You can wait in Jude's office.' I followed him through and sat down, pulling a Marge Piercy novel out of my bag and trying to look as if I were settled for the evening.

'Help yourself to a coffee,' he said, gesturing towards a tray containing all the paraphernalia for brewing up. 'Someone'll come down for you when we're ready. I'm afraid it'll be about three quarters of an hour at least.'

'Thanks,' I said absently, already appearing immersed

in my book. I waited till I heard his footsteps reach the top of the stairs, then I counted a hundred elephants. I put my book away and moved quietly across the room. I inched the door open and listened. There was a distant hum of conversation, too low to make out individual voices.

I pulled the door further open and stuck my head into the hall. If I'd seen anyone, I was looking for the loo. But the coast was clear. There was no one in the hall or on the stairs. I crept out of the room, closing the door quietly behind me, and moved quickly across the hall and down the side of the stairs towards the room where the records were kept. I paused outside the door.

My hands were slippery with nervous sweat, so I wiped them on my trousers before taking an out-of-date credit card from my pocket. I'm not bad at picking locks, thanks to Dennis the burglar, but with a simple Yale, the old credit card trick is quicker and leaves fewer traces if you're an amateur like me. I turned the door handle with one hand, and with the other, I slid the card between the door and the lintel. At first, it wouldn't budge and I could feel a trickle of sweat running down between my shoulder blades. I took the card out, took three deep breaths, listening all the time for noise from upstairs, then tried again.

This time, the lock slipped back and the door opened. I hurried into the room and closed the door behind me, flipping up the catch to double-lock it. I leaned against the door and found myself panting. I forced myself to breathe normally and took stock of my surroundings. First, I examined the filing cabinets. I soon found a drawer marked 'Clients. O-R'. It was locked.

Fortunately, the Seagull Project didn't just hand out charity. It had clearly been on the receiving end as far as the elderly filing cabinets were concerned. With new cabinets, you actually have to pick the locks. But with ones of this vintage, I could forget about the set of lock-picks I'd bought from Dennis. I inched the cabinet away from the wall and pushed the top, tipping it back. Cautiously, keeping it in place, I crouched down and slipped my hand underneath. I groped around till I found the lock bar and pushed it upwards. The sound of the bar releasing the locked drawers was sweet to my ears. I carefully let the cabinet down and pushed it back into place. It had taken me nearly five minutes. I flicked hastily through the files and found a cardboard folder marked 'Pollock, M'. I pulled it out. It was worryingly slim and when I opened it I discovered why. It contained only one sheet of paper. My heart sank as I read it. 'Moira Pollock. File transferred to computer 16th February.'

I swore under my breath and turned to the computer. The perfect end to a perfect day. I switched it on and sat down. As I'd expected, it wanted a password. I tried Seagull. No luck. Then Andrew. It's amazing how many people are stupid enough to use their own names as security passwords. Andy wasn't one of them. I thought hard. My next try had to be right. Like copy-protected games, most security programs only give you three attempts before they crash. I sat and stared into the screen, desperately racking my brains for inspiration.

Then it came to me. I crossed my fingers, said a swift prayer to the gods of the New Age and typed in JONA-THAN. 'Thank you, Richard Bach,' I said softly as the menu appeared before me.

Once I was into the program, it didn't take me long to find Moira's records. I didn't have time to plough through them all then and there, but realizing I might have to steal some data from the computer, I'd taken the precaution of bringing a couple of blank floppies with me. I quickly made two copies of the file to be on the safe side, pocketed the discs and switched off the computer. So much for the Data

Protection Act. I checked my watch and saw that it was nearly ten past eight. Time to get a move on.

At the door, I paused and listened. It seemed quiet, so I carefully released the lock catch and opened the door. I stepped into the hall with a sigh of relief and pulled the door to behind me. The noise of the lock snapping home sounded like a thunderclap. I didn't wait to see if that's how it sounded to anyone else. I raced down the hall and out of the front door. I didn't stop running till I got to the car.

I didn't like leaving the Seagull Project minus their new volunteer. But at least I'd managed to avoid the collective meeting. Besides, I figured that now she'd flown the nest, Moira might need my help more than them.

I arrived home just as Richard was leaving. When he saw me, his face lit up in my favourite cute smile and he leapt across the low fence that separates our front gardens. He pulled me into his arms in a comforting hug. Until I tried to relax into him, I hadn't realized how tense I still was after my burglary at Seagull.

'Hey, Brannigan!' he exclaimed. 'I'd given you up for dead. Come on, get your glad rags on and we'll go and paint the town.'

It was a tempting offer. I didn't keep the full range of software at home that we have in the office, and I knew that I couldn't read the disc I'd copied at the Seagull Project with what I had on my machine. I certainly couldn't face going into the office this late. Besides, it was Friday night and I felt entitled to time off for bad behaviour. 'Sounds like a good game,' I agreed.

I took a quick shower and blissfully pulled on a pair of clean toffee-coloured silk trousers that were my bargain of the year – a tenner in a reject shop. I added a cream camisole and a linen jacket, and half an hour after I got home, I was climbing into the passenger seat of Richard's hot pink Beetle convertible. I wriggled uncomfortably, then pulled out a handful of scrunched up papers from under me and tossed them on to the rest of the detritus in the back seat.

'This car's a health hazard,' I grumbled as I kicked Diet Coke cans, old newspapers and cigarette packets aside in a bid to find some floor space for my feet.

'It's my office,' he replied, as if that was some kind of reason for driving round in a dustbin.

'You leave it sitting around with the top down, and somebody's going to come along and mistake it for a skip. You'll come out one morning to find a mattress and a pile of builder's rubble in it,' I teased him, only half-joking.

Luckily for my eardrums, Richard was having a night off, so we avoided anywhere with live music. We ended up dancing the night away at one of the city's more intimate clubs. Afterwards, we went for a late Chinese, so it was after three when we finally crawled into bed, hungry for one thing only. And I don't mean sex.

11

I woke around noon to the electronic music of a computer game, and found Richard sitting naked in front of the screen playing Tetris. It's a game that sounds simple, but isn't. The object is to build a solid wall out of a random succession of differently shaped coloured bricks. Sounds boring, but the game has outsold every other computer game ever invented. Richard, like half the high-powered traders in the City, is addicted to it. Unlike the City super-stars, however, Tetris is about Richard's limit when it comes to computers.

I pried him away from the screen not with the tempta-tions of my body but with the offer of a pub lunch. He got up eagerly and went off to his house to have a shower, a shave and a change of clothes. What I had omitted to mention was that this was to be a working lunch. A couple of weeks ago, I had followed one of Billy Smart's customers to a pub on the outskirts of Manchester. I wanted to take a look and see what was going on there. But a woman on her own would be both conspicuous and a target for the kind of assholes who think that a woman alone is desperate for their company. What better camouflage in a trendy young people's fun pub than Richard?

We took my car, partly on environmental health grounds and partly so that Richard could have a drink. It took about twenty minutes to drive out to the pub in

Worsley, a large 1950s tavern with a bowling green and a beer garden that ran down to the canal. The car park told me all I needed to know. Every car had its string of poser's initials – GTI, XR3i, Turbo. I felt like a second-class citizen with a mere SR. Inside was no better. The interior had been completely revamped according to the chapter of the brewery bible headed 'fun pub'. My first impression as we walked through the door was of pink neon and chrome. It looked like a tacky version of every New York bar featured in the teen movies of the last decade. I half-expected to find Tom Cruise throwing bottles around behind the bar.

I was out of luck. The barman who shimmied up to serve us looked more like a cruiserweight. While Richard ordered the drinks, I took a good look around. The pub was busy for a lunchtime. 'Plenty of Traceys,' Richard commented as he glanced round.

He wasn't wrong. The women looked as if collectively they might just scrape together enough neurons for a synapse. The men looked as if they desperately wanted to be taken for readers of *GQ* magazine. One day, I'm going to find a pub where I feel equally comfortable with the staff, the decor, the clientele and the menu. I rate the chances of that as high as coming home to find Richard doing the spring-cleaning.

Richard handed me my orange juice and soda and I steered him over to a crowded corner of the lounge where I'd spotted my man. I'd briefed Richard on the way so he was happy to oblige. We sat down a few yards away at a table that gave me a good view of what my target was up to. He was sitting at a table with a bunch of eager young men and women around him. There was nothing particularly discreet about his operation. For a start, he was wearing a bright green Sergio Tacchini shell suit. In front of him on the table were half a dozen watches. I could identify the fake Rolexes and Guccis from that distance. Within minutes, all of them had been bought. He appeared to be charging fifty pounds a time, and getting it without a quibble. But he didn't seem to be passing them off as the real thing. Realistically, though, anyone trying that routine would have to be a lot more discreet, dealing one on one to make it look like an exclusive.

Another half dozen watches appeared from Billy's contact's pockets, and most of them vanished as quickly as the others. He shuffled the remaining two back into his jacket then burrowed under the table. He surfaced with three cellophane packets containing shell suits. Surprise surprise. The suit he was wearing was a schneid.

'Sometimes this job is a pain in the arse,' I muttered to Richard.

He looked surprised. 'Did I hear right?' he asked in tones of wonderment. 'Did I hear you say you were less than one hundred per cent thrilled with your life in crime?'

'Piss off,' I quipped wittily. 'Just look at those shell suits! They're the business. If this wasn't a surveillance operation, I'd be over there right now buying those suits. Take a look at the colours!' I couldn't take my eyes off two of the suits, one gold, one teal blue. I just knew I'd look wonderful in those colours.

Richard got to his feet. 'Poor old Brannigan,' he teased. 'But I'm not working.' He moved towards the neighbouring table.

'Richard!' I wailed. A couple of heads turned and I lowered my voice to a piercing whisper. 'Don't you dare!'

He shrugged. 'Who's to know? Anybody asks you, I bought them for you as a present. You didn't have to know they were copies, did you?'

'That's not the point,' I hissed. 'I *do* know. Sit down right now before you blow me out of the water.'

Richard reluctantly did as I asked him. His face had

sulk written all over it. 'I thought you wanted one,' he muttered.

'Of course I do. I also want a Cartier tank watch, but I can't afford the real thing. I dare say if Dennis had offered me a copy before I got involved in this assignment, I'd have bought it. But this job changes things. I'm sorry, Richard, I know you were trying to please me. And if you want one for yourself, I won't mind.'

Richard shook his head. 'You and your bloody morals,' he commented darkly.

'Oh, come on! Who was it who read me a lecture a couple of months ago about how immoral it is to make tapes of my albums for my friends when it means taking the bread out of the mouths of poor, starving rock stars like Jett?' I reminded him.

He grinned. 'OK, Brannigan, you win. Now, have you seen enough, or do I have to spend the whole day in this dump?'

I glanced over at the next table. The man had got to his feet, empty-handed, and was heading over towards the door, followed by most of his audience. I guessed the rest of his stock was in his car outside. 'I'm nearly done,' I told him. 'Let's just tag along with the kids and see what he's got hiding in his boot.'

We trailed behind at a discreet distance, and I managed to get a good look as we passed. The boot was full of shell suits in a wide choice of colours, but there were no rolls of watches that I could see. Nevertheless, it had been worth the trip, I pointed out as I drove Richard home. And there was a bonus too. If we pulled off the watches job, we might well be able to interest Sergio Tacchini in doing something similar for them. I'd been surprised to see the suits. I knew that schneid designer clothing was big business, but it was the first time I'd come across it connected, however tangentially, to the Smarts' business. I said as much to Richard.

92

'There's a lot of it about,' he said, to my surprise. 'I've seen all sorts of stuff on sale at gigs in the clubs. Anyway, I'm glad it worked out. Always happy to oblige the Sam Spade of Chorlton-on-Medlock.'

Poor sod, I thought. In reality, we live in Ardwick, one of those addresses that makes insurance companies blench. But Richard still believes the propaganda that the property developers came up with to convince us that we were moving somewhere select. 'Ardwick,' I corrected him absently. He ignored me and asked what my plans were for the afternoon. 'Work, I'm afraid. And this evening too, probably. Why?'

'Just wondered,' he said, too innocently for my liking.

'Tell, Barclay. Or else I'll tidy your study,' I threatened.

'Oh no, not that!' he pleaded. 'It's just that I've got the chance of a ticket for this afternoon's match at Old Trafford. But if you were free, I was going to suggest we went to the movies.'

The scale of the sacrifice made me realize he really does love me. I pulled up at the lights and impulsively leaned across to kiss him. 'Greater love has no man,' I remarked as I drove off.

'So will you drop me at that pub opposite the ground? I said I'd meet the lads there if I could make it,' he asked.

How could I refuse?

Moira's file made fascinating reading. The first interesting nugget came under the heading of 'Referral'. The entry read, 'Brought in by unidentified black male, who made donation of £500 and described her as a former employee in need of urgent help.' It sounded as if Stick had a bigger heart than he wanted anyone to know about. It also explained why he wanted five hundred pounds for his information.

Moira had apparently reached the point in her addiction

where she realized that she wasn't going to have too many more last chances to kick the smack and change her life. As a result, she'd been a model patient. She had opted to go down the hardest road, kicking the drug with minimal maintenance doses of methadone. After her cold turkey, she had been extremely co-operative, joining in willingly with group therapy and responding well in personal counselling. After a four-week stay at the project, she had signed herself out, but had continued to turn up for her therapy appointments.

The sting in the tail for me came at the very end. Instead of going to the halfway house after her initial intensive treatment, she had moved in with a woman called Maggie Rossiter. The notes on the file said that Maggie Rossiter was a social worker with Leeds City Council and a volunteer worker at the Seagull Project.

That was unusual enough to raise my eyebrows. But a separate report by Seagull's full-time psychiatrist was even more revealing. According to Dr Briggs, Maggie and Moira had formed a highly charged emotional attachment while Moira was still at Seagull. Following her discharge, they had become lovers and were now living together as a couple. In the doctor's opinion, this relationship was a significant contributory factor in Moira's commitment to staying off heroin.

Jett was going to love this, I thought to myself as I made a note of Maggie Rossiter's address. It's one thing to know with your head that a lot of whores prefer relationships with women. I can't say I blame them. If the only men I ever encountered were johns or pimps, I'd probably feel the same way. But when the woman concerned was your former soul mate . . . That was a whole different ball game.

I reluctantly called Colcutt Manor to give Jett an up-to-date report, but Gloria informed me gleefully that he was out. No, she didn't know where he could be reached. No, she didn't know when he'd be back. Yes, he would be back that night. I was almost relieved that I'd missed him. I felt sure that once he knew I had Moira's address he'd want to come with me himself. I couldn't help thinking that would be the messiest possible way to handle things. All that raw emotion would get us nowhere. I settled for typing up a current report and faxed it through to Gloria for her to pass it on to Jett as soon as he returned.

I copied Moira's files on to the disc where I was storing Jett's information, then switched off the computer. The office seemed unnaturally quiet, not just because I was alone in it, but because all the other offices in the building are occupied by sensible people who think working from Monday to Friday is quite enough to be going on with. I locked up behind me and walked down to the ground floor. Luckily, I emerged on Oxford Road just before the afternoon matinee at the Palace Theatre spilled its crowds on to the pavement. I'd left the car at home since parking near the office is impossible thanks to Saturday afternoon theatregoers and shoppers. Besides, the walk would do me good, I'd thought. That was before the rain came on.

I plodded up past the BBC and headed across to Upper Brook Street. By the time I got home, I was wet through. I hoped Richard had been sitting far enough back in the stands to avoid a soaking. I had a quick shower to warm me up, then I stood in front of the wardrobe wondering which outfit would be the key that would get me across Maggie Rossiter's doorstep.

I settled on my favourite Levis and a cream lambswool cowl-necked sweater. Thoroughly inoffensive, making no statement that a lesbian social worker could disagree with, I hoped. I went through to the kitchen to fix myself a plate of snacks from my supermarket blitz, and washed it down with a small vodka and grapefruit juice. I was in no real hurry. I was aiming to get to Maggie's home in Bradford between six thirty and seven. With any luck I'd catch them before they went out for the evening.

As it turned out, my timing was diabolical. I found Maggie's house easily enough, a neat brick terrace in a quiet street only a mile away from the motorway. I parked outside with a sinking heart as I registered that the house was in darkness. I walked up the crazy paved path and knocked on the stripped pine front door anyway. There was, of course, no response.

As I walked back down the path, a small calico cat rubbed itself against my legs. I crouched down to stroke it. 'Don't suppose you know where they've gone, do you?' I asked softly.

'Darsett Trades and Labour Club,' a deep male voice said from behind me. I nearly fell over in shock.

I stood up hastily and stared in the direction of the voice. A tall dark hunk was standing by the gate with a box of groceries. 'I'm sorry?' I asked inadequately.

'I'm the one who should be sorry, startling you like that,' he apologized with a smile that lit up twinkling eyes. I shrugged. Eyes like that I'd forgive most things. 'If you're looking for Maggie and Moira, they've gone to Darsett Trades and Labour Club,' he said.

'Oh, right,' I hedged. 'I didn't realize they were out tonight. I'll catch up with them later.'

'You a friend of theirs?' the hunk asked.

'Friend of a friend, really,' I replied, walking down the path towards him. 'I know Maggie from Seagull.'

'I'm Gavin,' he said. 'I live next door. We would have been going with them tonight except that we've got people coming for dinner. Still, I'm sure there will be plenty more chances to hear Moira sing in public.'

My heart jolted. Moira was singing? I swallowed hard and spoke before Gavin's helpful garrulity gave out. 'I didn't know it was tonight,' I improvised.

'Oh yeah, the big night. Her first engagement. She's going to be a big success. I should know, I hear her rehearsing enough!'

I smiled politely and thanked him for his help. 'I'll catch them another time,' I said, getting back into my car. Gavin sketched a half-wave from under his box and turned into the next house. I pulled out my atlas. I groaned. Darsett was a good twenty miles away. With a sigh, I headed back towards the motorway.

12

Within three minutes of entering Darsett Trades and Labour Club, I knew that not even double rates could compensate me for spending Saturday night there. I don't know enough about the northern club circuit to know if it's typical, but if it is, then my heartfelt sympathy goes out to the poor sods who make their living performing there. The building itself was a 1960s concrete box with all the charm of a dead dog. I parked among an assortment of old Cortinas and Datsuns and headed for the brightly lit entrance.

Being a woman, I already had problems on my hands. In their infinite wisdom, working men's clubs don't allow women to be members in their own right. Strange women trying to get in alone are a complete no-no. The doorman, face marked with the blue hairline scars of a miner, wasn't impressed with my story that I was an agent there to see Moira perform, not even when I produced the business card that carefully doesn't specify what Mortensen and Brannigan are. Eventually, he grudgingly called the club secretary, who finally agreed to let me in, after informing me at great length that I would not be able to purchase alcoholic beverages.

I regretted this rule and the fact that I was driving as soon as I crossed the threshold. The only way to make an evening at Darsett Trades and Labour Club tolerable was to be so pissed I wouldn't notice it. The bar, on my left, was brightly lit, packed and already blue with smoke. It sounded like a riot was in progress, an impression increased by the rugby scrum at the bar.

I carried on through double doors under a blue neon sign that said Cabaret Room. Like the bar, the room shimmered under the glare of lights and the haze of cigarette smoke. It was crammed with small, round tables, two-thirds of which were occupied with chattering groups of men and women. Their gaiety was infectious, and I mentally ticked myself off for my patronizing response to the club.

At the far end of the room was a small stage. A trio of electronic organ, drums and bass were listlessly playing 'The Girl From Ipanema'. No one was listening. I looked around intently, trying to pick out Maggie in the crowd. At first, I couldn't see any woman on her own, but on the second sweep of the room, I spotted her.

She was standing in the shadows right at the edge of the room about halfway back. Her clothes as much as her isolation marked her out. Unlike the other women in the room apart from me, she wasn't dressed up to the nines in teetering heels and a bright dress. Maggie wore jeans, a chambray shirt and a pair of trainers. From where I was standing, it looked like she had also avoided the cosmetic excesses of the rest of the room. She was about my height, with curly, shoulder-length pepper and salt hair. She was carrying about ten pounds overweight, but she looked sturdy rather than flabby.

For a moment, I toyed with the idea of making the first approach to her, but decided against it. I suspected she'd leap immediately to Moira's defence and give me the elbow without actually weighing up what I had to say, and I couldn't blame her for that. Even if I'd been going to approach her, I was cut off at the pass. The organist finished the Stan Getz piece with a flourish and played a fanfare. A burly man leapt on to the stage and peppered the audience with a few risqué jokes, then announced, 'Ladies and animals, put your hands together for tonight's star attraction, a young lady who's going all the way to the top. Let's hear it for Moira Moore!'

With another fanfare on the organ, he vanished into the wings. The band played the opening chords of 'To Be With You Tonight' and Moira walked out on to the stage. As she moved forward into the fixed spotlight, she looked nervously from side to side, as if searching for an escape route that wasn't there. She was wearing a tight blue lurex dress which came to just above her knees. She looked painfully thin.

As the band finished the intro, Moira leaned forward to the mike and began to sing. To say I was astonished would be putting it mildly. Could this really be the woman who'd been happy to take a back-seat, lyricist's role because her voice wasn't up to scratch? OK, she didn't have the silky richness of Jett, but by any other standards Moira's was quite a voice. Slightly husky, almost bluesy, she hit the notes perfectly, and the nerves that were obvious in her body language didn't transmit themselves into her singing. Even the louts in the audience shut up to listen to Moira sing.

She followed Jett's first hit with an unadventurous selection of torch songs, ending up with a version of 'Who Will I Turn To' that almost had tough old Brannigan in tears. The audience loved it, clapping and cheering and demanding more. Moira looked dazed and surprised by her reception, and after a few minutes of applause, she turned and asked the organist something inaudible. He nodded and she launched into Tina Turner's whore's anthem, 'Private Dancer', with the kind of bitter attack that could only come from experience. The crowd went wild. If it had been up to them, she would have been there all night, but she looked exhausted by the end of the song and escaped gratefully to the wings.

Like the audience, I'd been mesmerized by Moira and when I looked back to where Maggie had been standing, I realized I'd been letting pleasure interfere with work. Maggie had gone. Furious with myself, I hurried down the side of the room and through a pass door at the side of the stage.

I was in a narrow corridor. Two doors on the left were marked Ladies and Gents, and on my right were steps leading up to the stage. Round a corner, I found three more doors. No reply to my knock on the first. Same with the second. On the third attempt, I hit pay dirt. The door opened six inches and Maggie's face appeared in the crack. Close up, she was a pretty woman. She had small, neat features and intelligent blue eyes with laughter lines at the corners. I put her in the mid thirties. 'Can I help you?' she asked pleasantly.

I smiled. 'You must be Maggie. Hi. I'd like to see Moira.'

She frowned. 'I'm sorry, have we met?' Without waiting for a reply, she went on. 'Look, she's too tired. If it's an autograph you want, I can get her to sign one for you.'

I shook my head. 'Thanks, but I need to see her. It's a personal matter,' I stated calmly.

'Who is it?' a voice from inside the room called out.

'No one we know,' Maggie remarked over her shoulder. She turned back to me and said, 'Look, this is not a good time. She's just done a show, and she needs to rest.'

'What I have to say won't take long. I don't like to be difficult, but I'm not going till I've spoken to Moira.' I spoke firmly, with more confidence than I actually felt. I was in no doubt that Maggie could have me thrown out of there so fast my feet wouldn't touch the sticky carpets. However, to do that, she'd have to leave Moira. I couldn't see Darsett Trades and Labour Club being the kind of place that had a house phone in the star dressing room.

'What the hell's going on?' Moira demanded, pulling the door open and staring belligerently at me. It should have been a moment of triumph for me, to come face to face with my quarry like this, but any satisfaction was destroyed by the irritation in her voice. 'Are you deaf or what? She told you, I'm too tired to talk to anybody.'

'I'm sorry it's a bad time, but I need to talk to you,' I apologized. 'It's taken me a long time to find you, and it's important for you that you listen to what I have to say.' I tried a conciliatory smile which produced a scowl from Maggie, standing like a bulldog in front of Moira.

Moira sighed and pulled her white bathrobe more tightly round her. 'You're damn right, it's a bad time. I suppose you'd better come in. Let me tell you, sister, this better not be bad news.'

I waited for Maggie to move reluctantly away from the door before I entered the tiny dressing room. There were two small formica topped tables in front of mirrors, a corner sink unit, three chairs and several hooks on the wall. Moira sat down in one chair facing a mirror and carried on removing her make-up. Maggie leaned against the wall, arms folded.

I pulled a chair over beside Moira and sat down. 'I don't think it's bad news, but that's for you to decide. My name's Kate Brannigan and I'm a private investigator.' Moira flashed a quick look at me, fear in her eyes, then forced herself to look back in the mirror.

'So what's your interest in me?' she challenged.

'Jett asked me to find you,' I told her, watching for her reaction. The hand with the make-up removal pad shook and she quickly lowered it to the table.

'I don't know what you're talking about,' she said in a low voice.

102

'He wants to work with you again. He bitterly regrets what happened all those years ago,' I tried. My instincts told me that with Maggie in the room, I should steer well clear of the emotional arguments.

Moira shrugged. 'I haven't a clue what you're on about.'

'I think you should go now,' Maggie piped up.

I ignored her. 'Look, Moira, Jett is desperate to reach you. He says his work has gone down the tube since the two of you stopped writing songs together. As a fan, I have to agree with him. And I bet you do too. He just wants to meet you, to talk about the possibilities of making music together again. That's all. No strings.'

Moira laughed, a harsh bark. 'Oh yeah? And what's Kevin going to say about that? If you've been looking for me, you know what my life's been like the last few years. I'd be too much of a skeleton in the cupboard for Mr Clean. Never mind what Jett will think.'

'Jett knows all about it. And he didn't tell me to stop looking just because you'd been on the game, or on smack. He wants to talk to you. He doesn't care what's happened in between,' I argued as fiercely as I could.

Moira ran a hand through her short curls. 'I don't think so,' she said softly. 'Too much water under the bridge.'

'You heard her,' Maggie interjected. 'I really think you'd better go now before you upset her any more.'

I shrugged. 'If that's what Moira wants, I'll go. I told Jett he might be wasting his money, asking me to find you. I told him you might not want to be found. But he's not going to be satisfied with that. And the next private eye he hires might not do things my way.'

'Don't you threaten us!' Maggie exploded.

'I'm not threatening you,' I flashed back. 'I'm simply trying to be straight with you. Jett wants to find you. Whatever that takes. You might do a runner after tonight, but you've got to leave traces. Someone else will track you down, just like I did. And next time, it could be Jett knocking on your door. Don't you think it would be better to meet him on your terms, when you're prepared for it, rather than have him catching you by surprise?'

Moira's head dropped into her hands. 'You say he knows already?' she mumbled.

'He knows about everything except the singing.' And I don't think that's going to give him the screaming habdabs, I thought wryly.

Moira's head came up and she stared at her face in the mirror. 'I don't know,' she said doubtfully, lighting up a pungent Gauloise.

Maggie crossed the room, all two paces of it, and put a protective arm round Moira. 'You don't need him any more,' she declared. 'Where was he when you really needed help? If he'd been so bloody keen to find you, why didn't he do it when you left? He's just being selfish. His career's a disaster area, and he wants you to get him out of the shit. You don't owe him anything, Moira.'

'Oh, I see,' I remarked. 'There's a statute of limitations on feeling guilty now, is there? Just because Jett didn't act right away, then he can only be out for himself? Is that it?'

Maggie glowered at me, but Moira actually smiled as she reached up to squeeze her lover's hand. 'He's really not like that, Maggie. He's one of the good guys. I didn't expect him to come after me. I'd been doing his head in for so long he must have been glad of the peace.'

'So what's it to be?' I asked. 'Will you at least listen to what he's got to say?'

Moira took a deep drag on her cigarette. Maggie looked as if she was holding her breath and praying. Moira blew two streams of smoke down her nose and nodded at me. 'I'll listen. When can you set it up?'

'The sooner the better. He's at home working on his

new album. Believe me, he needs your help yesterday.'

Moira smiled, a wide grin that lit up her whole face and took ten years off her. 'I'll bet,' she said. 'What about tonight? Might as well get it over with.'

'But it's past ten o'clock!' Maggie protested. 'You can't go off there now.'

'Maggie, unless Jett has had a personality transplant, he'll be up watching videos and listening to music till three or four o'clock. He doesn't get up to listen to the Archers omnibus on Sunday mornings,' Moira replied, a gentle tease in her voice.

Maggie flushed. 'I still think you should leave it till tomorrow,' she said stubbornly. 'You're tired. You need a night's rest after the show.'

She still had a lot to learn, I thought sadly. Every performer I've ever met is so high after a show that they need half the night to come down to a point where sleep's possible. That's why so many of them get hooked on a mixture of uppers and downers.

As if reading my thoughts, Moira said, 'No, Maggie. Right now, I'm on a high. All that applause! Tonight, I feel like I could meet Jett as an equal. And if I sleep on it, I'll probably bottle out. Or else I'll let you talk me out of it.'

Moira got to her feet and put an arm round Maggie's waist. 'Kate, if you'll give me ten minutes, we'll meet you in the car park. Ours is the red 2CV. I'll have to go home and change into something more suitable,' she added, waving at her blue lurex dress and a jogging suit. 'If you follow us back there, then you can take me over to see Jett. If that's OK with you.'

'Fine by me,' I confirmed, feeling exultant. There's no better feeling in the world than the moment when you know you've cracked a difficult job. Moira wasn't the only one who was on a high.

An hour later, Moira and I were heading back down the motorway towards Manchester. 'I feel like I've spent more time on this motorway in the last couple of weeks than I've spent in my own bed,' I muttered to break the silence that had fallen on us since Maggie had waved a mournful farewell on the doorstep.

Moira chuckled. 'I'm sorry I've given you so much trouble,' she remarked.

'Oh, it's not just you. It's another case I've been working on. A team that's flooding the country with fake watches. You know, Rolex copies, all that sort of thing.'

Moira nodded. 'I know exactly what you mean. A lot of the guys in Bradford are into that kind of thing. It's a nice little earner. They do a lot of fake jogging suits and t-shirts. You know, any big thing like the Batman movie, or the Teenage Mutant Turtles. They just copy the legit stuff and flog it round the pubs and the markets. The guy I worked for in Bradford even had us selling fake perfume to johns for their wives, can you believe it?'

I laughed. 'Wonderful. I love the psychology.' I put Everything But The Girl's *Language Of Life* in the cassette and we both settled in a companionable silence to listen to Tracy Thorn's sensuous tones.

'So how did you track me down?' Moira asked finally as I turned on to the M6, heading south towards Jett's mansion. The home she'd never seen, I reminded myself.

When I got to the bit about Stick asking for his four hundred pounds, she laughed out loud. 'You know,' she said, 'if this does work out, I might just pay him back. Mind you, he'd die of embarrassment if word got out that he took me to Seagull. Stick the hard man! He'd never live it down.'

I turned into the gateway of Colcutt Manor and wound down the window and leaned out to press the intercom button. When it crackled back at me, I said clearly, 'It's

Kate Brannigan to see Jett. Don't fuck with me, Gloria, let me in.'

As the gates opened, I caught Moira's expression out of the corner of my eye. She looked stunned. I headed up the long drive, and the house appeared in my headlights. 'Shit,' she breathed. 'You might have warned me, Kate.'

I pulled up at the foot of the steps that led up to the front door and said, 'You ready?'

Moira took a deep breath and said, 'Ready as I'll ever be.'

We got out of the car and I led the way up towards the door. Three steps from the top, it opened and a pool of light flooded out. Jett himself stood silhouetted in the doorway. It took only a moment for him to realize I wasn't alone. Then he saw who my companion was. 'Moira?' he said in tones of wonder, as if he couldn't believe his eyes.

I paused, and she walked past me. 'Hi, babe,' she said, stopping a few feet short of him.

Jett's hesitation was only momentary. Then he stepped forward and folded her into his arms. Moira buried her head in his shoulder.

Me, I headed back into the night, trying to start the car as quietly as possible. Some things don't need witnesses. Besides, I had a huge invoice to dictate before I could sleep.

Part Two

13

The sound of the phone jerked me awake. 'Kate? It's Jett. It's an emergency. Get over here right away.' Then the phone slammed down. The clock said 01:32. Happy Monday. I leapt out of bed and dressed on automatic pilot. I was halfway to the car before I remembered it had been six weeks since I'd stopped working for Jett. What the hell was he playing at? By then, I was awake anyway, so I figured I might as well drive out and see.

The gates stood open, and Jett was waiting for me on the doorstep. He looked stoned out of his box. I asked what was going on and he simply handed me the key and said, 'The rehearsal room.'

It was my first dead body. The private eyes in books fall over corpses every other day, but Manchester's a long way from Chicago in more ways than one. My first reaction was to get out of the room as fast as my legs would carry me and keep on running till I was safe inside my car.

Instead, I tried to fight my nausea by breathing in deeply. That was my second mistake. Nobody ever told me that freshly spilled blood has such a strong smell. My only experience with the stuff was when half a pound of liver leaked all over my cheque book. That hadn't been too pleasant either.

I tried to behave like a professional and forget that I

111

knew the person who was lying dead on the polished wooden floor. If I was going to get through this experience, I'd have to convince myself it was no more real than the Kensington Gore in a Hammer Horror film.

Moira's body lay a few yards inside the door of the rehearsal room. Her limbs were splayed at angles too awkward for comfort. That alone would have been enough to show something was badly wrong. But there was more. The back of her head was matted with blood, which had trickled into a congealed pool behind her. A few yards away lay a tenor sax, its gleaming golden horn smeared with blood. I left it alone. My only direct experience with murder weapons was Cluedo, but even I knew enough not to mess with it.

I walked cautiously towards the body, and noticed that her face looked mildly surprised. I crouched down, forcing myself not to think of this as Moira, and noticed that her hands were empty, palms upwards. No clues there. Feeling foolish because I couldn't think of anything else to do, I picked up her wrist and felt vainly for a pulse. Nothing. Her skin felt warmish – not quite normal temperature, but not cold either. I got to my feet and glanced at my watch. It was forty minutes since Jett had woken me. What the hell was keeping the police?

With a deep sigh, I left the room and locked it behind me. I found Jett in the blue drawing room, huddled in a corner of the sofa. I sat down beside him and put a hand on his shoulder. His skin felt cold and clammy through the thin silk shirt.

His eyes were frightened. I realized now he was in shock rather than stoned.

'She's dead, isn't she?' he whispered hoarsely.

'I'm afraid so.'

He nodded, and kept on nodding as if he had a tic. 'I should never have brought her here,' he muttered.

'What happened, Jett?' I asked as gently as I could. It looked pretty obvious even to me, but I wanted to hear it from his own lips.

'I don't know,' he replied, his voice breaking like a teenager. 'We were supposed to be working on a new song tonight, and when I went in, she was lying there.' He cleared his throat and sniffed. 'So I came out and locked the door and called you.'

Gee, thanks. 'Did you try her pulse?' I asked.

'No need. The spirit had left. I knew that right away.'

Thank you, Dr Kildare. 'Why aren't the police here yet?' I asked, refraining from pointing out that she just might have been still alive when he made his New Age diagnosis.

'I didn't call the police. I only called you. I thought you'd know what to do.'

I couldn't credit what I was hearing. He'd found his ex-lover's murdered body in his house and he hadn't called the police? If Jett wanted to throw suspicion on himself, the only way he could have made a better job of it would have been to call his lawyer as well. 'You'll have to call them now, Jett. You should have done that first, before you called me.'

He shook his head obstinately. 'No. I want you to handle it. I can trust you.'

'Jett, you can't hush up a murder. You have to call the police. Look, I'll make the call if you don't feel up to it,' I offered desperately. The last thing I needed was for the police to get it into their heads that I was involved in concealing a crime.

He shrugged. 'Please yourself. But I want you to handle it.'

'We'll talk about it in a minute.' I stood up. There was a phone in the room, but I wanted some privacy to gather my thoughts so I headed for Gloria's office down the hall. Neil was coming down the stairs as I reached the door. He looked as surprised to see me as I was to see him. 'Kate!' he exclaimed. 'I didn't know you were here.'

'Jett needed a meeting,' I offered lamely, not feeling up to breaking the news.

'Maybe see you later,' he said, sketching a wave as he walked down the corridor into the far wing. Clearly he saw nothing odd about business meetings in the small hours.

I closed Gloria's door behind me, picked up the phone and dialled 999. I was quickly connected to the police emergency line. 'I'm calling to report a murder,' I said. To my amazement, I could feel a giggle welling up inside me. I must have been more shocked than I'd realized.

The copper on the other end of the phone wasn't amused. 'Is this some kind of hoax?' he demanded.

I pulled myself together and said, 'I'm sorry. Unfortunately not. A woman has been killed at Colcutt Manor, just outside Colcutt village.'

'When did this happen, madam?' His voice was hard and cool.

'We're not sure. The body's only just been discovered.' I gave him the details. It seemed to take forever. When I returned, Jett was sitting exactly as I'd left him, hugging himself and rocking gently to and fro. What he needed was a cup of strong, sweet tea, but I didn't rate my chances of finding my way to the kitchen and back again without a ball of string or a map. Instead, I sat down and put an arm round him. 'Jett,' I said softly. 'We're going to have to get our story straight or the cops are going to get very heavy with you. Listen. I was passing on my way home from a job and I dropped in for a drink. We were talking for the best part of an hour, then you went down to the rehearsal room to get Moira to join us, and that's when you found the body. I was already here. Understand?' I could only pray that the pathologist wouldn't come up with a time of death that made a nonsense of the alibi I was handing him.

'I got nothing to say to the cops,' he informed me.

'Jett, unless you want to spend tonight in a cell, you're going to have to stick to our story. In their eyes, you're the number one suspect, especially if we tell them the truth. Promise me you'll keep to my version.' I repeated the tale to him and made him recite it back to me.

We were interrupted by the distant sound of the gate intercom. Jett showed no signs of moving, so I headed back towards the hall. Gloria had beaten me to it. She was wearing a heavy red silk kimono with, appropriately enough, black and gold dragons embroidered all over it. Either she had ears like a bat or she'd been on her way downstairs anyway when the intercom sounded. She was carrying out her usual friendly interrogation over the entryphone when I butted in and said curtly, 'Let them in. Jett knows all about it.'

She pressed the gate release button then turned furiously towards me. 'I don't know what you think you're playing at, police in the middle of the night. I suppose Moira's doing drugs or something. I wish he'd never hired you in the first place. Then we would all have been happy.'

I already felt put upon, which is the only excuse I can offer for snapping back at her, 'Moira won't be doing drugs or anything else ever again. Somebody made very sure of that tonight. Moira's dead.'

Before I could properly judge her reaction, there was a tattoo of knocks on the front door. I pushed past Gloria and opened the door. Two uniformed officers stood on the doorstep, the flashing blue light on top of their car washing them in an eerie glow. 'Miss Brannigan, is it?' the older of the two asked politely.

'That's me. You'd better come in. Are the CID on their way?'

'That's right, miss,' he said as they walked into the hall, looking around them curiously. They'd drink out on this for months, murder in the rock star's den. 'Can you show me where the uhh . . .'

'You'd better wait here, Gloria,' I said loftily. 'Someone will have to let the other officers in.'

As I turned away to lead them to the rehearsal room, a man's voice echoed down the stairwell. 'What the fuck is going down?' I glanced up to see Kevin leaning over the gilt banister, looking as spruce as if he was heading for a meeting with his bank manager. Didn't anybody ever sleep in this house?

'You'd better get yourself down here,' I called back.

'What the hell are you doing here, Brannigan?' he ranted as he turned the corner of the stairs. Then he saw the cops and stopped dead. 'Oh shit, what are they doing here? What's going on?'

'Moira's been killed,' I blurted out before anyone else could speak.

Kevin missed a step and almost tumbled to the foot of the stairs, just catching himself in time on the banister. 'You what?' he gasped. 'There's got to be some mistake. Gloria, what's she playing at?'

'I don't know, Kevin. I just came downstairs and found her here.'

'No mistake, I'm afraid,' I interrupted. 'I've seen the body. You'd better go and sit with Jett. He's in the drawing room.'

Kevin shook his head like a man who thinks he's trapped in a bad dream and moved across the hall towards the door. Gloria took a couple of steps after him, then hesitated. The policemen conferred almost inaudibly, then the younger one stepped back towards the front door. 'I'll have to ask you not to leave the building, sir,' he said to Kevin.

'Listen, sonny, I'm not going anywhere. I've got an artiste to look after,' he said self-importantly. 'I've got a right to be here. Why don't you ask her what the hell she's doing on the premises? She's the outsider here,' he complained sharply, pointing to me.

The older policeman looked exasperated. All he wanted to do was get to the murder scene before the CID arrived and started treating him like a turnip. At this rate, he'd end up looking like a complete wally who hadn't even managed to keep tabs on the occupants of the house. Ignoring Kevin's histrionic gesture, he said, 'Miss, if you could just show me the way?'

I led him to the door. Wild horses wouldn't have dragged me across the threshold again. I handed him the key and nodded at the door. 'In there. I checked for a pulse, but there wasn't one.'

'Touch anything else, miss?' he asked as he unlocked the door.

'No.' I leaned against the wall as he let himself in. All I wanted was to climb back into bed and pull the duvet over my head. It didn't seem to be an available option. Wearily, I pushed myself back into action. Apart from the young constable, whose radio was crackling like an egg in a hot frying pan, the front hall was empty. I didn't feel up to Kevin and Gloria, so I sat on the bottom step of the stairs and wondered gloomily why I'd already stuck my neck out to protect Jett. He wasn't a friend, simply a client who'd paid his bill promptly. I know that's rarer than a socialist at a Labour Party meeting, but it still wasn't reason enough for my quixotic behaviour.

The sound of the intercom brought Gloria scuttling back from the drawing room. This time, the door opened to reveal two plain clothes officers, a uniformed sergeant and an inspector. They hadn't wasted any time. They had a brief conference with the officer on the door, and the CID disappeared in the direction of the rehearsal room. The inspector went off to the drawing room. The sergeant turned to Gloria and me, pulled out his notebook and asked, 'Who else is in the house?'

I shrugged and Gloria pursed her mouth in a self-satisfied smirk. She didn't care if it took murder to keep me in my place. Then she rattled off efficiently, 'Jett is in the drawing room with his manager, Mr Kleinman. Mr Webster, Jett's official biographer, will either be in his office or in bed. Miss Spenser, Jett's companion, is in her room upstairs.'

'Thank you,' the officer interjected, desperately trying to keep up with her flow. He scribbled on for a moment then said, 'And you ladies are . . . ?'

'I'm Gloria Seward, Jett's personal assistant and private secretary. And this is Kate Brannigan,' she added, her tone spelling out that I was an insignificant menial, there to make up the numbers. I held my tongue. The time to reveal my profession would come soon enough. Once they knew I was a private eye, it would be straight into quarantine for me, and I wasn't ready for that yet.

The sergeant, a hard-eyed man in his late thirties, finished writing and said, 'So that's everyone, is it?'

Gloria ran through her mental checklist, then her hand flew to her mouth. I really didn't think anyone did that any more. 'I forgot Micky,' she wailed. 'I'm sorry. Micky Hampton is Jett's record producer. He'll probably be in the studio – that's in the cellar.'

'Don't worry, it's hard to remember everything at a time like this. You've obviously had a bit of a shock. I'm sorry to ask this, but we're going to have to interview everyone as soon as possible. I'd appreciate it if one of you ladies could get everyone together,' he said.

'I'll go,' I piped up. 'I think Gloria should be with Jett right now.'

The look she shot at me was pure poison, but there was really nothing she could do about it. After all, she was the one who'd set herself up as Jett's little helper. The policeman nodded and I swiftly got directions from Gloria. Jett clearly wasn't going to let me walk away from this murder. And if I was going to have to investigate these choice specimens, I at least wanted to see how they reacted to the news.

14

Tamar was my first target. For obvious reasons, her reaction to Moira's death was the one that interested me most. I didn't know what had been happening at Colcutt Manor in the six weeks since I'd dutifully delivered Moira, but the corpse downstairs told me plenty. Not everyone had been as thrilled by her return as Jett. At least one person had taken extreme measures to try to return things to the status quo ante. (I love legalese. Sometimes it sums things up so beautifully.) And even if Jett and Moira had no longer been an item, it can't have been Easy Street for Tamar having Jett's alleged soul mate under the same roof.

I knocked sharply on the panelled door Gloria had directed me to and didn't wait for a reply. Crossing the threshold gave me the answer to one question at least. Jett and Tamar might be lovers, but he was clearly a man who liked his own sleeping space. This room was Tamar's, no question.

It looked like a guest room where someone was camping out. The only light came from a flickering TV screen, but it was enough to show me the room was decorated in white and gold, with some very nasty still-life oils on the walls. Lots of dead pheasants and fruit. It was furnished in Louis Quinze style. The only straight edges were on the television, which was even housed in a hideous gilt cabinet. If someone had put me up there, I think I would have preferred to sleep in the bath.

Tamar was lying on one of the twin beds wearing a pair of silk lounging pyjamas. She hadn't noticed my entrance because she was glued to the television, watching a video of 9½ Weeks. A pair of headphones were clamped to her head as she studied Kim Basinger and Mickey Rourke indulging in the ultimate nice work if you can get it. I walked across her line of vision and she sat bolt upright in annoyance.

She pulled the headphones off and snapped the bedside lamp on. More gilt horror.

'What the hell do you think you're doing, walking into my bedroom?' she snapped.

'Sorry to butt in on you,' I apologized insincerely.

'So you bloody should be. What are you doing here, anyway?'

I was beginning to get the message. Maybe I should change my deodorant. 'I'm afraid I've got bad news for you,' I said.

She scowled and pushed her tangled blonde hair back from her face. 'OK,' she sighed, swinging her legs over the side of the bed and standing up. 'Message received and understood. He means it this time.' She walked across the room and dramatically pulled open a wardrobe door. 'I was getting pissed off with having to be a little goody two shoes anyway. I'm too old to be sneaking off to the loo every time I want a joint.' She rattled the hangers noisily.

Then she turned back to me and shouted, 'So what are you hanging around for? Enjoying the cabaret, are you? My God, he didn't have to send you to do his dirty work.'

Crossed wires are, in my experience, the kind that provide most illumination. Unfortunately, it looked like this set had finally short-circuited. 'I think we're at cross

121

purposes, Tamar. It's not Jett who asked me to come and get you. It's the police.'

'The police?' The puzzlement on her face looked genuine. 'What d'you mean?'

'Like I said, I've got some bad news. Moira's dead,' I said.

It was as if I'd pressed the freeze-frame button. Tamar stopped dead, her face immobile. At first, she said nothing. Then a slow smile curled her lips. 'Well, what a shame,' she said sarcastically. 'I suppose she just couldn't stay away from the stuff.'

Tamar might have been a blonde, but I was far from convinced that she was dumb. And if she was guilty, she was choosing a very clever way of hiding it.

'You're right off track,' I commented. 'Moira's been murdered. In the rehearsal room.'

That got a reaction. Tamar flushed scarlet. 'I . . . I don't understand,' she whispered.

'I don't know any more than that myself,' I said. 'I called in to see Jett, and he went to fetch Moira. He discovered the body, and we called the police. They're waiting downstairs. You'd better get down there now. Everyone's in the blue drawing room.' I know I'm not going to win any points from bereavement counsellors for my attitude, but as far as I was concerned, Tamar lost all rights to my sympathy with that smile.

I moved towards the door. 'Wait,' she called. I turned back. 'Do you know who did it?' she asked.

I shook my head. 'Not up to me, Tamar. It's the police who work that sort of thing out. And they want to see you now,' I added, twisting the knife as I closed the door behind me.

I didn't hang around to see if she was following me. I tripped back down the curving stairs, half-expecting a Busby Berkeley chorus to break into song. But all I could hear was the police radio chatter. As I reached the hall, the intercom sounded again. This time, the constable on the door dealt with it so I made my way to the cellar door at the end of a short side-passage. I opened the door which led to a tiny vestibule with a flight of steps. I descended and found myself facing a heavy steel door. Above it was a red light. I know what happens in computer games if you ignore warnings like that, but I thought the chances of being zapped by an android were pretty remote, so I opened the door. Just shows how wrong you can be.

I was in a large recording studio, walls and ceiling covered in acoustic tiling. Keyboards, drum machines and mikes filled most of the available space. At the far end of the room there was a wall of glass. Behind it, a man sat hunched over a series of control consoles, a cigarette hanging out of one corner of his mouth. I could actually feel in my chest and stomach the throbbing bass line that emerged from tall speakers. I walked down the studio and waved to catch his attention. Abruptly the music stopped and a deafening voice yelled over the intercom, 'Get the fuck out of here! You blind, or what?'

I didn't know if he could hear me, but I spoke anyway. 'I'm sorry to interrupt, but you have to come upstairs.' I was beginning to wish I'd left this to Gloria.

'Look, sweetheart, it might have escaped your obviously limited intelligence, but I'm working. I don't stop on the say-so of anybody's bimbo, so just fuck off and find someone else to bug,' he snarled back at me, stubbing out his cigarette and immediately lighting another.

'Please yourself,' I said angrily. 'The next interruption you'll get will be the cops. They don't like being pissed about by little boys with expensive toys when they're investigating a murder.' I turned on my heel and marched off towards the door, feeling strangely satisfied with my childish response. Two steps later, I regretted it. I'd thrown away the chance of watching his reaction to my news. I turned back quickly and saw he'd stood up.

The resemblance to a chimp was overwhelming. The long arms, the jutting jaw, the flat nose all gave Micky Hampton a startlingly simian appearance. His blond-streaked hair had been carefully cut, but it couldn't altogether hide the Prince Charles ears. He'd have made a wonderful extra for *Planet of the Apes*. At least the make-up department wouldn't have had much work to do.

As I watched, he disappeared from my sight then emerged from a small door at the back of the studio. 'Wait a minute,' he said. 'You'd better explain yourself. For a kick-off, who the hell are you?'

'I'm Kate Brannigan.'

Understanding flooded his face. His soft brown eyes were unexpectedly intelligent. 'You're the one who dug Moira up,' he acknowledged. 'What did you mean about a murder?'

'Moira's been killed. I'm sorry to be the bearer of bad tidings, but the police want to see everyone who was in the house tonight,' I parroted.

Micky's eyebrows shot up. 'They're wasting their time with me. A bomb could drop up there and I wouldn't know. I've worked in top-class studios the world over and I've never found one that was better soundproofed than this.'

His concern for Moira was overwhelming. I hid my contempt and simply said, 'Nevertheless, they want to see everyone. The blue drawing room,' I added as I left him.

The hall had suddenly begun to resemble a police station. The scene-of-crime team had arrived with their cameras and fingerprint cases. Half a dozen uniformed constables were being directed to search the outside of the house and the grounds, to check for any signs of a break-in and to cover all exits. No one seemed to be paying any attention to me, so I slipped past them and crossed the hall. I headed down the corridor to Neil's domain. According to Gloria, he'd been given an office on the ground floor near the dining room.

I knocked on his door and heard him call, 'Come in, open all hours.' I closed the door behind me and leaned against it. The wood panelling obviously deadened any noise from outside. The small room looked remarkably like Richard's study. I wondered if journalists are born untidy or if they think the appearance of complete chaos is a necessary part of the image. Neil sat at the eye of the storm of paper, facing a computer screen, a small tape recorder beside him. He leaned back in his chair and grinned at me. 'Kate! Glad you could find the time to pop in on a humble scribe. Sorted out your business with Jett?'

'I'm afraid this isn't just a social call,' I said. 'I've been asked to come and fetch you.'

His hooded eyes half-closed as a guarded expression crossed his face. 'Fetch me?' he queried. 'Who wants me?'

'The police,' I said.

I could see the muscles in his jaw clench. 'What's all this about, Kate?' he forced out in a light tone.

'Bad news. Moira's dead.'

His eyes opened wide in horror. 'Oh no!' he exclaimed. 'Moira? Dead? How? What happened? Has there been an accident?' His questions spilled out, the professional habit attaching itself to his obvious personal shock.

'No accident, I'm afraid. Look, Neil, you'd better get along to the blue drawing room. The police want to see everyone who was in the house. They'll be able to fill you in on the details.'

'You mean, it happened here?'

'Why? Where did you think it had happened?'

'I don't know. She said something earlier about going down to the village to see someone. I suppose I assumed she was attacked on her way back or something. Oh God, poor Jett. He must be in a hell of a state.' At last, someone had finally spared a thought for the boss. Neil jumped to his feet and pushed past me to the door. 'The blue room, you said?' he demanded as he pulled it open.

'That's right,' I replied as I followed him.

As I re-emerged in the hall, a plain clothes policeman pounced. 'Kate Brannigan?' he demanded.

'That's me,' I agreed.

'You didn't tell us you're a private investigator,' he accused.

'No one asked me,' I replied, unable to resist. I don't know why I get this urge to be a smartass round coppers.

'The inspector wants to see you right now,' he told me, steering me down the hall into a smaller room next to the blue drawing room. It was wood panelled and stuffed with leather chairs. It looked like I've always imagined a gentlemen's club to be. A small writing desk had been moved away from the wall, and behind it sat a slim, dark-haired man in his mid thirties, his eyes indistinct behind a pair of glasses with tinted lenses. He was the last man in England wearing a pale blue shirt with white collar and cuffs under his dark blue suit. His striped tie was neatly knotted. He didn't look as if he'd been called out of bed in the middle of the night, but equally, he didn't look crumpled enough to have been on duty.

'I'm Inspector Cliff Jackson,' he introduced himself. 'And you must be our elusive private eye.'

'Good morning, Inspector,' I replied politely. 'I'm Kate Brannigan, of Mortensen and Brannigan.'

'I know exactly who you are, Miss Brannigan,' he countered, a note of irritation in his gravelly Lancashire voice. 'What I want to know is why you felt it necessary to go round interfering with witnesses.'

'I haven't been interfering with anyone,' I returned. 'If

126

you mean rounding up the inhabitants, I was simply doing what your sergeant asked.'

'As you well know, he wouldn't have let you near one of them if he'd known the way you earn a living.'

'Inspector, if anyone had bothered to ask what I do, I'd have been happy to tell them. Don't give me a bad time because one of your lads didn't do his job properly. I really don't want to fall out with you.'

'That's the first sensible thing you've said so far,' he grumbled as he made a note on his pad. We went through the formal routine that prefaces the taking of a statement, then he pushed his glasses up and massaged the bridge of his nose with surprisingly well-manicured fingers. 'So, what were you doing here tonight?' he asked.

'It was a social call. We did a job for Jett some time ago, and he told me to drop in whenever I was passing. So I did.' It sounded thin, even to me, but I could only hope he thought I was a bit starstruck.

'You were just passing at this time of night?' he challenged sarcastically, letting his glasses slip back into place. 'You normally drop in on people this late?'

'Of course not,' I countered. 'But I knew Jett keeps late hours. I'd been working and I was wide awake, so rather than go home and bounce off the walls I thought I'd stop off for a coffee. Besides, it wasn't that late when I got here. It can't have been that much after midnight.'

He clearly wasn't happy with the scenario, but he didn't have anything to contradict it yet, so he let it go for now. I outlined the version of events I'd agreed with Jett, hoping he'd remembered what he was supposed to say. I had plenty of time to think between sentences, since the detective who'd collared me was carefully writing it into a statement.

After we'd exhausted the subject of the discovery of the body, Jackson asked plenty of questions about the household and their movements, but I didn't have any answers. Frustrated, he gave up on that line and asked, 'What was the nature of this job your firm did for Jett?'

I'd hoped we wouldn't get to that till I'd had a chance to discuss the matter with Bill. I took a deep breath and recited, 'The nature of our business is confidential. I am afraid that is a private matter between Mortensen and Brannigan and our client.'

Jackson pushed his glasses up and rubbed the bridge of his nose again. It looked like he had a sinus headache, and I began to feel the slight stirrings of sympathy. He wouldn't be getting much sleep over the next few days unless they got a very lucky break. However, my sympathy didn't override my professional ethics.

'You are withholding information that could be material to a murder inquiry,' he sighed.

I was waiting with bated breath for him to say something, anything, that wasn't a cliché. I was destined for another disappointment.

'I don't have to tell you that it's an offence to obstruct the police. Frankly, I could do without the hassle of charging you, Miss Brannigan, but you make it very tempting.'

'I could do without the hassle too, Inspector. If it's any help, the answer will be the same whether you charge me or not.' I tried not to sound as defiant as I felt. A night in the cells would be both uncomfortable and bad for business.

'Get her out of my sight, Sergeant Bradley,' Jackson said, getting to his feet. 'Get her to sign her statement first,' he continued as he crossed the room and left.

The sergeant proffered the sheets of my statement and I read through it quickly. It never ceases to amaze me that no matter what you actually say in a police statement, it always comes out in a strangulated officialese. In spite of the jargon, Sergeant Bradley appeared to have got the gist of what I'd said, so I signed dutifully.

I was escorted back to the hall, where Jackson was earnestly talking to the uniformed sergeant. When he saw me, he scowled and said, 'Miss Brannigan's leaving now, sergeant. Get one of the lads to see her off the premises. And I mean right off.' Then he turned to me and said, 'I don't want you discussing the circumstances of this case with anyone. And I don't just mean the press. I mean you are not to talk to anyone about the method or timing of this incident. Is that understood?' I nodded. Then he added, 'We'll let you know when we want to see you again. And keep your nose out. Leave this to the professionals.'

I'd be only too happy to do just that, I thought as I drove down the drive. But somehow, I had the feeling Jett wasn't going to give me that option.

It was just after three a.m. when the electronic gates opened silently before me and I drove out into the lane, waving goodbye to the patrol car that had followed me down the drive. I slowed down as I approached Colcutt village, searching in the glove box for something more soothing than Tina Turner. As I hit the bend, a figure appeared in my headlights. It froze momentarily, then disappeared into the darkness of the verge.

I braked the car to a halt and jumped out. I ran back the few yards where the figure had disappeared. There was no trace of anyone. The only sound to break the silence of the night was the soft mutter of my engine. I might have been dreaming, but I didn't think so. I had only seen Moira's lover once, but I'd have recognized Maggie Rossiter anywhere.

15

When people find out what I do for a living, they always ask if it's dangerous. They usually seem disappointed when I confess that the hardest thing to deal with is lack of sleep. I get very ratty if I'm kept away from my bed. I'd been asleep for a mere four hours after my run-in with Jackson when the phone rang insistently.

I picked up the phone. 'Who is it?' I growled.

'Good morning to you, too,' Shelley replied. 'Bill wants to talk to you. Are you coming in or do you want to speak to him now?'

'Both,' I replied. Bill's no stickler for regular office hours, and he knows me well enough to know that if I'm not in the office at nine there's a good reason. So for him to get Shelley to roust me out of bed, it had to be important.

'Kate,' his voice boomed in my ear as Shelley connected us. 'What's this you've been up to now?'

'How did you get to hear about it?' I asked wearily, climbing out of bed and heading for the kitchen.

'The news about Moira was on the radio this morning, and I got into the office to find a string of increasingly hysterical messages from Jett and a demand for a meeting from a pompous asshole called Inspector Cliff Jackson. It didn't take a lot of working out,' he reported.

'What did Jett want?'

'You, basically. A lot of moaning about why did you

run out on him when he needed you and instructions to get yourself back over there asap. I think you'd better come in and brief me on what's been going on before we decide whether we want to have any further involvement. OK?' It was the nearest Bill was ever going to get to a direct order.

Twenty minutes later, I was filling him in. When I got to the bit about the story I'd concocted for the police about the body's discovery, he shifted uneasily in his chair. 'I don't think that was one of your brightest moves, Kate,' he complained.

'I know. But anything else made Jett look like the killer.'

'And how do you know he wasn't?' Bill challenged me.

'I saw the state he was in. It wasn't the kind of reaction I'd expect from a man who had just killed his so-called soul mate. It was more like he couldn't believe it till someone else had confirmed it. Besides, if I'd told the truth, Jett wouldn't have been cluttering up our answering machine all night. He'd be down the nick in an interrogation room.' I knew it sounded weak even as I told it, but the strength of my own gut feeling about Jett's innocence didn't allow for compromise.

'I trust your instincts, Kate. But the cops sure as hell won't. We'll have to make damn sure they don't find out the truth. And I suppose that means you'll have to stay close to whatever's going on,' he added. He chewed his beard restlessly, a sure sign that he's worried.

'At least Jett seems to want that,' I tried. It wasn't much of a consolation, but it was the only one I could see right then.

'Jett might, but I don't,' Bill flashed back. 'We don't do murders, Kate. We do white-collar crime. We're not geared up to compete with the police on something like this. Besides, I'm not happy about putting you in the front line when there's someone out there killing people.'

'I can handle myself,' I replied huffily.

'I know you can. It's the other poor fuckers I'm worried about,' he said with a tired smile. 'Seriously, though. I really wish you hadn't got us involved. But now we are, you'd better brief me fully.'

I gave him a quick résumé of events, leaving out only my glimpse of Maggie. I don't know why I held that back; maybe I was worried about her being the obvious scapegoat, even to a supposedly new man like Bill.

'Jackson wanted to know the nature of the job we did for Jett,' I finished up. 'I hid behind client confidentiality.'

'You did right. Leave Jackson to me. You'd better have a listen to Jett's messages then get yourself over to Colcutt.'

It was after eleven when I drew up outside the electronic gates. Half a dozen cars were parked along the verge, and I recognized a couple of national newspaper reporters. The news of Moira's death had broken too late for that morning's editions, but they were determined to make up for lost time. As I pulled up to speak to the police constable, who looked cold and miserable in the thin drizzle of rain, car doors suddenly opened and the pack descended. Luckily, Jett had had the sense to tell the police I should be admitted. He'd also remembered to leave me the security code for the gate in one of his messages. I was halfway through the gates before the first journalist reached me. I put my foot down and left him shaking off the spray from my tyres.

At the house, another freezing copper let me in. There was no one in sight, but the constable on duty at the door of the rehearsal room grudgingly told me that Jett was in the kitchen. I found him there alone, slumped at an old pine farmhouse table, a mug of tea sitting in front of him. He barely glanced at me when I crossed the room to the kettle. I put it on to boil and picked up his mug. Nothing like making yourself at home. His untouched tea was stone cold, so I made us both fresh.

'You shouldn't have gone,' he greeted me. 'I wanted you here.'

'I didn't have any choice,' I explained patiently, like I would to Davy, Richard's five-year-old. 'The cops bounced me as soon as they found out who I was.'

Jett lifted his mug to his lips, but lowered it untasted. His skin had taken on a strange dullness, the colour of slate. His eyes were bloodshot, but not puffy with tears. 'You liked her, didn't you?' he asked.

'Moira? I hardly knew her, but yes, I liked what I saw of her. She had courage, and a sense of humour,' I replied.

He nodded, as if I'd confirmed something. 'That's why I want you to find out who killed her. Somebody in this house, somebody I trusted, took her life away. You're going to find out who.'

I felt like I'd stumbled on to the set of an episode of *Murder, She Wrote*. I took a deep breath and tried to bring the conversation down to earth. 'Don't you think you should leave this to the police? They've got the manpower and the facilities to investigate murder, Jett. I haven't.'

He warmed his hands on the mug. 'You don't understand, Kate. This isn't going to be solved by fingerprints and alibis. This is going to be solved by understanding people. The Old Bill, they didn't know Moira. And they sure as hell don't understand any of us. The people in this house, we don't talk the same language as these cops. Not even Mr Respectable Kevin. But you're different. You live with Richard, you know this life. You can speak to them, make them open up like they won't to the Old Bill.' It was a long speech for a man as close to the edge as Jett obviously was. He leaned back in his chair and squeezed his eyes shut.

'I don't know, Jett. I've never had to investigate a murder before.'

His eyes opened abruptly and he stared at me, brows

drawn down in a scowl. 'Listen, Kate. To those cops, I'm just a piece of black shit. A rich piece, but still shit. Moira was just a junkie hooker to them. They'd love to pin this on me and walk away, because that would fit. I grew up in the Moss, I know how their minds work. I don't trust them and they sure as hell won't trust me. There's only you between me and the nick, Kate, and I need your help to stay out of it.' His bottom lip thrust out defiantly.

I pushed my mug away and reached out for his hand. 'OK, Jett. No promises, but I'll give it my best shot.'

He clasped my hand in both of his. There were tears shining in his eyes. 'That's good enough for me.' A single tear trickled down his cheek and he brushed it away as impatiently as if it were a troublesome fly.

'What happened after I left?' I asked.

'They kept us all shut up together till gone four o'clock. Didn't leave us alone for a minute, though. They had a kid copper keeping his ears open. That guy Jackson, he told me to say nothing about how I found her, or anything else. They all wanted to know, though,' he added bitterly.

'They'll be hoping they can trip up the killer,' I explained. 'You know, someone knowing more than they're supposed to.' Amazing that the police still rely on that after they spent three years barking up the wrong tree on the Yorkshire Ripper investigation because of a hoax tape that revealed details only the killer should supposedly have known.

'What time is it?' he asked incongruously.

I glanced at my watch. 'Five to twelve.'

Jett got to his feet and swallowed most of his tea in a oner. 'I told them all to be in the blue room at twelve. I knew you'd be here. You have an intuitive spirit. I knew you'd know I needed you.'

I refrained from pointing out that it had more to do with the office answering machine than my psychic powers. 'I'm going to have to talk to you about the last six weeks, Jett,' I protested as he walked out of the room.

'You're going to have to talk to all of us about the last six weeks,' he said over his shoulder as I followed him. 'I just want them all to know they have to co-operate with you. They can be as bloody-minded as they like with the cops, but it's me that puts the bread in their mouths and they'll do what I tell them.'

It was strange to see how quickly his natural authority had returned to him. I couldn't believe it was my agreeing to work for him that had done the trick. If he was capable of such mercurial mood shifts, maybe my initial assessment of his innocence had been way off-beam.

Jett threw open the drawing room door just on the stroke of twelve. They were all there except Neil. None of them looked as if they'd had much sleep. Equally, none of them looked like they'd shed too many tears.

As I entered behind Jett, Kevin groaned. 'Oh God, Jett, I told you to leave her out of this. We don't need an extra nosy parker round here. The cops have already turned this place into a goldfish bowl.'

'He's right, Jett,' Gloria chipped in. 'You need to come to terms with your grief. Having her around the place isn't going to help.'

Jett threw himself into a spindly-legged chair. Miraculously, it withstood the impact. 'I can't be doing any grieving while I know Moira's killer is under my roof, eating my food and drinking my booze. Kate's here to find out which one of you is my enemy. Any of you that doesn't want to be part of my team, you can go now. But you want to stick around, then you co-operate with Kate one hundred per cent. She'll be reporting directly to me, and I don't want her interfered with. Is that clear?'

Kevin cast his eyes up to heaven and muttered, 'Give me strength!' I knew exactly how he felt. Melodrama was never my favourite art form. But it was Tamar who was right on the ball. She crossed the room and hugged him. 'Whatever you need is all right by me, Jett.' I tried not to vomit, but it was hard.

Before anyone else could chip in with their tuppence worth, Neil came in. 'Sorry I'm late, Jett,' he apologized. 'I've been issuing full press statements to all the nationals, and it took longer than I thought.'

'Enter stage left, the in-house vulture,' Micky sneered.

'Somebody's got to handle them,' Neil replied mildly. 'Better that it's someone who can string two sentences together.'

'Meaning what?' Micky demanded belligerently.

'My God, can't you two stop bickering for once? Have some respect for the dead,' Tamar shouted. Her shameless hypocrisy left me gasping, but no one else seemed to notice. Micky mumbled an apology and walked over to the window to watch the rain falling.

'You on the payroll, then?' Neil asked me *sotto voce*. I nodded. He smiled conspiratorially. 'Glad I'm not the only one making a shilling out of Moira's death.'

I'd only been there an hour and already I was heartily sick of the lot of them. Some jobs should come stamped with a government health warning. Something like: 'You lie down with dogs, you get up with fleas.'

I decided it was time to start asking questions. But in the great tradition of the best-laid plans, I was thwarted by the arrival of Inspector Jackson and his merry men. Jackson marched in as if he'd taken a long lease on the place. He'd found time for a fresh suit and shirt, though the tie was the same. Maybe it held some Masonic significance I didn't recognize. Hot on his heels was an older man, who moved to Jackson's side and announced, 'Good day, ladies and gentlemen. I am Detective Superintendent Ron Arbuthnot and I will be in overall charge of this inquiry. I know some of you have given my officers initial statements, but we will be requiring you for further interviews in the course of the day. Please arrange to keep yourselves available.' The Royal Command having been delivered, Arbuthnot wheeled his tubby body round past Jackson and left us.

As soon as he'd gone, Jackson turned on me. 'Have you got some kind of death wish, Brannigan?' he hissed as he took me by the arm and led me to the door. 'I've already thrown you out of here once. Is business so bad you've got to come touting?'

'I was invited here,' I told him through clenched teeth. 'Get your hands off me. Now.'

He reluctantly let me go, then opened the door and tried to usher me through it. I stood my ground. Jett called, 'You OK, Kate? The lady's a friend, Inspector. I want her here.'

Jackson turned to Jett and flashed an insincere smile. 'I'm afraid that won't be possible, Mr Franklin. We have some questions for Miss Brannigan, and after that, we'll be needing to talk to you again. Perhaps it would be better if she came back tomorrow.'

Jett glared at Jackson. I wasn't sure if that was on my account or because Jackson had used his real name. Jett doesn't like to be reminded of its patriotic overtones. Let's face it, which of us outside the Tory Cabinet would like to be saddled with Winston Gladstone Franklin?

'It's OK, Jett,' I said reassuringly. 'I'll come back tomorrow morning, OK?' There were things I wanted to do, and none of this lot were going anywhere. They would keep. Maggie Rossiter might not be so keen to talk if I waited till she'd got her emotions under control.

16

I was in the Colcutt Arms by half-past twelve. It turned out that the only questions Jackson had for me related to what I was doing back at the manor and what I'd done for Jett in the past, nudge nudge, wink wink. I didn't like his innuendoes, and suspected he was trying to needle me into an admission of some sort. Obviously, he'd got no more change out of Bill than he had out of me. At least he wasn't challenging my version of the discovery of the body yet.

It wasn't just relief that drove me to the local pub. I was after information. I spotted the members of Her Majesty's Gutter Press in the lounge bar, and gave it a body-swerve. What the saloon bar lacked in creature comforts it made up for by the complete absence of journos. If I was going to go into my chatty passing-motorist act, I didn't want an audience.

The harried barmaid who served me seemed as glad to escape from them as I was. She bustled through from the lounge when I pressed a bell on the bar and pushed a strand of bottle blonde hair from her forehead. She was in her forties, and looked shell-shocked to find herself in the throes of a lunchtime rush.

'Busy today,' I said sympathetically as she poured me a St Clement's.

'You're not wrong,' she replied. 'Ice?' I nodded. 'Last

time we were this busy of a dinner time was Boxing Day.'

'Bad business up the road,' I remarked as I sipped my drink. She was happily leaning against the bar, relieved to escape the clod-hopping probings of the press. I hoped my questions fitted in the category of Great British Pub Gossip.

'That poor woman!' she exclaimed. 'Do you know, she was in here last night with a friend of hers, sitting in a corner of my lounge bar! And next thing you know, she's murdered in her own home. You're not safe anywhere these days. You'd think with all the security they've got up there they'd be all right. I said to my Geoff, it's like Fort Knox up there, and they're not safe. Makes you wonder.'

My ears pricked up at the news of Moira's meeting in the pub, but I didn't want to pounce too eagerly. 'I sometimes wonder if it's all the security that attracts them,' I responded, playing along with the Passing Vagabond theory. 'You know, like a challenge or something.'

'Well, all I can say is we've never had any trouble in this village till we had so-called rock stars living here.' Her mouth pursed, revealing a nest of wrinkles she'd have been mortified to see in a mirror.

'Do they come in here much?' I asked casually.

'One or two of them. They've got a journalist living up there, writing some book about Jett, he's never out of here normally. I don't know when he gets his writing done. He's in here for a couple of hours most dinner times and he gets through half a dozen pints every session. Not that I'm complaining – I'm glad of the custom in the winter months. Sometimes I wonder why we bother opening up in the middle of the day. What we take across the bar hardly covers the electricity,' she grumbled.

'Nice place, though,' I complimented her. 'Been here long?'

'Five years. My husband used to be a mining engineer,

but we got tired of living abroad, so we bought this place. It's hard work, especially doing the bed and breakfast, but it's better than living with a load of foreigners,' she replied. Before I could ask more, the bell from the lounge summoned her.

To ensure her return, I called, 'Do you do food?'

'Just sandwiches.'

I ordered a round of roast beef, and when she returned, I said, 'It must have been a shock for you, one of your regulars getting murdered.'

'Well, she wasn't exactly a regular. She's been in a few times the last couple of days when her friend was staying here. But she'd only been in the once before that, with a crowd of them. The only way I knew it was her was with her being black. Not that I'm racist,' she added hastily. 'It's just that we don't get many of them round here.'

I could believe her. I remembered only too well how the police inspector in one of the nearby Cheshire towns had defended his policy of arresting any blacks he saw on the street by announcing, 'None of them live around here so if they're walking our streets they're probably up to no good.'

'Her friend must have been in a hell of a state when she heard the news,' I tried, checking the gender of the friend. I was pretty sure it must have been Maggie, but it would be nice to make sure. I took a bite out of the sandwich. Even without the information about Moira's visit, the trip had been worthwhile. The bread was fresh and crusty, the meat pink, sliced wafer thin and piled thick, with a generous smear of horseradish. I nearly choked on it when I heard her reply.

'I don't even know if she has heard the news,' the landlady replied. 'When I got up this morning, there was an envelope on the hall table with the money she owed and a note saying she'd had to leave early. I knew she was

140

checking out today, but I didn't expect her to be off at the crack of dawn.' She sounded slightly aggrieved, as if she'd been done out of a good piece of drama.

'You mean she just cleared off in the middle of the night? Funny, that,' I remarked, trying not to sound like a private eye who's one happy step ahead of the police.

'No, not the middle of the night. She didn't actually leave till about half-past six. Our bedroom's at the back, you see. The car woke me up, and I got up because I thought she might have gone off without paying. I didn't even know about the murder myself then.' She clearly saw nothing suspicious in Maggie's behaviour, and I was grateful for that. There would be at least one suspect I'd get to before the police.

'Perhaps she had a phone call or something,' I hazarded.

'Not while she was here,' the landlady replied positively. 'I'd have known. I think she probably just woke up early and decided to get an early start. To be honest, I was surprised she wasn't staying at the manor. Their friends don't usually put up here.'

I could have come up with a couple of good reasons why Maggie Rossiter hadn't been willing to accept Jett's hospitality, but I wasn't about to share them. I finished my sandwich, exchanged a few routine complaints about the weather, and set off for Leeds.

It was still drizzling when I pulled up outside Maggie's terraced house. Crossing the Pennines hadn't worked its usual trick of transforming the weather. Through the drift of rain, the house looked miserable and unwelcoming. There were no lights on to combat the gloom. Mind you, if my lover was lying dead in a morgue somewhere, I don't think I'd feel like a hundred watt glare.

Maggie took her time answering the door. I'd just decided she wasn't home when the door opened. When

141

she saw me, she started to close it again. I moved forward quickly enough to insinuate my shoulder in the gap.

'What the hell do you think you're playing at?' she demanded feebly, her voice cracked and shaky.

'We need to talk, Maggie,' I said. 'I know it's the last thing you feel like, but I think I can help.'

'Help? You do resurrections?' Her voice was bitter, and tears shone in her red-rimmed eyes. My professional satisfaction at getting to her first withered in the face of her obvious grief.

'I'm trying to find out who killed Moira,' I told her.

'What's the use? It's not going to bring her back, is it?' Maggie rubbed her eyes impatiently with her free hand, as if she hated showing me her humanity.

'No, it's not. But you've got to grieve. You know that. And finding out what happened is the first step in the process. Maggie, let me come in and talk to you.'

Her straight shoulders seemed to sag and she stood back from the door. It opened straight on to her living room, and I sat down before she could change her mind. Behind me, Maggie closed the door firmly and went through to the kitchen. I could hear the sound of a kettle being filled. I took the chance to take stock of the room. It was large, occupying most of the ground floor of the house. One of the alcoves by the chimney breast held an assortment of books, from science fiction to sociology texts. The other held a small TV and a stereo system with a collection of tapes, CDs and LPs. The only decoration on the walls was a large reproduction of Klimt's Judith. The room contained two sofas and, in the bay, a small pine dining table with four chairs. It looked like home, but only one person's idea of it.

She came through with a pot of tea on a tray with two mugs, a bottle of milk and a bowl of sugar. 'I've got this terrible thirst. I can't seem to stop drinking tea,' she said

142

absently as she poured. Her hair looked dishevelled, as did the sweatshirt and jeans she was wearing. The room was unbearably warm, the gas fire on full, yet Maggie shivered as she lifted her mug to her lips.

'I'm sorry,' I said, knowing how hollow it would sound, but feeling the need nevertheless. 'I hardly knew her, but I liked what I did know.'

Maggie walked over to the window and stared out at the silent rain falling on the grey roofs. 'Let's get one thing straight, Kate,' she observed. 'I am not going to discuss my feelings with you. I have friends for that. I'll tell you anything I can about what happened after she left with you that night, but our feelings for each other and the way I feel right now is nothing to do with you.'

'That's fine by me,' I said, feeling like I'd been reprieved. After Jett's histrionics, I didn't know how much more I could take.

She turned back into the room and sat on the other sofa, as far from me as it was possible to be. 'I suppose Jett's hired you to discover I did it?' she challenged.

'I'm working for Jett, but he hasn't pointed the finger at anyone. I think he's still too upset to have given it much thought. It was him who found the body, you know.'

'I didn't know,' she sighed. 'You should never have tried to find her. If Jett had let the past rest in peace, she'd still be here now.'

I couldn't deny it. And I saw no point in trying to justify my own part in the process. 'Suppose we go back to the beginning and work forward?' I asked. 'What happened after I took her over to see Jett?'

Maggie sighed again. She pulled a small tin out of her pocket and with trembling fingers rolled a cigarette. 'She rang the morning after. She said that she and Jett had had a long talk.' A half-smile flickered across her lips as she went on. 'She'd learned the hard way not to take any prisoners. She went in there with an agenda, and she wasn't prepared to make any compromises. She said she'd work with him on the songs for his new album, and if that worked out, then she'd consider future collaborations. But that was it. No going back to their old relationship. She wanted a room of her own, all the back royalties that were due to her, and a new deal for the new album. She wanted a percentage share of the profits as well as her songwriting royalties. After all, he'd be doing well out of it too.' Maggie paused, looking to me for a response.

'It doesn't sound unreasonable to me. I'd guess that Jett could afford it,' I agreed.

'Jett was over the moon, according to Moira. He said she'd have to work out the money details with Kevin, but it was fine by him. She was laughing, you know? She said he'd got into all this New Age stuff, and kept telling her they were soul mates and must be together. She'd told him that only extended to work and he could forget sex. Then he went all huffy and started on about spiritual love. She was very funny about it all.' Memories overwhelmed Maggie suddenly and she looked away.

Awkwardly, I said, 'I liked her sense of humour, too. Maggie, did she say anything about the reactions of the others at the manor to her arrival?'

Maggie relit her cigarette and took a deep drag. 'Not then. But she had plenty to say later. Only Neil seemed really pleased that she was there. He seemed to think she'd be able to fill in any gaps from the early days. I know he talked to her about what it was like before Jett hit the big time. She said Gloria was always trying to bust up their conversations. She wanted to come across as the only significant person in Jett's life. Pathetic, really.

'Tamar hated her on sight, of course. Her and Jett have been having this on-off relationship for a few months now, and I guess she saw Moira as a threat. Moira couldn't stand her, thought she was just a stupid bimbo, and she told me she used to wind her up by flirting with Jett when Tamar was around. But there was nothing in it. She told me that, and I believe her. I trust . . .' she gulped. 'I trusted her.'

'What about Kevin? How did he take it?' I probed.

'She said he wasn't thrilled, but that she wasn't surprised because the idea of parting with any money, even if it's not his own, gives him a physical pain. She said if he gave you his shit for fertilizer he'd want the roses. And there was a lot of money coming to her. All those years of royalties from the first three albums.'

'Did she get the money?' I suspected I knew the answer before I asked the question.

'Not yet. Kevin said it was tied up in some account where he had to wait three months before he could get access to it.'

I'd been right. Moira had died before she'd cost anyone a penny. I wondered if anyone would ever be able to untangle things now she was dead. 'Do you happen to know if she left a will?' I asked.

Maggie's mouth twisted into an ironic smile. 'Jett tell you to ask that? Yes, she left a will. We both made wills in favour of each other about two months ago.'

'Do you mind if I ask you why?'

'Because a friend of mine was killed in a car crash and she hadn't left a will. The house was in her name, and her family kicked her lover out on the street the day before the funeral. Gay couples don't have any rights. We have to make our own. That's why we made the wills. At that point, Moira didn't even think she had anything to leave,' Maggie said bitterly.

But when she'd died, it had been a different picture. I knew I'd want to come back to this, but I needed to hear more from other people before I'd have any useful leverage. So I changed the subject. 'Surely Micky was pleased?

He must have been happy that they were all working together again, just like the good old days?'

'You'd have thought so, wouldn't you? But not according to Moira. She said he was always nit-picking. She thought he wanted to take all the credit for Jett's great comeback album – they hadn't worked together for the last four, you see.'

'I'm beginning to wonder why she stuck it,' I remarked.

'I wondered myself. But she really enjoyed the work she was doing with Jett. She loved the writing. And she was even doing some of the backing vocals. She kept telling me that when the money came rolling in, I could give up work and we'd go and live in the sun somewhere.' Maggie's face crumpled and she pulled a soggy handkerchief out of her pocket. She blew her nose. 'If she hadn't been doing it for us, maybe she'd never have been tempted to stay.'

'Had you seen her much in the last few weeks?' I asked.

'Not really. She hasn't been home at all. We had a couple of weekends in a hotel in Manchester. Jett had gone to Paris with Tamar, and he'd given her some money and told her to show me a good time.' Her eyes lit up, then the light died. 'We had a good time, too,' she said softly.

'Why did you go to Colcutt this week?' I asked.

She looked at me in surprise. 'What do you mean?'

'I saw you. I was driving the car that nearly ran you over in the early hours of the morning. The landlady at the Colcutt Arms told me you'd been staying there. I just wondered, you know? With you two not having seen very much of each other lately.' I let my words hang in the air. Maggie was no fool. She must have realized it would only be a matter of time before the police would be at her door.

'Now I see why you wanted to talk to me,' she accused. 'You really are trying to pin it on me.'

146

I shook my head. 'Maggie, I'm not trying to pin it on anybody. I'm trying to find Moira's killer.'

'If that's true, you'd be better off back in Colcutt,' she said angrily. 'Someone there had it in for her. That's why I went over to see her, to try to persuade her to come home with me.'

'What do you mean?' I asked. My antennae were quivering. I had the feeling we were really getting somewhere at last.

'Someone there wanted her dead. They'd already tried once.'

17

I took a deep breath and said very slowly, 'What do you mean, they'd already tried?'

'I don't know how much you know about heroin addiction,' Maggie replied.

'Lay person's knowledge only. Assume I'm ignorant.'

'OK. Coming off is hell. But once an addict is off, they often get a strange kind of confidence that one little hit wouldn't do any harm. Like the smoker who's been stopped for three years and fancies a fag at a party. Only with heroin addicts, that can be fatal a lot faster than with smokers. Anyway, someone at Colcutt Manor kept leaving a set of works in Moira's room. Every couple of days, she'd come upstairs to find a nice little hit sitting there waiting for her.' Maggie stopped dead, her anger making her voice a growl.

'That is evil,' I breathed.

'So now you see why I wanted her to leave. So far, she'd just flushed the smack down the loo and shoved the syringes in the bin. But sooner or later there was going to come a time when she'd be low, when she couldn't ring me up for reassurance, when she was going to go for it. I couldn't stand the thought of it.'

I swallowed hard. Now for the nasty question. 'So why did you leave when you did? In the middle of the night like that?'

Maggie rolled another cigarette while she pondered my question. I couldn't help feeling she was using me as the rehearsal for the harder interrogation she knew was on the horizon. 'We'd had a drink together that evening in the pub. Moira promised me that her work would be over in another two weeks and then we'd go on holiday together. She said she could hold out, and begged me not to make her choose. I gave in, God help me.

'Afterwards, we went up to my room and made love. She left about eleven, saying she was going back to work with Jett. I tried to sleep, but I couldn't. I know it sounds pathetic, but I had a dreadful feeling in the pit of my stomach that something terrible was going to happen. Eventually, I got up and went for a walk. Then I saw all those police cars up at the manor and I panicked. Whatever was going on, I knew I would only be in Moira's way if I turned up on the doorstep, so I went back to the pub. That's when you nearly ran me over.' Maggie lit her cigarette and ran a hand through her greying curls.

'I tried to ring from the phone in the pub, but it was constantly engaged. I didn't know what else to do, so I set off for home. Moira knew I was coming home today, and I knew she'd call me as soon as she could. The first I knew she was dead was when I heard the news on Radio One at half-past nine.' She couldn't hold the tears back any longer, and they streamed down her face. Her shoulders shook.

I got up and tentatively put a hand on her arm, but she shook me off and huddled into a ball. Feeling helpless, I retreated to the sofa. While I waited for her to compose herself, I thought about what I'd heard. It sounded incredibly thin to me. I couldn't imagine any circumstances in which I'd behave as Maggie had done unless I was running from something. But equally, I couldn't see why she'd have killed Moira if she was telling the truth about their relationship.

149

After a few minutes, Maggie managed to find the strength from somewhere to dry her tears, clear her throat and look me in the eye. 'I didn't kill her. I'd have cheerfully killed the bastard who was trying to destroy her with the smack, but not Moira. Never Moira.'

Her denial was vehement. But I've heard good performances before. I didn't have enough information to try to get beyond that right now, but if I uncovered it, I'd be back. This was one case where I couldn't let sentiment get in the way. 'I believe you,' I said, almost convinced. 'Is there anything else, however trivial, that Moira said that might shed some light on what happened?'

Maggie got up and poured herself another mug of tea. She leaned against the table, eyebrows twisted in concentration. 'There was one thing,' she said uncertainly.

'Yes?' I asked expectantly.

'It's probably nothing, but last night in the pub, she asked me about one of the guys she used to know in Bradford. A bloke called Fat Freddy. She wanted me to ask around and see what he was into just now that might be connected to Jett in some way,' Maggie said hesitantly.

'Did she say why?'

Maggie shrugged. 'To be honest, I wasn't paying a lot of attention. She said something like, she'd seen him talking to someone from the manor who shouldn't be mixing with small-time villains like Fat Freddy.'

The whiff of red herring was getting pretty strong. If I'd been trying to divert suspicion away from myself, that was exactly the kind of unprovable line I'd come up with.

'Did she say who it was she'd seen with this Fat Freddy?' I asked cautiously.

Maggie shook her head. 'I'm sorry, she didn't. She said she wanted to find out what the connection was before she said anything more.'

I felt frustrated. Why couldn't Maggie have shown a bit

more interest in something other than her own relationship with Moira? Had she no natural curiosity? If I'd dropped something like that on Richard, he'd have been on it like a rat up a drain, demanding chapter and verse on everything I'd seen and heard. 'What do you know about Fat Freddy?' I asked without much hope.

'He's a bit of a wide-boy. Moira knew him from when she was working in Bradford. She told me he was into buying and selling – whatever came along. I met him once. Moira bought a couple of jogging suits from him.'

'Would you know where to find him?'

Maggie pulled a face. 'Not really. Why? Do you think it might be important?'

'Yes, I do. I don't know how yet, but it could be.'

'OK. I'll see if I can find out what he's up to and get in touch with you. It's what Moira asked me to do.'

I tried not to show my surprise at her co-operation, and fished a card out of my wallet. I wrote my home number on the back. 'If you remember anything more or come up with something on Fat Freddy, give me a call any time, day or night.' I got to my feet. 'Thanks for being so helpful. I know it can't have been easy.'

'Believe me, the worst is yet to come. And I'm not talking about the police.' Maggie's face had frozen into a cold mask. 'There's no framework for grief when you're gay.'

'I'm sorry,' I said inadequately.

'Spare me the bleeding-heart liberal shit,' Maggie flashed back, suddenly angry. 'Just leave me alone.'

It wasn't hard to do exactly as she asked.

I spent what was left of the afternoon back at the office. I'd recorded my notes on tape on the way back from Leeds, so I didn't even have that to keep me occupied. I hate those spells in an investigation where everything is stalled.

I didn't want to go back to the manor for another confrontation with Jackson. I'd rather wait till tomorrow, when the police presence would have eased off, and the initial shock would have worn off for the inhabitants.

So I did the paperwork on the Smart brothers that had been hanging over me for the last couple of weeks since our clients had passed our dossier on to the police. I was providing them with more details on my surveillance, so they'd be fully prepared for the raid they were planning for some unspecified date in the future when they got their act together. I ploughed through my diary for the relevant weeks, and there, in the middle of it all, I found the notes of my search for Moira. I couldn't help agreeing with Maggie that it was a pity I'd ever found her. Bill had been right. Missing persons' jobs produce more trouble than they're worth.

Before I left the office, I helped myself to a couple of Raymond Chandlers and a Dashiell Hammett from Bill's bookcase. I was going to need all the help I could get, and somehow I had the feeling that wandering down to Waterstone's for a book on how to solve a murder wasn't going to be a lot of use.

I got home just after six. For once, my heart sank when I saw Richard's car outside the house. I wasn't looking forward to telling him about the secrets I'd been keeping. But I couldn't hide my involvement in the murder investigation, not without moving out while it went on. There would be too many incoming phone calls and answering-machine messages from people connected to the case.

I decided to get it over with as quickly as possible, so I poured myself a drink and crossed the conservatory. Halfway across, Jett's first album hit me right between the ears. Richard's living room was empty, so I followed the music down to his study. He was so absorbed in the screen of his word processor that he didn't hear me enter.

Over his shoulder, I read, 'Moira got her second chance at the dream ticket just six weeks ago when she turned up at Jett's luxury mansion, a world away from the mean streets where they started off.' I don't know, even the journalists I trust can't get their facts right.

I tapped him gently on the shoulder and he glanced up at me with a distracted smile. 'Hiya, Brannigan.'

I leaned over and kissed him. 'Busy?'

'Ten minutes. You hear about Moira Pollock?' I nodded. 'I'm doing a piece for the *Sunday Tribune* – you know, wringing their withers, lots of colour, plenty of topspin. Be right with you.'

I left him to it. True to his word, ten minutes later he joined me in the conservatory, where I was watching the rain on the glass making rivers against the darkness. Richard threw himself into a basket chair and popped the top of a Michelob Dry.

'I have a confession to make,' I announced.

Richard's eyebrows rose and he gave me his cute smile. 'You wore the same clothes two days running? You forgot to hoover the lounge before you went out this morning? You ate a yoghurt that was two days past its sell-by date?'

I don't know who told him he was funny. It certainly wasn't me. 'This is serious,' I explained.

'Oh, shit! You left a ring round the bath!' he teased.

Sometimes I wish I lived with a grown-up.

'Moira Pollock didn't just turn up on Jett's doorstep out of the blue,' I announced bluntly. It was the only way to get his attention.

'How d'you know that?' he demanded, suddenly serious now his professional world was involved.

'Because it was me who drove her there.'

I had the momentary satisfaction of seeing his jaw drop. 'You what?' he exclaimed.

'I'm sorry. I couldn't tell you about it at the time. Jett

153

swore me to secrecy, with particular reference to you. He hired us to find Moira for him. So I did. And now he's hired me to find Moira's killer.'

I'd dropped my bombshell, and it seemed to have left Richard momentarily speechless. He just stared at me, mouth open like a drunken actor who's forgotten his lines. Eventually, he closed his mouth, swallowed hard and said, 'You're at the wind-up.'

'Never been more serious.'

He looked at me suspiciously. 'So how come you're telling me now? How come client confidentiality goes out the window at this precise moment?'

'Because when murder's on the agenda, I'm entitled to grab all the extra help I can get,' I explained.

'Shee-it,' he drawled. Then the journalist in him jumped out like a jack-in-the-box. 'That's great. You'll be able to give me the inside track on the story.'

I shook my head wonderingly. 'That's not the idea, Richard. We'll happily pay you a consultancy fee, but I don't let the cat out of the bag for anyone except my client. And besides, whatever I could give you would be old hat anyway. Your old mate Neil Webster is sitting there in Colcutt Manor, feeding the world what it wants to hear, straight from the horses' mouths.'

He covered his disappointment with a wry grin. 'Anybody should have been murdered up there, it should have been that piece of shit,' he complained. 'OK, Brannigan. You got it. Any help I can give you, it's yours. So why don't you take me right back to the beginning and tell me how you tracked Moira down. Surely you can at least give me that teensy weensy exclusive?'

I grinned back at him. One day I'm going to learn how to put up a resistance to his charms. With any luck, it's a long way off.

18

There was still a policeman at the gates of Colcutt Manor when I arrived the following morning. But half-past ten was too early for the press, who, judging by the number of cars in the pub car park, had invaded the guest rooms of the Colcutt Arms and were still sleeping off their expense account excesses.

It was also too early for the household. Now the bulk of the police had left, life was slowly returning to normal. The kitchen was empty, as was the blue drawing room, the television room, the dining room, the billiard room and Neil's office. I was beginning to feel like a National Trust curator on a rainy Wednesday as I trudged back to the hall. This time, one of the crew of the Marie Celeste had appeared.

Gloria was just walking out of her office when she heard my heels clattering on the terrazzo tiles and turned sharply round. 'Oh, it's you,' she said with her usual grace and charm. She ignored me and carried on walking, closing the door behind her.

Undaunted, I followed her down the hall to the rear porch. As she pulled on a tan leather blouson, she eyed me warily, and I returned the compliment. I know that white is the colour of mourning in oriental cultures, but I've never encountered the civilization where they show their feelings for the departed in coral and cream jogging suits. I guess Valkyries do things differently.

'I'm busy,' she informed me, opening the back door and heading for the stable block.

'Must be a lot to do,' I said. 'Organizing the funeral and all.'

She had the good grace to blush, a reaction that strangely did nothing for her English Rose colouring. She zapped the up-and-over garage door with the little black box on her keyring and the door slid quietly open.

'That's being arranged by Moira's mother. We decided Jett was in no fit state to cope with it,' she informed me.

And Ms Pollock indubitably will be, I thought, but didn't say. There was already enough animosity between us. 'In that case,' I insisted, following her to the driver's door of a Volkswagen Golf, 'I'm sure you can find a few minutes of your time to answer a few questions.' She climbed in the car, ignoring me, and started the engine. I had to jump back to avoid her rear wheels amputating my toes.

'Bitch,' I yelled as the GTi shot out of the garage, leaving me gagging on her exhaust fumes. I hesitated for a moment, then my anger got the better of me. I raced back to the house, clattered down the hall and jumped behind the wheel of my Nova. I hit the drive at fifty, and reached the gates in time to see Gloria turn right.

By the time I got through the gates, she was out of sight. I put my foot to the floor and screamed down the winding lane, standing on my brakes like a boy racer. I prayed she hadn't taken one of the narrow lanes that turned off at irregular intervals. I was nearly at the main road when I caught a glimpse of her across the angle of a field. She was heading for Wilmslow.

'Gotcha,' I yelled triumphantly as I shot across the oncoming traffic to make a right turn and get on her tail.

I assumed she didn't know my car, but hung back a little just in case.

She seemed to know where she was going, moving between lanes with no hesitation. Just before she hit the town centre, she suddenly swung left without indicating, leaving me to make a hair-raising manoeuvre, cutting up a coach who was really too big to argue with. I found myself in a narrow street of terraced houses. I drove down as fast as I dared, slowing at the junctions to check she hadn't turned off. I was almost at the end when she headed back down the street, well in excess of the speed limit. I had to swerve to avoid her.

She clearly wasn't afraid to let me know she'd spotted me. I wrenched the wheel round in a tight turn, hitting the pavement as I went. Another thousand miles off the tyres. I screeched back after her, reaching the junction in time to see her continue on her way to Wilmslow. I sat at the corner long enough to see her turn right down the side of Sainsbury's. I followed, and found a space in the car park near the back entrance to the supermarket. I was afraid I'd lost her, but I picked her up by the Pay And Display ticket machine and got back on her tail.

I felt like a complete moron when she walked into Sainsbury's and helped herself to a trolley. I tried to console myself that she'd spotted me and was trying to throw me off the scent again, but by the time she'd reached the breakfast cereals and her trolley was almost full, I had to concede I'd overreacted. I strolled alongside as she grabbed a packet of Weetabix.

'I said I wanted you to answer a few questions,' I remarked casually. She nearly jumped out of her skin, so I added, 'Just like Jett invited you to yesterday.'

She was torn between the desire to piss me off in good style, and the sure and certain knowledge that if she did, I'd go straight to Jett, reporting on the merry dance she'd just led me. Her adulation of the boss won. 'You've got till the check out,' she said, trying to sound tough and almost succeeding.

'It may take longer than that, but I'll be as quick as I can,' I replied calmly. 'Where were you between eleven and two the night before last?'

'I've already told the police all this,' she complained, moving ahead down the aisle.

'I'm sure you have. So it should all be clear in your mind.'

Gloria's blue eyes narrowed in a glare. If looks could kill, the corn-fed chicken would have been well past its sell-by date. 'I was in the TV room watching *The Late Show* on BBC2 till quarter to midnight. Then I came into the office to check the answering machine. There were no messages, so I went straight up to bed. I was reading till the sound of the intercom disturbed me.'

'You got there very quickly,' I commented.

'My bedroom is right at the top of the stairs,' she replied defensively.

'I thought you'd have a TV in your room,' I said.

'I do. But it doesn't have stereo speakers and there was a band performing that I wanted to listen to. And before you ask, I didn't see anyone except Kevin. He came into the TV room and watched the band with me, then he left. Now, if that's all, I've got stuff to do.'

I shook my head. 'It's a long way short of being all, Gloria. Why did you hate Moira so much?'

'I didn't hate her,' she blurted out. The woman standing next to her having the mental washing-powder debate was so riveted she began to follow us before she was withered by Gloria's hard stare and her muttered, 'Do you *mind*?'

A few feet further on, she said, 'I just didn't like the effect she had on everyone. We were all happy here together before she arrived. Since she got here, everyone's been bickering. And whatever anyone else says, she made Jett edgy with her constant demands. Everything had to be just the way she wanted it.'

'So you're not exactly sorry she's dead?'

Gloria banged her fabric conditioner on the side of the trolley. 'That's not what I said!' she flared. 'Just because I didn't think she was good for Jett doesn't mean I'm not upset about the way she died. I know you don't like me, Miss Brannigan, but don't think you can pick on me!'

I felt a pang of sympathy for her then. She was too young to be setting herself up as the devoted handmaiden to the great man. She should have been out there enjoying life, not stuck with a bunch of piranhas who fed off each other's emotions and talents. I mean, for God's sake, who sends a qualified secretary round the supermarket these days? Apart from anything else, it would be cheaper to hire a woman from the village.

'How long have you been with Jett?' I asked, hoping to defuse her anger.

'Three years and five months,' she replied, unable to keep a note of pride out of her voice. 'I was working at his record company, and I heard he needed a secretary. Of course, the job has grown a lot since I took over. Now I organize his schedule completely.'

This time my sympathy was all for Jett. Again, I switched the subject, hoping to catch her off guard. 'When I told you about Moira, you seemed convinced that she was doing drugs. Why did you think that?'

Gloria refused to meet my eyes. 'Everyone knew she'd been a drug addict,' she mumbled. 'It was the obvious conclusion. We all knew she'd be back on the drugs again as soon as she got half a chance.'

'And did you help to give her that half a chance?' I demanded, leaning over Gloria to study the assorted nuts, so close I could smell her fresh lemony perfume.

'No!' she cried desperately.

'Somebody did, Gloria,' I insisted.

'Well, it wasn't me. You've got to believe me,' she pleaded. 'If she was doing drugs, she was doing it of her own free will. Why else would she steal my syringes?'

19

I just stood staring at Gloria, who looked back at me with a mixture of triumph and defiance in her eyes. 'What do you mean?' I finally gasped.

'Somebody has been stealing my syringes over the last four weeks or so,' she said.

'What syringes?' I almost howled in my frustration. The snacks section had never seen drama like this.

'I'm a diabetic. I have to inject myself with insulin. I keep a supply of disposable syringes in my room. On three or four occasions, I've noticed that there were a couple missing. I have to keep a close eye on them, because I daren't run out.'

I took a deep breath. 'So why did you assume that Moira was responsible?'

She shrugged. The shopping was forgotten now. We'd gravitated to the end of the aisle, and neither of us was showing any inclination to hit the soft drinks.

Gloria dropped her voice and said, 'Well, who else would want needles except a drug addict? And in spite of what you might think about the rock business, nobody in the house is a junkie. Jett just wouldn't stand for it. He's got very strict views on the subject. I know some of the others sneak away and do some coke, but none of them are stupid enough to get into heroin. Especially after what happened when Moira got hooked.'

'Any other reason why you were sure it was Moira?' I asked.

'Well, for one thing, they'd never gone missing before she moved in. Then one day I came upstairs and caught her with her hand on my doorknob. She said she'd just knocked to see if she could borrow a book, but I wasn't falling for that. I knew by then what she was after.'

'And did she borrow a book?'

'Yes,' Gloria acknowledged reluctantly. 'The new Judith Krantz.'

'Was she in the habit of borrowing books from you?'

Gloria shrugged. 'She'd done it a couple of times.'

'And did she know you were a diabetic?' I asked.

'There's no secret about it. She never actually discussed it with me, if that's what you're getting at.'

The next question was obvious, though I knew she wouldn't like it. That was just tough luck. 'Who else comes into your room either regularly or occasionally?' I demanded.

I was right. 'Just what are you trying to suggest?' Gloria flashed back, outraged.

'I'm not trying to suggest anything. I asked a straightforward question, and I'd appreciate a straightforward answer.'

Gloria pointedly turned away from my stare. 'No one uses my room except me,' she mumbled. 'Moira was the only person apart from the cleaner who's been in there.'

I took pity on her. I couldn't see being madly in love with Jett as an emotionally rewarding pastime, and I didn't want to rub in the fruitlessness of her passion. 'Given that it wasn't a drug overdose that killed her, have you any ideas about who might have wanted rid of Moira?'

'How should I know?' Gloria snapped.

'I would have thought there was no one better placed to have a few theories,' I replied. 'You're right at the nerve centre of the household. You're in Jett's confidence. I can't imagine there's much goes on around here that you don't know about.' When in doubt, flatter.

Gloria rose to the bait. 'If I had to choose one person, I'd pick Tamar,' she bitched right back at me. 'If Jett wasn't such a nice guy, she'd have been out of here weeks ago. They've been rowing for ages, and when Moira arrived, Tamar's nose was put right out of joint. Jett needs a woman who understands him, who really appreciates how demanding his work is. But Tamar just wants to have a good time, and Jett's just the means to that end for her. When Moira turned up, he saw how many of his needs weren't being met by Tamar, and it was obvious he didn't have much time for her any more. And now Moira's dead, Tamar's been all over him, trying to get back in his good books.'

It was a long speech for Gloria, and her efforts to make it sound objective rather than vitriolic would have been funny under any other circumstances. I nodded sagely, and said, 'I see what you mean. But do you really think she's capable of a crime of violence like that?'

'She's capable of anything,' Gloria retorted. 'She saw her position under threat, and I think she acted on the spur of the moment to protect herself.'

'What about the others? Micky? Kevin?' I inquired.

'Kevin wasn't thrilled that she was back. He was worried about the press getting hold of the details of her past and using that to smear Jett. And she was always chasing him about money, as if he was trying to do her out of her share, which is just ridiculous. I mean, if Kevin was dishonest, Jett would have found out and got rid of him years ago. He had nothing to fear from Moira's silly allegations, so why would he kill her? All her murder's achieved is to stir up the very stuff he wanted kept quiet,' Gloria informed me.

'And Micky?'

'You wouldn't be very thrilled if someone who had been out of the business for years came along and started telling you how to do your job, would you? She was very pushy, you know. She had her own ideas and God help anyone who didn't go along with them. I felt really sorry for Micky. She was always pushing Jett into taking her side over the album, and he was so scared that she'd take off again that he went along with her. But Micky wouldn't have killed her. I mean, she might have been driving him demented, but she couldn't do his career any damage,' Gloria stated. She pointedly made for the check-out queue. In her eyes, she'd clearly decided she'd told me all I was going to get.

I cut round in front of her, making her brake sharply. 'One last question,' I promised. 'You said cocaine was the drug of choice around Colcutt. Who uses it?'

'It's not my place to say,' she replied huffily, her eyes on the display of cookery books beside us.

'If you don't tell me, someone else will. And if no one else will, I'll just have to go to Jett,' I retaliated, fed up with fencing.

Gloria gave me a look that should have reduced me to a smouldering heap of ashes. Clearly she thought threats were as pleasant a form of communication as I did. 'Ask Micky about it,' she finally offered.

'I'll do just that,' I replied. 'Thanks for your help, Gloria. I'll mention to Jett how co-operative you've been.' I smiled sweetly and walked away. If I were a store detective, I'd never have let me out of there without a body search. There can't be that many complete weirdos walking around looking like they're rehearsing scenes from *Inspector Morse* in Sainsbury's in a nice *Country Life* town like Wilmslow.

Back in the car park, I found that an officious traffic warden had decided to make my day. Peeling off the ticket, I crumpled it into a ball and tossed it on the floor of the car. Clearly Richard's disgusting motoring habits were beginning to rub off on me. Grumbling quietly in a highly satisfactory sort of way, I eased the car into the traffic and headed back towards Colcutt.

I was stopped at the lights when I spotted Kevin. He was coming out of the bank, and I nearly peeped the horn to let him know I was there. Luckily, my reflexes were a little slow that morning. He was joined immediately by a burly guy in a padded leather body warmer over a navy blue rugby shirt. His Levis were tight enough to show he wasn't wearing boxer shorts. I grabbed my tape recorder, depressed the record button and said, 'White male, mid-forties, straight grey hair, thinning on top, neatly cut. Wide mouth, plump cheeks and chin, beer gut.' The lights changed and I had to go with the flow. What I did see as I drove off, apart from the bulky gold flash of a Rolex on Kevin's pal's wrist, was the thick manila envelope that changed hands on the steps of the bank. I could think of a dozen reasons why Kevin should be paying someone off in cash. At least half of them made me feel very uncomfortable indeed.

I swung the car right into a narrow side street and doubled back towards the lights. At the junction, I paused, eyes flicking from side to side, trying to spot Kevin's contact. I caught sight of him as he rounded the arcade of shops opposite, heading for the leisure centre car park. An impatient driver behind me sounded his horn, so I committed myself to a left turn, then turned off for the leisure centre. I reversed the car into a side turn and waited. I'd made the right gamble, not keeping my quarry in sight every inch of the way. A couple of minutes later, a red XJS shot past my turning. The driver was unmistakably Kevin's contact. I waited till he'd moved out into the traffic heading back towards Manchester, then I slipped out behind him and took up station a couple of cars behind.

The guy was the worst kind of driver to tail. He was a show-off, determined that everyone sharing the same bit of road as him would see he was a big man with a flashy Jag. Never mind that it was four years old, it was the real thing, not some souped-up piece of Jap crap. I could just hear him laying down the law in the wine bar. I reckoned he and Kevin were probably a pair out of the same box.

He drove like a man with serious sexual problems, cutting people up, overtaking in the craziest places, flashing his lights like the Blackpool illuminations. Interestingly, I drove no differently from normal, and I was never in any danger of losing him. As we shot through the lights on the dual carriageway at Cheadle, he made a kamikaze run across three lanes of traffic to hit the motorway intersection. I said one of those words that men like my dad think women shouldn't know and followed, praying he wasn't keeping too close an eye on his rear-view mirror.

Out on the motorway he let rip. He either wasn't a local or he didn't give a toss about the video cameras mounted every couple of miles along the motorway to catch the speeders. I was forced into the kind of driving that terrifies me, never mind the rest of the drivers on the road, zooming right up behind lorries, nipping into the outside lane to overtake, then cutting back in as soon as I was clear of their front bumper. It made for an interesting journey.

Then the volume of traffic built up and things got a little less traumatic. By the time we were heading east on the M62, I had stopped sweating and started breathing again. I slid Sinead O'Connor into the cassette deck and had a little wonder to myself about my friend in the XJS with the envelope full of readies. He looked definitely iffy to me, but not the sort of bad lad who carries out hits. On the other hand, he might well know a man who could . . . As we headed up Hartshead Moor, I checked my fuel gauge and started sweating again. I'd be OK if Bradford was the destination. I might just make Leeds. But if we were heading for Wakefield or Hull, I'd be making the acquaintance of the AA man.

For once, my luck was holding well. He repeated his suicide run across the lanes again to take the Bradford exit. But this time I was prepared, hiding in the inside lane. I stayed with him in the heavy traffic round the ring road, skirting the city centre and out towards Bingley. Then I lost him. He jumped an amber as it turned red and shot off, leaving me law abiding at the lights. I watched helplessly as he hung a right about half a mile ahead. Of course, by the time I made it to that corner, he was long gone. I drove back to the nearest petrol station in a seriously bad mood and filled up.

I signalled to turn back in the direction of the motorway, then I changed my mind. What the hell was I playing at? I'd schlepped all the way over the Pennines, taken more risks behind the wheel in one morning than I normally handle in a week, and I was even thinking about leaving it at that? I swear to God, two days in the world of sax 'n' drugs 'n' rock 'n' roll and my brain was getting as soft as theirs.

I went straight back to the street corner where I'd lost him and started the slow cruise. Within a few yards of the main road, I was in the kind of tangle of narrow streets where the wide-boys operate. Terraced houses, small warehouses, the odd little sweatshop factory, corner grocers converted into auto spares shops, lock-up garages filled with everything except cars. It was the kind of district I'd become familiar with recently, thanks to the Smart brothers. I didn't need a map to have a pretty clear idea of how the streets would be laid out, and I carefully started to quarter them, eyes peeled for the scarlet Jag.

As it was, I nearly missed it. I was taking it slowly when I caught a flash of red on the edge of my peripheral vision.

I'd overshot the narrow alley before it registered properly. I parked up and strolled back along the street. On the corner of the alley, I stopped and glanced down. The Jag blocked the whole alleyway, barely leaving enough room for someone to sidle past it. It was parked outside the back entrance to a two-storey building. I counted from the end of the alleyway down to it, then walked on to the next corner.

The building had once been a double-fronted shop. Now, the windows were whitewashed over, and the signboards over them were weathered illegible. A Transit van with its doors open was parked outside. I turned the corner and continued my leisurely stroll. Before I drew level, the door opened and a youth waddled uncomfortably in the general direction of the van. He couldn't actually see it since he was struggling to balance four cardboard cartons stacked on top of each other. 'Left a bit,' I suggested.

He threw a grateful half-smile at me, sidestepped and swivelled on one heel. The top box started to slide, and I moved forward to grab it as it fell.

'Cheers, love,' he gasped as he leaned forward to tip the boxes into the van. He stepped back, hands on hips, head dropping forward.

'What you got in there anyway? Bricks?' I said as I stowed the other box for him.

He looked up at me and gave me the once over. 'Designer gear, love. Top-class stuff. None of your market stall rubbish. Hang on a minute, I'll get you a sample. Just a little thank you.' He winked and headed back to the door. I followed him and stood in the doorway. To my right, cardboard boxes were stacked ceiling high. Beyond them, a couple of women stood at long tables, folding shell suits, putting them in plastic bags and filling more boxes with the bags.

On my left, two machines clattered. The further one

seemed to be printing t-shirts, while the other was embroidering shell suits. Before I could get a closer look, the van driver drew everyone's attention to me. 'Oy, Freddy,' he shouted.

From a small office at the back of the warehouse, my quarry emerged. 'Do what, Dazza?' he asked in a deep voice, the cockney revealing itself even in those couple of words.

'T-shirt for the lady,' Dazza said, waving an arm at me. 'Saved my stock from the gutter.'

'Pity she couldn't do the same for you,' Freddy grunted. He gave me an appraising look, then picked out a white t-shirt from a pile on a trestle table by his cubbyhole. He threw it at Dazza, then turned on his heel and pulled his flimsy door shut behind him.

'I see he's been to the Mike Tyson school of charm and diplomacy,' I remarked as Dazza returned.

'Don't pay no never mind to Fat Freddy,' he said. 'He don't take to strangers. Here you are, love.'

I reached out for the t-shirt. I picked it up by the neck and let the folds drop out. His face gazed moodily into mine. Across the chest, in vivid electric blue was the *Midnight Stranger* logo, straight from the last album and the tour promotional posters. Jett was alive and well and being ripped off in Bradford.

20

I sat in the car and stared at the t-shirt. I wasn't quite sure what it amounted to. If Kevin was responsible for official merchandising, there was no reason why he shouldn't farm it out to Fat Freddy, even if some of the guy's other business was well on the wrong side of the legal borderline. What I needed to find out was whether this particular t-shirt was the real thing.

I also owed Maggie the courtesy of letting her know I didn't need her to do my legwork any longer. I thought of phoning, but decided against it. Face to face, there was always a chance that she'd come across with some more information, and her house was only a twenty-minute drive away.

The house looked much the same, except that a sheaf of cream and red tulips had suddenly bloomed by the front door. For some reason, it made me think of Moira, something I'd been determinedly avoiding. I didn't think I could get through this job if I allowed myself to dwell on my own anger and the guilty fear that I'd delivered her to her killer. The vivid memory of her singing 'Private Dancer' filled my head. The grip of her voice on my mind didn't make it any easier to walk up the path to face her lover.

I rang the bell and waited. Then I knocked and waited. Then I peered through the letter box. No lights, no sign of life. I thought about writing a note and decided to try the neighbours instead. Next door there was someone home. I could hear the operatic screeching five feet from the door. I had no confidence that whoever was inside would hear the doorbell above the earsplitting soprano that was going through my head like cheesewire.

Abruptly the music stopped, though the ringing in my ears continued. The door opened to reveal the twinkling blue eyes of the neighbour I'd encountered before. He frowned at me, in spite of my smile.

'Hi,' I said. 'It's Gavin, isn't it?' I amaze myself sometimes.

He nodded, and the frown deepened into a scowl. 'You're the private eye,' he said. It wasn't a question. Obviously the jungle drums had been busy after my first visit.

There didn't seem a lot of point in getting into a debate about it. 'That's right. I'm looking for Maggie. I just wondered if you happened to know when she'll be back.'

'You're too late,' he said.

'I'm sorry?'

'The cops took her off about two hours ago. They let her come round and tell me, so I could feed the cat if she's not back. But the policewoman who was with her didn't make any reassuring noises about her getting home in a hurry. Looks like your friends in the cops have gone for the easy option,' Gavin said angrily.

There were things I wanted to say. Like the cops aren't my friends. Like did she know a good criminal lawyer. Instead, I gambled that Maggie would have picked on a nice, reliable chap like Gavin as the concerned person who would be informed of her whereabouts. So I simply asked, 'Do you know where she's being held?'

He nodded grudgingly. 'They rang me about half an hour ago. They've got her at Macclesfield cop shop. I asked about lawyers, but they said they would be arranging that with Maggie.'

'Thanks. I'll make sure she's got a good one.'

'Don't you think you've done enough?' he said bitterly. There didn't seem much I could say to that, so I turned and walked back down the path.

I made good time back over the motorway. I'd rung Macclesfield police station from the motorway services. I regretted the impulse as soon as I was connected to Cliff Jackson.

'I'm glad you rang,' he growled. He didn't sound it. 'I want a word with you.'

'How can I help, Inspector?' I said. It's a lot easier to sound sweet and helpful when there's forty miles of road between you.

'There's nothing gets on my threepennies more than people like you who think there's something clever about obstructing the police. One more stroke like this, Ms Brannigan, and you're going to be in a cell. And if you remember your law, under PACE I can keep you there for thirty-six hours before I have to get round to charging you with obstructing my investigation.' Now he'd got that off his chest, I hoped he felt better. I sure as hell didn't.

'If I knew what you were referring to, Inspector, I might be able to offer you some reassurance as to my future conduct.' He really brought out the lawyer in me.

'The way you conveniently forgot to mention that Maggie Rossiter was not only in the vicinity of Colcutt Manor at the time of Moira Pollock's death but was also out and about in the highways and by-ways of Cheshire at the relevant time,' he snarled.

'Well, for one thing, Inspector, I wasn't even sure what the relevant time was. The fact that she was in the lane a good hour after Jett and I discovered the body didn't seem especially revelant to me, I have to admit.'

'Don't try to be clever with me, Ms Brannigan. I'm not making idle threats here. If you interfere with the course of

172

my investigation again, or if I find you've been withholding evidence, I'm going to come down on you so hard it'll make your eyes water. Do I make myself plain?'

'As the proverbial pikestaff, Inspector.'

'Right. And I think I'll be wanting another word with you about your version of events around the time of the murder. You seem rather more hazy than I'd expect from someone who thinks she's as sharp as you do. I'd appreciate it if you could come into my office tomorrow morning at nine.'

Before I could refuse, the line went dead. Going back to Colcutt could only be an improvement on the day.

'Kate!' Neil exclaimed as I stuck my head round the door of his office. 'Come in!' I'd caught a glimpse of his retreating back as I'd entered the manor and followed him.

He was standing by his desk pouring a mug of coffee from a Thermos jug. His face had the bleary, unfocused look of a hangover. 'Fancy a cuppa? I've no milk here, I'm afraid.'

'Black's fine,' I replied. He opened his desk drawer and took out a second mug, which he filled and handed to me.

'Fancy a little something to keep the cold out?' he asked. I shook my head with a mental shudder, and watched in revulsion as he pulled a bottle of Grouse from his desk drawer and poured a generous slug into his mug. He took a long swallow of the brew, and as it went down, his face seemed to regain definition. 'Aah,' he sighed comfortably. 'That's better.'

Neil slouched across the room and collapsed into a leather armchair in a corner. 'So,' he said with a crooked smile, 'how's Hawkshaw the Detective getting on? Ready to finger the culprit yet?'

'Hardly,' I replied, sitting down on the typist's chair in front of the desk. I was in two minds whether or not to

173

tell him about Maggie's arrest. On the one hand, I didn't want to help him earn a shilling out of selling the story. But on the other, I was convinced Jackson was so far off-beam that I wanted him to end up looking like the fool he was. In the end, I decided I wanted to get my own back on Neil more than I did on Jackson, so I kept the news to myself.

'I've only just started my inquiries,' I said. 'And if Gloria's anything to go by, I'd have more joy panning for gold in the Mersey than extracting information out of you lot.'

Neil pulled a face. 'I don't envy you the lovely Gloria. But if it's good gossip you're after, you've come to the right place. My encyclopaedic knowledge of the occupants of Colcutt Manor is entirely at your disposal. Fire away.' My relief must have shown in my face, for Neil chuckled. 'Bit of a shock to the system, eh, finding someone who actually wants to talk.'

'Just a bit,' I said. 'Before we get down to the serious gossip, though, I have to do the proper detective bit. You know, where were you on the night of, etc.'

He lit a cigarette and blew out a cloud of smoke with an appreciative smile. 'Eat your heart out, Miss Marple. Well, I'd been nattering to Kevin earlier, then about ten I went down the local pub for a few sherbets before closing time. I must have got back about half-past eleven, then I came through here and did a couple of hours' work, transcribing tapes and knocking them into shape. I went up to bed around half-past one. Didn't see a soul, before you ask.' It was hard to gauge his truthfulness from his hooded eyes. Like most journalists I know, he'd carefully cultivated the appearance of total sincerity to encourage the public to fly in the face of all the evidence and trust him.

I asked a few more questions, and soon elicited the fact

that he hadn't seen Moira in the pub. Presumably she and Maggie had gone up to her room before he'd arrived. I decided to change to a more profitable line of questioning. 'So, if you were a gambling man, who would you be putting money on?'

His eyes crinkled up in concentration for a moment, then he rattled off the odds: '2–1 Tamar, 3–1 Gloria and Kevin, 7–2 Jett, 4–1 Micky and 10–1 the girlfriend.'

I couldn't help smiling. I hadn't expected such a literal answer. 'And what about you?'

Neil stroked his moustache. 'Me? I'm the dark horse. An outsider in more ways than one. You'd have to put me down at 100–1. After all, I was the only one who had nothing to gain and everything to lose from her death.'

I was intrigued. On the face of it, what he said was plausible. But since my only experience of murder is in the pages of Agatha Christie, that made him number one suspect in my book. I said as much.

He roared with laughter, and got up to refill his mug. This time, the tot of whisky was noticeably smaller. 'Sorry to disappoint you, Kate,' he remarked, 'but I meant what I said. Moira was the best possible source for early material on Jett. I mean, we all know how showbiz biogs steer well clear of scandal. And Jett's life has been well-documented. The only genuinely new angle I could hope for was finally lifting the lid on what happened between Jett and Moira all those years ago. I couldn't get an on-the-record word out of anybody about the reasons for the partnership splitting up. Her arrival on the scene was a godsend. She was willing to talk, and we'd only just begun to get into it. So I had a vested interest in her being around to talk to me. Forget the doctrine of the "least likely person".'

'OK. So you didn't have a motive. But you obviously think the others did. Suppose you run them past me?' I flipped my bag open and on the pretext of getting my notebook out, I switched on my tape recorder. I'd meant to tape all my interviews, but finding a strategy to deal with Gloria had driven the thought from my mind.

Neil stretched out in his chair and crossed his legs at the ankle, revealing odd socks above his scuffed leather loafers. 'First, Tamar,' he said, a note of relish in his tone that made me feel slightly uncomfortable. Life with Richard has shown me that journalists are the biggest bitches on two legs, but I still can't get off on listening to them dishing the dirt. 'They were on the rocks long before you found Moira. She'd actually taken a walk a week or two before that gig when I met you, but when Jett didn't chase her, she came back off her own bat. If he hadn't been so distracted with the work on the album, she'd have been on her bike a long time ago. But she was putting a lot of work in on making herself indispensable. When Moira turned up, Tamar could see all that good work going down the tubes.'

'What d'you mean, good work? All I've seen her do so far is doss around,' I interrupted.

Neil grinned. 'I mean, "Yes, Jett, no, Jett, three bags full, Jett". And all those evenings in the kitchen rustling up tasty little gourmet dinners for her hard-working man. Not to mention the horizontal work. Once Moira arrived, she used to wind Tamar up something rotten, flirting with Jett whenever Tamar was around. As long as Moira was around, Tamar was living on borrowed time. And hell hath no fury. But now Moira's gone, Tamar's wasting no time consolidating her position. As you no doubt noticed for yourself yesterday.'

'I can't see Tamar choosing a tenor sax as her murder weapon,' I objected.

Neil crushed out his cigarette. 'All the more reason for her to use it,' he countered. 'Though I agree it is a bizarre image.'

We both paused for a moment to contemplate the idea.

For me, it didn't work, but judging by the satisfied smirk on Neil's face, he was having less trouble with it. 'Next,' I demanded. 'Gloria at 3–1.'

'Obvious motive. She is obsessive about Jett. Madly in love with him, and all she is to him is a housekeeper with word-processing skills. She didn't approve of Moira's presence, reckoned she was disruptive and ultimately bad news for Jett, trapping him in a time warp. And if she thought Moira was going to spill any dirt on her idol, Gloria would have a double motive for getting her out of the way,' Neil summed up with an air of having said all there was to be said on the subject.

'And you think Kevin's motive is as strong?' I challenged him.

'We-ell, that depends on how straight you think he is. There's been a lot of argument in this house over the past few weeks about money and contracts. Jett was pissed off with Kevin for signing me up, you know. He wanted your boyfriend.'

'I know,' I said stiffly. That had already tagged Kevin in my mind as a shit. I had to be careful not to let my personal reactions interfere with my professional judgement, something which Neil seemed to be deliberately trying to provoke. 'But I hardly think that would give Kevin a motive for killing Moira.'

'Well, there was a lot more going down between the three of them than that. Moira was convinced that Kevin had been systematically ripping Jett off. She kept egging him on to straighten out his finances, to get Kevin to give him a detailed breakdown of his earnings and his assets. Kevin was being awkward about it. Now, whether that is because he genuinely had something to hide or because Moira just pissed him off and made him stubborn, I don't know. I do know that she was having a hell of a lot of trouble getting her hands on all her back royalties.' That confirmed what Maggie had already told me. Things were beginning to fall into place. Nothing like a bit of corroboration, though.

'There were a lot of rows about touring, too,' Neil added. 'Moira kept telling Jett that he shouldn't be having to do so much touring, that he should be concentrating on short tours of big venues like Wembley and the NEC. Kevin was furious. He seemed to think that she didn't know what she was talking about, and she had no right to interfere after being away for so long. She really was making his life a misery. If I'd been in his shoes, I'd probably have taken a meat axe to her weeks ago.'

Neil certainly wasn't stinting himself when it came to putting the poison in. In spite of my misgivings, I knew I had to milk it for all it was worth. 'Micky?' I asked, leaning over to pour myself the last cup of coffee.

'Micky produced Jett's first four albums, and that was the springboard that put him on the map as a producer.' Neil paused to light another cigarette, and I had time to reflect that he even spoke like a tabloid newspaper. 'But the last two years have seen him plummet from the top of the tree, thanks to the old nose candy.'

'Coke?' I asked.

'The same. Just like Jett, Micky's had too many flops for comfort, and he knows it. The collaboration was supposed to work the old magic and produce a classic album. Till Moira came along, it was shaping up to be classic dross. She encouraged Jett to shout Micky down and go back to their old style. Micky kept ranting that they were five years out of date. But then, as Moira sweetly pointed out, so are most of Jett's fans. She also wasn't scared of badmouthing him over his habit. Given Jett's views on drugs, that was a serious no-no for him.'

'You're not seriously trying to tell me Jett doesn't know about Micky?' That I couldn't believe.

'Yes and no. I mean, theoretically, he probably does. But Micky's very careful to keep it under wraps. You won't ever walk into a room here and find somebody doing a line or two. It's all behind-locked-doors stuff. Everybody goes along with Jett's little fantasies about this being a clean house. Moira was using that as a lever to put pressure on Kevin to make her joint producer. Micky was really running scared.'

'Scared enough to kill her?' I asked. Maybe I'm too naïve for this game, but even my naturally suspicious mind was having trouble getting round that idea.

Neil shrugged. 'Coke makes you very paranoid. It's a fact.'

'And the girlfriend? What exactly do you mean?' I demanded.

'I'm presuming you knew Moira had become a dyke, since it was you who tracked her down? Well, she'd been shacked up with some social worker called Maggie over in Bradford. The girlfriend wasn't exactly chuffed as little mint balls when Moira upped sticks and moved in here. According to Moira, Maggie was constantly kicking off about it, sending out ultimata in every post. So, Moira told her it was Good night, Vienna,' Neil replied.

'And you think being given the big E is a motive for murder?' I said sceptically.

'If she thought Moira was packing her in to go back to Jett, yeah. Helluva blow to the ego. And she's the only outsider you could reasonably expect Moira to let into the house.'

And she stood to inherit a substantial amount of money. I could see why Jackson was in love with the idea of Maggie. 'You seemed to think Jett had a motive. But he has an alibi. He was with me, remember?'

'And I am Marie of Romania! Come on, Kate, I know that was all bullshit. And I know you believe he couldn't have had anything to do with it. But just think on. Moira had turned his comfortable life on its head. That might have been OK if they had been lovers. But she wasn't having any, and he really wasn't handling that. I mean, you've heard all his New Age stuff about them being soul mates destined for each other. He wanted them to be together and make babies, for God's sake. Maybe she just turned him down once too often. I mean, the guy has got one helluva quick temper. Maybe he thought that if he couldn't have her, then no one else would. In spite of the front he puts up, he's no pussycat.'

'One big happy family,' I remarked ironically. 'All for one and one for all.'

'I tell you, if I wasn't working for Jett, I could make a fortune with the shit I've picked up round here in the last few weeks.'

I got to my feet. I might still be able to learn more from Neil, but I'd had enough for one helping. 'Thanks for the info,' I said. 'You've given me a lot to think about.' I wasn't bullshitting, either. Neil's reminder of Jett's quick mood changes niggled in my mind like biscuit crumbs in the bed. I almost missed his parting remarks.

'You sound like you're surprised by the catalogue of motives. Listen, I thought journos were backstabbers till I got into rock. Just don't run into any of them in a dark alley.'

With Neil's gypsy warning ringing in my ears, I stood in the hall and wondered which one of Moira's enemies I should go after next. Before I could take another step, the pager went off. In the echoing stillness of the hall at Colcutt Manor it sounded like the four-minute warning. I pulled it out of my pocket and hit the button that silenced it. The message said, 'Back to base. Double Urgent.'

That's not the kind of message you argue with. Not if your boss is a foot taller than you.

21

I made it back to the office in record time. The driver of the traffic car I'd zipped past at 110 m.p.h. had clearly been convinced he'd been hallucinating since he didn't get on my tail with sirens blasting. I dumped the car on a single yellow outside the chemist's shop, left the note that says, 'picking up urgent prescription' on the dashboard and hit the stairs running.

I burst through the outer door, red-faced and sweating. Very chic. Shelley looked me up and down and shook her head in a mockery of disapproving motherhood. 'Three deep breaths,' she told me. 'Then you're wanted in there.' She gestured with her head at Bill's closed office door.

'What's going on?' I demanded in a stage whisper. I know just how thin the walls in this place are.

'The cops raided Billy Smart's warehouse this morning. The place was clean as a whistle,' Shelley replied, her voice so low I had to lean close and risk my crowns on her Rasta beads.

'Oh shit,' I sighed. 'So who . . . ?'

'Bill's having a post-mortem with Clive Abercrombie from the jewellers' group and DI Redfern. He's been stalling them till you got here.'

Some days I wish I did something simple for a living. Like brain surgery. I flashed a hopeless smile at Shelley, made a throat-cutting gesture and headed for the Spanish Inquisition.

Tony Redfern was sitting on the broad window sill, looking more like a depressed golden retriever than ever. Wavy blond hair, soulful brown eyes, drooping mouth. For all I knew, a wet nose too. He nodded gloomily as I entered. Clive Abercrombie leapt smartly to his feet and inclined his head towards me, every inch the Eton and New College gentleman. You'd never have guessed he was actually educated at a secondary modern in Blackpool followed by Salford Tech.

'Sorry to drag you back, Kate,' Bill said. 'But we really did need your expertise here.' Translation: Someone's going to come out of this looking like a prize asshole, and it's not going to be us.

'I was only down the road. Just routine,' I said.

Tony grinned. 'Giving Cliff Jackson a headache, so I hear.'

'The feeling's mutual, Tony,' I replied, returning the grin. I've known Tony since he was a DS on the burglary squad. He's one of the few coppers I have any professional respect for. 'Is there some kind of a problem with the Smarts?'

'That would be one way of putting it,' said Clive, stuffy as ever. 'It would appear that when Inspector Redfern and his colleagues from the Trading Standards department executed their warrant on Mr Smart's warehouse premises, they drew a blank.' See what I mean? You'd never guess.

I looked questioningly at Tony. He nodded, looking as if he'd just lost the five closest members of his family. 'He's not wrong. We'd had a team watching the place all day, and not a sausage came out that front door. There's no back entrance, no side entrance. The place was clean, Kate. Billy and Gary stood there watching us with a grin on their faces like a pair of Cheshire cats. I don't know where you got your info, but it's a duffy.'

I couldn't believe it. 'We were hoping you would be able to furnish us with some explanation, Miss Brannigan,' Clive said icily. 'You had mounted surveillance personally for some time, I believe.'

'Over a period of four weeks, to be precise,' Bill weighed in. 'Averaging a sixteen-hour day. You were sent our detailed reports, including photographs, Clive.' There was a warning note in Bill's voice. I hoped Clive was alert to it. It's hell getting bloodstains out of grey carpet.

'I don't understand it,' I said, going for the note of genuine puzzlement. 'Unless they've changed warehouses. But there's no reason why they should.' I frowned. 'Tony, how long have you had someone on them? Could they have cottoned on and shifted the gear?'

Tony shook his head. 'Nice try, Kate. But we didn't move on them till yesterday morning, and all we did was put a team outside the warehouse. They couldn't have cleared the stuff since then.'

'Perhaps there is a leak inside your organization, Mr Mortensen?' Clive suggested.

I thought Bill was going to explode. He leaned forward in his chair, put his rather large hands flat on the desk and snarled, 'No way, Clive. If there is a leak, it's not from here. People in glass houses, Clive. I've always wondered how the thieves knew exactly which cupboard wasn't wired.'

Clive looked petulant. 'That's an outrageous suggestion,' he complained. 'Besides, it was your company that installed the alarm system.'

'Bickering isn't going to get us anywhere,' I said, my reflexes geared as ever to stopping the boys squabbling. But I couldn't help feeling Clive had a point about a leak. Unless there had been a tip-off, I couldn't see how Billy and Gary had got away with it. And until I did, Mortensen and Brannigan were going to be the fall guys, that much was clear. 'Look, something has clearly gone down here that needs looking into. Will you give me twenty-four hours to see what I can come up with?'

Clive looked triumphant. 'This will of course be at your own expense?'

Bill scowled. 'I don't see why it should be.'

I stepped in again. They were like a pair of stags in the rut. 'The reward when the Smarts are convicted will more than pay for a day of my time,' I said sweetly. Out of the corner of my eye, I could see Tony grin.

'I can't pull my team off,' he said, 'but I won't pursue any active line for another twenty-four hours.' It wasn't much, but it was a small concession. At least I wouldn't be falling over PC Plod on every street corner.

Now the deal was struck, our guests couldn't get out of the door fast enough.

'The guy's a toad,' Bill grumbled loudly as the door closed behind them. I knew he didn't mean Tony. 'None of us is in Billy Smart's pocket. So, what are we going to do?'

'To be honest, I'm not sure. I thought I'd just go walkabout and see what I can dig up. The Smarts are going to be on their guard after last night, so God knows if I'll get anywhere. But I had to say something to stop Clive sniping away at us.'

Bill nodded. 'Noted and appreciated. What are you going to do about the murder investigation? D'you need anything from me?'

'Cliff Jackson and his merry men have pulled in Maggie Rossiter. It might be worth checking whether she's sorted with a good lawyer. If not, maybe you could give Diana Russell a bell? Jackson also wants to see me tomorrow morning, but I can handle it. Other than that, put it on hold. If Jett calls, tell him I'm pursuing some leads among the people she was hanging out with before she came back to the manor. OK?'

'No problem. I really am sorry to have dragged you back like that, but it was one of those situations where you have to put on a show of strength. Besides, if you hadn't been there, that shithead Clive would have spent the whole time putting the knife into you.'

I knew Bill had enough on his plate right now without having to put up with Clive whingeing for England, so I gave him a reassuring smile and said, 'As my grannie always said, if they're talking about me, they're leaving some other poor soul alone. I'll let you know when I get somewhere, OK?'

He looked relieved. 'Thanks, Kate. And, by the way – Clive's full of shit. I know you did that job properly. If anyone fucked up, it wasn't you.'

Now all I had to do was prove that.

I spotted Tony Redfern's surveillance team on my first pass of the Smarts' warehouse. In that area, any child over two and a half would have clocked them straight off. Newish Cavalier, base model, with a whiplash radio aerial. Two clowns in suits trying to look tough. Pathetic. They blended in like Dolly Parton in a Masonic lodge.

I cruised round the block. Tony had been right about the absence of other obvious exits. The Smarts' warehouse was flanked by two others. All three of them backed on to one big warehouse that was now a tyre and exhaust outlet, staffed by a constantly changing team of no-hopers in really practical sunshine yellow overalls. I slowed down, but studying the Fastfit premises told me nothing.

I pulled up near the corner and studied the layout in my rear-view mirror. As I watched, a Transit van reversed into Fastfit's loading area. The driver opened his door and got out. For some reason, I wasn't too surprised to see it was Gary Smart.

Three minutes later, my car was in one of Fastfit's bays, while I did the foreman's head in with a series of inquiries about the prices of tyres, shock absorbers and exhausts for my Nova. And my boyfriend's Beetle. And my dad's Montego. And, incidentally, while I got a good look at what Gary was up to.

Cardboard cartons about the size of a case of wine were being unloaded from the back of the van, then carried down between the stacks of tyres to the foot of a flight of wooden steps leading up to the exhaust storage area. I began to see a tiny glimmer of light.

Stopping the foreman in mid-sentence, I thanked him profusely, and climbed back behind the wheel. I couldn't help admiring Billy Smart's forward planning. I drove about half a mile through the back streets before I found what I was looking for. I took my camera case out of the boot and walked into the block of council flats and headed for the lifts. I was in luck. I had to wait nearly three minutes, but at least the lift was working. I got in, trying to breathe through my mouth only, and got out on the top floor.

It took me a moment to get my bearings, then I chose my door. I knocked politely, and breathed a sigh of relief when an elderly woman answered the door. It opened three inches on the chain and she looked out suspiciously. 'Yes?' she said.

I gave her the uncertain smile. 'I'm terribly sorry to trouble you,' I started. 'I'm a photography student at the Poly and I'm doing a project for my finals. I've got to get photographs of the Manchester city centre skyline from lots of different angles, and this block is just perfect for me. I know it's a terrible imposition, but I wondered if I could possibly step out on your balcony for five minutes to do some pictures?' I looked hopeful.

She looked suspicious and craned her neck to see past me. I stepped back obligingly so she could see I was alone. 'I could pay you a small fee,' I said, deliberately sounding reluctant.

'How small?' she asked belligerently.

'I could manage ten pounds,' I replied hesitantly, taking my wallet from my pocket and opening it.

The money made her decision for her, and I could see why as soon as I stepped inside. The whole place was threadbare – carpets, curtains, furniture. Even her cardigan was darned on the elbows. There was a pervasive smell of staleness, as if fresh air cost as much as every other commodity that made life worth living. I didn't like deceiving her, but consoled myself that it was in a good cause, and besides, she was a tenner richer than she'd been this morning.

She offered me a cup of tea, but I declined and waited patiently while she unfastened the two locks on the balcony door. Maybe she'd been watching too much television and really believed in Spiderman.

The balcony was perfect. I opened my case and took out a 400mm lens. I twisted it into my Nikon body and leaned the heavy assembly on the balcony rail. I looked through the viewfinder. Perfect. Now I could see exactly how it had been done. I started shooting, then, to prove the gods were really smiling on me, Gary Smart appeared in shot. I kept my finger on the trigger and let the motor drive do the work.

An hour later, I was surveying the results with a feeling of deep satisfaction. I marched through to Bill with a sheaf of prints and dumped them on his desk.

'Elementary, my dear Mortensen,' I announced.

Bill tore himself away from his screen and picked up the pictures. He thumbed through them with a puzzled frown, then, as he reached the ones with Gary, he laughed out loud.

'Bang to rights, Kate,' he chuckled. 'Tony Redfern will be kicking some arses tonight.' He picked up the phone and said, 'Shelley, can you get me Tony Redfern, please.' He covered the mouthpiece and said, 'Well done, Kate. After I've put Tony in the picture, I'm going round to see Clive and tell him myself. I can't wait to see the grief on his face . . . Hello, Tony? Bill Mortensen.

'Kate's just walked through the door with your answer.' I knew Tony would be squirming at the glee in Bill's voice. 'Listen to this for a scam. The Smarts' warehouse is the middle one of three, right? They all have pitched roofs, right? And all three back on to Fastfit. Which has a flat roof behind a parapet so you can't see it from the street. Still with me? The gear comes out of the window in the gable end of the warehouse, on to the Fastfit roof, down to the Fastfit loading bay then over the hills and far away . . . Yes, Kate has it all on film. They've been moving gear back in today. They must have spotted your surveillance team and shifted everything out in advance of the raid. And of course, you wouldn't be moving on them again till you saw something going in. And long before you did, you'd lose interest.'

Nothing like making someone's day. I headed back for Colcutt hoping that someone would make mine.

22

By the time I got to Colcutt, the buzz of tracking the Smarts' scam had worn off and my stomach seemed to think it was time for something a little more substantial than black coffee. I headed for the kitchen, planning to take some of my wages in kind. On the way, I noticed that the rehearsal room was taped up with police seals. I wondered how long it would be before Jett felt like making music again.

I poked around in the kitchen, checking out the fridge, the freezer and the cupboards. I opened a can of Heinz tomato soup, the ultimate comfort food, emptied it into a bowl and put it in the microwave. I'd only managed to get a couple of spoonfuls down when the door leading into the stable yard opened and Micky walked in, shaking the drops of rain off his waxed jacket. It was the first time I've ever seen anyone with arms so long their wrists actually stuck out of the sleeves of a Barbour.

He nodded at me and headed for the kettle, pulling off a tweed cap which had left a circular impression on his thin blond-streaked brown hair. The effect was quite bizarre. 'Bloody awful weather,' he complained, the cigarette in the corner of his mouth bobbing up and down like a conductor's baton.

'You're not wrong. You wouldn't have caught me out in it unless I'd been working,' I fished. He didn't rise. All

189

I got for my pains was a grunt that fitted well with his simian features. I tried again. 'Have you got a minute? I need to ask you some questions.'

Micky sighed deeply and tossed his cigarette end into the sink. 'It's doing my head in, this business. Questions, questions, questions. And Plod all over the sodding place. All I want to do is get on with my job. Some of us have got deadlines to meet,' he grumbled.

'Inconsiderate of Moira, really,' I replied. 'But the sooner you answer my questions, the sooner it'll all be sorted,' I added with a confidence I didn't feel.

'Might as well get it over and done with,' he muttered irritably, tossing a teabag into a mug and swirling it around viciously with a teaspoon. He removed his jacket and threw it over a chair, then brought his tea over to the table. He perched on the edge of a chair and immediately lit another cigarette which he continuously dabbed nervously at his lips. Apart from the cigarette, he looked just like those chimps they dress up for the PG Tips adverts. I half-expected him to answer my questions in Donald Sinden's fruity tones.

'I need to know your movements around the time of Moira's death,' I said bluntly.

'I didn't make any,' he replied belligerently, his fingers beating a silent tattoo on the side of the mug. I gave him the benefit of my quizzical look. I couldn't do words because I had a mouthful of soup. 'I was in the studio all evening,' he finally volunteered.

'Doing what, exactly?' I pursued.

'Doing what I do, exactly. Jett and Moira had been in earlier, around eight, listening to what we'd been working on that afternoon. Moira was full of bright ideas about the mixing, and some synth effects she wanted me to lay down. I was fiddling around with a couple of tracks, trying various things. I wanted to have a selection of versions for them to hear the next day. Time passes fast when you've got your head down.' Micky took a swig of tea and sniffed loudly as the steam hit his cold nose. It was far from incontrovertible evidence of what Gloria had suggested and Neil had confirmed.

Even the cloud of smoke slowly filling the kitchen couldn't put me off my soup. I finished it, and the sound of my spoon scraping on the bottom of the bowl made him wince. 'I understand Moira had pretty firm ideas on what she wanted the album to be like,' I remarked.

He crushed out his cigarette, swallowed some more tea, sniffed again, blew his nose on a large, paisley patterned handkerchief and lit another cigarette before he answered. 'She was a royal pain,' Micky informed me. 'Let's try it this way, no, maybe not, let's go back to what you wanted to do in the first place,' he mimicked with cruel accuracy. 'She'd been out of the game too long to have a bloody clue what she was talking about.'

'Doesn't sound like you're too sorry that she's dead,' I said.

The look of astonishment that crossed his face came as a genuine surprise to me.

'Of course I'm bloody sorry,' he shouted. 'She was a bloody great songwriter. Just because she couldn't do my job doesn't mean I didn't respect the way she did hers. She might have been bloody difficult to work with, but at least she gave you something you could get your teeth into in the first place.' He subsided as quickly as he'd erupted and slouched even deeper in the chair. 'For fuck's sake,' he muttered.

'I'm sorry,' I said, meaning it. 'Did anyone else come down to the studio while you were there?'

He rubbed the bridge of his nose with his fingers, screwing up his eyes in concentration. 'Kevin came in. I've been trying to remember if it was once or twice, but I'm not sure. He wanted to hear how it was going, but I wasn't really in the mood. I was into the music, you know? I didn't have a lot left over for small talk.'

'Screws your memory up, doesn't it?' I said sympathetically.

'What d'you mean?'

'Charlie. Destroys the short-term memory.'

'I don't know what you're on about,' came the reflex answer.

'Coke. And I don't mean the brown fizzy stuff. It's OK, Micky, I'm not a copper's nark. I don't give a shit what you do to yourself. Everybody's got the right to go to hell in the handcart of their choice. I'm just concerned about finding out what happened to Moira. And if you were out of your box, your evidence on Kevin's movements isn't worth a damn,' I informed him, aware even as I spoke how bloody sanctimonious I sounded. At least I'd managed to restrain myself from dishing out the standard Brannigan anti drugs sermon.

'So I do the odd line. So what? I'd had a bit, but I wasn't flying. I just don't remember if he came in once or twice, OK?' The belligerent edge was back in his voice.

'You ever use heroin?'

'No way. I've seen too many talented kids go down that road. No, all I do is a bit of recreational coke.'

'But you'd know where to get heroin if someone else wanted it?'

He shook his head in wide, disbelieving sweeps. 'Oh no, you don't pin that one on me. I don't deal, not for anybody, not for my nearest and dearest. Personal use, that's all.'

'But you'd know where to get it?' I persisted.

'I'd have a shrewd idea who to ask. If you work in this business, you get to hear things like that. But if you're nosing into heroin dealers, I'm not the one you should be asking.' Micky lit his next cigarette. I was beginning to feel like a herring in a smokehouse. I'd be a kipper before morning if I hung around Micky.

'So who should I be asking?'

He shrugged, and a malicious gleam crept into his eyes. 'A certain little lady who's got nothing better to do with her time. Ask her why she was so fascinated by Paki Paulie at the Hassy the other week.'

He obviously meant Tamar. The description certainly didn't fit Gloria. And where better to meet a dealer than the Hacienda, full as it always is of kids looking for the next kick? I filed the hint away for further investigation.

'Have you got any idea who killed Moira?' I asked.

'I can't imagine any of them having the bottle, frankly,' Micky said contemptuously. 'Except Neil. That bastard would do anything for a few bob. He must have made a fucking fortune out of her death already, all the stories he's been selling to the papers. Fucking vulture.' The venom in his voice was shocking.

'Sounds like there's not a lot of love lost between the two of you,' I observed. When it comes to spotting the obvious, I'm an Olympic contender.

'Let's just say he's not the person I'd choose to write my biography.'

'Why's that?'

'He's too fond of seeing his name in big letters in the papers. He turned over my brother-in-law, you know. Years ago, it was, but Des's never recovered. OK, Des was a bit dodgy, he ripped a few people off, but he wasn't a bad lad, not a proper villain, not when you compare him to those City bastards who rip people off to the tune of millions. Thanks to Neil fucking Webster, Des ended up inside for eighteen months. He used to have his own business, you know, but now he's just a bloody brickie working for buttons. Tell you what, an' all,' Micky continued, his accent losing its classlessness and becoming

193

pure East End, 'that fucker Webster won't have given him another thought. I bet he doesn't even realize why I hate his guts.'

All this was deeply fascinating, but I couldn't see its relevance. In spite of Micky's obvious conviction, I couldn't see Neil cold bloodedly planning murder for the sake of a byline. Before I could divert the conversation down more profitable paths, the door from the house opened and a wave of Giorgio cut through the smoky air.

I turned in my chair to watch Tamar sweep across the room in her silk pyjamas. Without a word of greeting, she made for the fridge. She bent over to peer inside, then slammed it shut with an air of bad temper. She started for the cupboards on the other side of the kitchen and caught Micky's eyes on her. 'Stop letching, sleazeball,' she threw at him on her way to the Weetabix.

Micky scrambled to his feet and hurried out of the room, grabbing his coat as he went. Thanks a bunch, Tamar, I thought to myself as I watched her tip two bars into a bowl and drench them with sugar. On her way back to the fridge, I remarked, 'Sleep well?'

'What the hell business is it of yours?' she grumbled as she poured milk on her cereal and perched on a stool at the breakfast bar. If she was always this charming first thing in the evening, it wasn't so surprising that Jett preferred to wake up alone.

'You can always tell good breeding,' I said airily. 'Plebs like me, we can never aspire to the courtesy of the moneyed classes.'

To my surprise, she spluttered with laughter, spraying the worktop with gobbets of coconut matting. 'OK, I'm sorry, Kate,' she conceded. It was the first time I'd seen a side of her that explained why Jett had put up with her for more than five minutes. 'I'm always a complete shit until I've had something to eat. I think I get low blood

194

sugar in the night. I guess all this business over Moira is just making it worse. And breakfast with Bonzo there was a prospect too dire for words.' Her upper-class drawl exaggerated her words, made them seem more amusing than they were.

'So what's the daughter of a baronet doing among the Neanderthals, then?' I asked, trying to pick up the tone of her own remarks. Richard's background info was still coming in handy.

She gave an ironic smile. 'Depends who you want to believe. According to my mother, I'm indulging in a belated teenage rebellion, having a bit of rough before I settle down. According to the lovely Gloria, I'm a gold-digger who likes having her name linked in the gossip columns with Jett. According to Kevin, I was useful in the early days because I kept Jett amused, but now I'm a pain because we keep rowing.'

'And according to you?'

'Me? I'm still here because I'm crazy about the guy. I'll admit that when I first met him, I thought he might be fun to play with for a while. But that changed. In a matter of days, that changed. I'm here because I love him and I want to make it work. In spite of all the efforts of his so-called friends to put a spanner in the works,' she added, with an edge of bitterness that nullified the light tone of her earlier remarks.

'Was Moira one of those?' I asked, getting up to make myself some coffee.

She nodded. 'In spades. Sorry, an unfortunate turn of phrase, but maybe not so inaccurate. She treated me like a brainless bimbo to the point where I felt like having my degree framed and hung on my door. Did you know I have an upper second in modern languages from Exeter?' she asked defensively. I waved an empty mug at Tamar and she nodded. 'Black, one sugar. Moira seemed to think that since I wasn't a black, working-class musician then I could have nothing to offer Jett. It was ironic. She didn't want him any more, but she was damned if she was going to let anyone else be part of his life.'

I was almost beginning to feel sorry for Tamar myself. Then I remembered the display in the drawing room the previous morning, and how insincere I'd instinctively felt it to be. 'Well, she won't be around to throw any more spanners,' I responded heartlessly.

'And if I'm being honest, I'd have to say I'm glad. If I'd heard one more sentimental conversation about "our roots" I think I'd have screamed. But I didn't kill her. You can't get away from the fact that they made good music together. And I wouldn't have taken that away from him. I know how much his work means to him.' Tamar stirred her coffee demurely. I nearly believed her. Then I remembered Micky's hints and their implications. Someone had been shoving heroin at Moira, and it looked like Tamar. I decided to wait till I had more evidence to hit her with, rather than waste the talkative mood she was in today. It hadn't escaped me that the reason for her co-operation might be nothing more than a desire to stay in Jett's good books.

'I hate to be a bore, but I have to ask you what you were doing on the night Moira was killed,' I said. 'I know you'll have run through it already with the police, but I have to go through the motions.' I gave what was supposed to be a winning smile.

Tamar ran a hand through her tousled hair and pulled a face. 'Bor-ring is right. OK. I'd been shopping in town all afternoon, then I met my sister Candida for a coffee in the Conservatory, you know, just off St Anne's Square. I got back around half-past seven. I bumped into Jett and Moira in the hall on their way down to the studio. Jett said they'd be about half an hour, and I decided to cook dinner.

196

'I did steaks in brandy and cream sauce with new potatoes and mangetout, and Jett and I ate in the TV room. I drank most of a bottle of burgundy, Jett had his usual Smirnoff Blue Label and Diet Coke. We watched the new Harrison Ford movie on video, then I went upstairs and had a bath. Jett came up and joined me just after ten. We made love in my room, then he went off downstairs some time after eleven. He said he was going to do some work with Moira. I couldn't sleep, so I read for a while then I started to watch the video. That's when you walked in.'

It all came out a bit too pat. I used to have a boyfriend who continually confounded me by his ability to remember the most trivial remarks weeks later. So when he lied to me, his stories were always so detailed it never crossed my mind to doubt their veracity. When I think of that, I thank God that Richard can barely recall what he ate for dinner the night before. Unless it impinges on his professional life, information passes through Richard's head without leaving a trace. But Tamar was trying to impress me very forcibly with her candour and her excellent memory. I didn't trust her an inch.

I tried the tired old question. 'So who do you think killed Moira?'

Tamar's eyes widened. 'Well, it wasn't Jett. But then, you know that, don't you?' she added, her voice heavy with irony.

'Leaving Jett aside, you must have given the matter some thought,' I pressed her.

She got to her feet and dumped her dishes in the dishwasher. With her back to me, she said, 'Gloria is a very stupid woman, you know. Stupid enough to think she's bright enough to get away with murder, if you understand me.' I caught the reflection of Tamar's face in the kitchen window. There was a tight smile on her lips.

She turned back to face me, her expression wiped clean.

197

'Why don't you ask her what she was doing running upstairs just before one o'clock?'

I could feel the pulse in my throat. 'What do you mean?'

'I heard someone running upstairs. I was coming through from my bathroom, so I stuck my head round the door. I saw Gloria's door closing. What was she up to? You're the detective. Maybe you should ask her.'

23

Tamar swept off to make herself fit for company after that final pleasantry, leaving me rejoicing at the prospect of another friendly little chat with Gloria. Luckily, I didn't have to scour the shopping centres of the north west for her. She was in her office, beating up her word processor as if the keyboard had my face on it.

'Sorry to interrupt,' I said. 'I just wondered where I might find Kevin.'

'He's got a suite in the west wing,' she said pompously, not even breaking her rhythm. 'Bedroom, bathroom, lounge and office. Turn left at the top of the stairs, then left again. The office is the double doors on the right. But you probably won't find him there at this time of day. He's more likely to be out and about.'

'Thanks. Oh, one other thing. When I asked you about your movements, you didn't mention that you'd gone downstairs again after you went up to bed.'

That brought her frenzied typing to a halt. 'I never did,' Gloria denied vehemently, her chin thrust out like a defiant child. 'Anyone who says I did is a liar.' She'd gone that ugly puce again.

'Are you sure?' I asked mildly.

Her lips seemed to tighten and shrink. 'Are you accusing me of lying?' she challenged.

'No. I simply wondered if it might have slipped your mind.'

'It couldn't have slipped my mind if I'd never done it, could it?'

I shrugged and said, 'See you around, Gloria.' I walked slowly up the stairs, pondering on her reaction. If I were Neil, I'd be laying odds of 2–1 that she'd been lying. Which meant one of two things. Either she was the killer, or she thought she was protecting the killer. And the only person I could imagine Gloria protecting was Jett.

I followed Gloria's instructions to the letter, but there was no reply when I knocked on the double doors. I tried each handle in turn. They moved, but both doors were locked. On the off chance that someone had been careless, I tried the pair of them together. The doors swung apart, the small gilt bolt in one grazing the pile of the carpet. Oh dear, someone hadn't fastened it properly. I remedied the oversight, carefully sliding the bolt into place as I shut the doors behind me. The lock clicked sharply into place. The Ramblers' Association would have been proud of me.

The contents of Kevin's office were a set of clichés that sat in that beautifully proportioned room like a Big Mac on Sèvres china. The walls were mushroom – sorry, taupe! – decorated with framed gold discs and photographs of Kevin with everyone from Mick Jagger to Margaret Thatcher. There was a Georgian repro stereo cabinet, and lots of those tricksy little repro low-level cupboards and sets of drawers. His desk was roughly the size of a championship snooker table. On top of it, two telephones flanked a Nintendo console. Naff toys for mindless boys. I laid a small bet with myself that he couldn't get beyond level two of Super Mario Brothers. Behind the desk was an executive swivel chair upholstered in glossy chestnut leather, and against the walls there were a couple of those deep sofas that leave your feet waving in the air like a toddler.

I wasn't sure what I was looking for, but that's never stopped me before. I started with the desk itself. It held few surprises. Top drawer, pens and executive gadgets, right down to the aerobasic calculator. (I only knew what it was because they sell them in the Science Museum's mail order goodie book, and I'm a catalogaholic.) Second drawer, scratch pads and packs of adhesive memos with album and record company logos on them. Also, black leather desk diary and telephone book. Bottom drawer, current issues of the music press, and men's mags from the navel-gazing *Esquire* to the nipple-gazing *Penthouse*.

I turned my attention to the nasty furniture. The unit immediately behind the desk looked like it had two drawers. But when I pulled it open, I realized they were fakes, disguising a file drawer. I quickly flipped through it, but as far as I could tell, it was a file of routine correspondence with record companies, promoters and tour venues. There was nothing at all relating to merchandising. The second looked more promising, if only because it was locked. I was assessing my chances of getting into it undetected when my worst nightmares came true. I heard voices outside the door.

It's amazing how quickly your mouth can get really dry. I straightened up as the key fumbled noisily into the lock. There weren't too many options. Under the desk was a sure way to be discovered inside thirty seconds. No room behind the sofas. That only left the door on the far wall. It could lead to a cupboard or a bedroom. As I shot across the room, grateful for the ostentation that had required ankle-risking deep-pile carpet, I prayed it wasn't locked. I yanked the door open and hit the threshold running. I hauled the door shut behind me, in time to see the office door opening.

Gloria's voice reached me across the office and through the door. 'If you'd just like to take a seat, Inspector, Mr Kleinman will be back in about ten minutes. If you see that Miss Brannigan, would you tell her that? She was looking for him a few minutes ago, but she's obviously found something more interesting to do than wait. Can I get you some tea?'

'No thanks, Miss. The constable and me are awash with tea. We'll keep an eye out for Miss Brannigan, though.' There was no mistaking that voice. It grated like an emery board on my nails. Cliff Jackson was sitting on the other side of the door, in the room I'd illegally entered not quarter of an hour before.

I looked around the room I'd registered subconsciously was a bathroom. That old villain Lord Elgin would have had it away on his toes with the whole room. Walls, floor and even the ceiling were marble. Not that cold, white marble with the grey veins. This was soft, pinky, with dark red veins running through it like a drinker's nose. The bath looked as if it had been hollowed out of a single lump of the stuff, with monstrous gold dolphins for taps. You could never be sure you'd got it really clean, that was for sure.

Luckily for me, there was another door on the far side. I slipped off my heels and tiptoed across the room. That was where my luck ran out. The door wouldn't budge. I crouched down, applying my eye to the crack. Situation hopeless. It was bolted on the far side. That left me two alternatives. Either I could sit it out and hope that no one would be caught short. Or I could brazen it out. If I was going to do that, better sooner rather than later. It would be a lot easier to talk my way out of it before Kevin arrived and started asking awkward questions about what I was doing in his office.

I tiptoed back to the loo and put my shoes back on.

Then, very noisily, I stood up, flushed the loo and clattered loudly over to the sink, where I committed an arrestable offence with the dolphin till I got a loud gush of water out of it. Then I made great play of fiddling with the door lock before I emerged.

I managed to stop short in the doorway with every appearance of surprise. 'Inspector Jackson!' I exclaimed as his head swivelled round to face me. Those tinted glasses of his were really sinister when the light was behind him.

'And what exactly are you doing here, Miss Brannigan?' he demanded, a note of weary irritation in his voice.

'Pretty much the same as you, by the looks of it. Waiting for Kevin. I heard he'd be back soon.' Well, it was true, sort of.

'And how, exactly, did you get through a locked door?' His voice was oilier than I'd have imagined possible. It's the voice they use, cops, when they think they've got you bang to rights. Doesn't matter if it's speeding or murder. I think they learn it in training.

'Locked? You must be mistaken, Inspector. I just turned the handle and walked through. After all, if I'd effected an illegal entry, I'd hardly be powdering my nose and touching up my mascara, now would I?'

Me and my big mouth. Jackson's hands moved up to the knot of his immaculate paisley tie and tightened the precise knot a fraction. I had the irresistible feeling he wanted to tighten his hands round my neck. 'And is Mr Kleinman expecting you?' he said through stiff lips.

'Only in the most general way. He knows I'll be wanting to talk to him sometime. Nothing urgent. I'll pop back another time, when I'm not in your way.' I headed for the door, doing the confident routine.

'While you're here, let's you and me have a little chat while we're waiting,' he commanded.

'Fine by me,' I said. 'It'll save me having to get up early

tomorrow for our little chat.' I can't help myself, I swear. Every time I run up against a copper who thinks he's in the last days of his apprenticeship to God, I get one on me. I walked over to the desk and leaned against it. Jackson squirmed forward on the sofa to try and get in a commanding position. I could have told him it was a waste of effort. 'Ask away, Inspector,' I invited him.

'In your statement, you said you'd been here, quote, about an hour, unquote, before you and Mr Franklin went in search of Miss Pollock.'

'That's right,' I confirmed.

'You can't be more precise than that? I'm sorry, but I find that very hard to believe, Miss Brannigan. I thought you private eyes prided yourselves on being accurate.' Had to get his little dig in, didn't he?

I shrugged. 'Don't you find that's so often the way it is, Inspector? People's memories are incredibly inconvenient. I'm constantly surprised when I'm interviewing people by the things they manage to be vague about.'

'Perhaps we can be more precise if we work backwards. Where did you come from? And what time did you leave there?'

'I had been working near Warrington. I finished there about half an hour after midnight, and decided that since I was only ten minutes or so away from Colcutt, I'd pop in for a nightcap.' Time to go on the offensive, I decided. I really couldn't afford to get into a detailed analysis of time and place. 'What's the big deal, anyway, Inspector? Still trying to get Jett in the frame? I'd have thought there wasn't a lot of point in that now you've got someone in custody.'

He pushed his glasses up and rubbed the bridge of his nose in an exasperated gesture. 'Why don't you just leave us to do the job we're paid to do, Miss Brannigan?'

'Are you denying you've arrested Maggie Rossiter?'

'If you're so keen to find out what we're up to, you should send that boyfriend of yours along to our press conferences,' he said sarcastically. Pity the police aren't as good at catching villains as they are at gossiping. 'At least that way you'd get hold of the right end of the stick. You still haven't answered me. What time was it when you got here?'

'I told you, I can't be sure. We chatted for about an hour, I'd guess, then Jett went to fetch Moira.'

'Why did he wait that long? Why didn't he go and get her before then?'

I took a deep breath. 'He went to get her then because they'd arranged to meet for a working session in the rehearsal room and he didn't want her hanging around waiting for him. I guess he didn't go and get her before because he didn't know where she was.'

'How long was he away?'

'A couple of minutes. Not long enough to kill her, if that's what you're trying to get at. Besides, I felt her skin temperature when I tried for a pulse. She was a lot cooler than she could have got in three or four minutes.'

'Don't tell me,' Jackson said sarcastically. 'Let me guess. And she wasn't as cold as she would have been if she'd been dead an hour, am I right?'

'That would be my judgement, yes,' I replied.

'I'm sure our pathologist will be fascinated by your expert opinion,' Jackson sighed. 'When you saw the girl-friend – was she going towards the house or away from it?'

'I can't be certain, but I think she was heading back towards the village.'

Jackson nodded. 'And she looked what? Startled? Afraid? Upset?'

'She looked pretty startled. But who wouldn't, nearly being run over in the small hours?'

'And when you went rushing off to interview her, did she happen to mention how Moira Pollock met her end?'

'No.' That I was sure about.

'And did you?' He was probing more firmly now. I began to wonder why he wasn't back at the station giving Maggie the third degree.

'No. You told me not to, remember?'

'And you always do what you're told? Spare me, Miss Brannigan.'

I pushed myself away from the desk. 'I don't know where this is getting us, Inspector, but I've got more important things to do with my time than sit here being insulted. If you've got some genuine questions to put to me, fine, we'll talk. But if you're just going over old ground, and trying to get me to change my testimony to incriminate my client, then you're wasting your time as well as mine.' I was halfway to the door as I finished. But Jackson was faster than me.

He blocked the doors, standing with his back to them. 'Not so fast,' he began. Then he stumbled forward, nearly cannoning into me as someone pushed the door behind him.

Kevin looked furious as he stomped into his office. 'What the hell is going on here?' he started. 'What is this? Why's everybody playing cops and robbers in my office?'

'I was just leaving,' I said haughtily, skirting the pair of them. 'I'll catch up with you another time, Kevin,' I threw over my shoulder as I pulled the door shut firmly behind me. Time to do some work on my timetables.

24

I found Jett in his private sitting room, on the opposite side of the house to Kevin's suite. I walked in through the open door, then paused till he noticed me. He was sitting on a tall stool by the window, picking out fragments of old melodies on a twelve string Yamaha. After a few minutes, he turned his head towards me and nodded. He reached the end of a phrase of 'Crying In The Sun', one of their collaborations from the second album, then stood up abruptly. 'Kate,' he said softly. It was impossible to see the expression on his face, silhouetted against the light as he was.

I sat down on a chaise longue and said, 'How're you doing?'

Jett carefully leaned the guitar against the wall then folded himself into the lotus position on the floor a few feet away from me. 'It's the hardest thing I've ever known,' he replied, his voice curiously lacking in its usual resonance. 'It's like losing half of myself. The better half. I've tried everything I know – meditation, self-hypnosis, booze. Even sex. But nothing makes it go away. I keep getting flashbacks of her lying there like that.'

I didn't have anything useful to say. Bereavement isn't something I've had a lot to do with. We sat in silence for a few moments, then Jett said, 'Do you know who killed her yet?'

I shook my head. 'I'm afraid not. I've asked a lot of questions, but I'm not a whole lot further forward. Anyone could have done it, and nearly everyone seems to have some kind of motive. But I've got a few interesting leads that I need to follow up. Then I might have a clearer idea.'

'You've got to find who did it, Kate. There's a really bad atmosphere round here. Everybody suspects everybody else. They might not admit it, but they do. It's poisoning everything.'

'I know. I'm doing my best, Jett. It would help if I could ask you a few questions.' I was treading gently. I didn't know how close to the edge he was and I didn't want to be the one to push him over. Besides, he was the client, therefore not up for any kind of badgering.

He sighed, and forced out a half smile that looked grotesque on his haggard features. 'I laid you on, so I guess I have to pay the price. Look, I have to go see Moira's mother. Why don't you drive me into town and we can talk on the way.'

'How will you get home?' I asked. Trust me to find the completely irrelevant question.

He shrugged. 'Gloria'll come and pick me up. Or Tamar. It's not a problem.'

I followed him out the door and down the stairs. On the front steps, he paused and said, 'You can ask me anything you want, you know. Don't worry about sparing my feelings.'

'Thanks.' I unlocked the car and kept an anxious eye on him as he squeezed into the passenger seat. The briefest of smiles flickered on his face as he strapped himself in.

'I've got too used to flash motors,' he remarked.

I revved the engine and headed off down the long drive. The tyres hissed on the wet road, the wipers struggled to keep the screen clear. 'Weather looks like I feel,' Jett said. 'OK, Kate, what d'you want to know?'

'Can you run through your own movements from about eight? I particularly want to know where and when you saw anyone else.'

Out of the corner of my eye, I saw Jett massage the back of his neck with one hand, then rotate his head a few times. 'Tamar came back from one of her shopping sprees, and said she'd cook us some dinner.'

'Was that usual?' I butted in.

He shrugged. 'We don't stick to formal routines round meals here. Everybody kind of fends for themselves, except for Sunday. Gloria always cooks a proper Sunday dinner and we all get together then. But Tamar often cooks for the two of us. Moira did dinner a few times the first couple of weeks she was here, but once we'd really got stuck into the work, she didn't bother.'

'Right. So what did you do then?' I opened the window and pressed the gate release button. A flurry of rain stung my face before the electric window could wind up again.

Ignoring the invasion of the weather, Jett said, 'Moira and I went down to the studio to see Micky about a couple of tracks we weren't happy with. He wanted to do some fancy stuff with drum machines and stuff, but we weren't thrilled with the idea. So we discussed it, and then I went up to have dinner with Tamar.'

'Did you and Moira come back upstairs together?'

Jett thought for a moment. 'No,' he eventually said. 'She was still there when I left, but she was upstairs a few minutes later, because I saw her going towards the front door as I came through from the kitchen. I thought she was going off to meet Maggie.'

'So you knew Maggie was staying in the village?' I asked, with a vague gesture in the general direction of the pub.

'Sure I knew,' he replied in surprise. 'Moira didn't broadcast it, but she had to tell me. I'd have been worried, you see, if I'd been looking for her and I hadn't been able to find her. I told her to bring Maggie up to the house to stay, but she wasn't having any of that. Said she didn't see why Maggie should have to put up with the shit she was getting from all sides.'

'OK, so after Moira left, what then?'

'We ate our steaks, and watched *Regarding Henry* on the video. Tamar went off to have a bath just before ten, and I came up here to make a couple of phone calls. There were a couple of session musicians I wanted for next week, and I needed to check they were available. Usually, Micky does that, but he's got such strong ideas about this album that I didn't trust him not to come back to me pretending they couldn't make the sessions. After that, I went along to Tamar's room and we went to bed together.' His voice dropped and he came to a halt.

'What exactly is the score between you and Tamar?' I prompted.

'That's a question I don't have the answer to. I'm fond of her, but sometimes she drives me crazy. She's so materialistic, so empty compared to Moira. I keep thinking I'll end it, then we go to bed together one last time and I remember all the good times and I can't let go. Maybe if Moira and me had been able to get it together in bed again, I'd have been able to free myself.'

You mean Tamar's a great lay, and you won't say goodbye till something better comes along, I thought cynically. 'I see,' was all I said. 'So where did you go after you left Tamar's room?'

'I went back to my room and had a shower. Then I went down to the rehearsal room. That must have been some time between half-eleven and midnight. Moira and I had planned to do a couple of hours' work on a couple of new songs, but we weren't meeting till half-past one.'

I said nothing for a moment, concentrating on the road

210

junction ahead. The traffic comes down that main A56 like it was a German autobahn and speed limits hadn't been invented. I spotted a gap in the cars and went for it. Thank God for the Nova's acceleration. It took Jett by surprise, I noticed. He was thrust back into his tight-fitting sports seat with a look of serious discomfort on his face.

'Isn't that a bit late to start work?' I asked.

Jett relaxed as my speed levelled out and the G-forces disappeared. His smile this time seemed genuine, though I couldn't see into his eyes. I adjusted the rear-view mirror slightly so I could see his face. 'We always did our best work in the early hours,' he told me. 'Sometimes we'd still be tossing lyrics and tunes around at dawn. In the early days, we used to drive off to a greasy spoon around five in the morning and have bacon butties and tea to celebrate our new songs.'

'So why did you go off to the rehearsal room so much earlier than you'd arranged?'

'I'd had a tune going round my head for a couple of hours, and I wanted to fiddle around with it a bit before Moira arrived. So I'd have something new to show to her, I guess. I tinkered with it for a while, then I decided to fix myself a sandwich, so I went off to the kitchen. That must have been just before one, because the news came on the radio while I was eating.' His speech had become notice-ably more jerky as he got closer to the discovery of the body, his shoulders tense and hunched.

I slowed for the roundabout but still managed to hit the motorway slip road at fifty-five. This time, Jett made it to the grab handle in plenty of time.

'Did you see anyone at all?'

'No. But then I probably wouldn't have noticed anyone unless they'd actually spoken to me. My head was full of music, I wasn't paying attention much to anything else. I don't know how to explain it to someone who's not a musician. I don't even remember what was on the radio. They could've announced World War Three and I wouldn't have taken it in.'

Which explained Gloria's behaviour. Great. I had a client in the right place at almost the right time. I had a witness who wasn't admitting it yet, but who could put him there. And it was my lies to the police which had given him his non-existent alibi. Never mind Inspector Jackson, Bill was going to love this.

'Did you go straight from the kitchen to the rehearsal room, then?'

Jett bowed his head in assent. 'That's when I found her. I was only a room away, and I didn't hear a damn thing.'

'Because the rehearsal room's so well soundproofed?'

'That's right. That's why the police had to believe you and me when we said we didn't hear a thing.'

There was no point in questioning him about what he'd seen in the room. I'd seen it too and it hadn't told me anything except that Moira was battered to death with a tenor sax. Besides, he seemed to be retreating inside himself, and I figured I'd have to move the conversation into different channels if I wasn't to lose him altogether. 'Who do you think it was, Jett?'

'I can't believe any of us did it,' he said in a tone that lacked conviction. 'Shit, we're always rowing in this business. Nobody ever got killed before.'

'She'd been arguing with Kevin, hadn't she? Do you know what that was all about?'

'She thought he was ripping her off over her royalties. But that was only a little bit of it. She made me stand up to him to get the deal she wanted – you know, a profit percentage on the album, an increased royalty rate, and now she was pushing for a production credit too. She kept telling me I wasn't getting my share either, that Kevin was taking too much of a rake-off. And she kept going on about

212

how I was being ripped off on the merchandising. She said there were loads of illicit copies of the tour merchandise all over the place, and Kevin should be doing something to put a stop to it, and why wasn't he.'

My ears pricked up. Moira knew about the schneids? I was so busy with my own thoughts I almost missed Jett's next comment. 'She was even hinting we should get shot of Kevin and manage ourselves. She said it wouldn't take her long to get the job sussed, then we could ditch him. I didn't want to, but she made me promise that if she got evidence that he was ripping me off, I'd go along with her.'

I took a deep breath. Could anyone be as naïve as Jett appeared to be? Here he was, handing me the strongest of motives on a plate, and he didn't even seem to notice.

'Did you know someone kept dropping heroin on Moira?' I asked. The motorway petered out into dual carriageway. I barely noticed, only my automatic-pilot reflexes making me slow to within ten miles an hour of the speed limit.

His face jerked up and his lips seemed to curl inwards in a snarl. 'What the hell do you mean?' he demanded.

'Someone had been leaving fixes and syringes in her room, according to Maggie. And Gloria said she'd noticed some of her disposable syringes had gone missing.'

'Jesus Christ!' he exploded. 'What kind of bastard would do that? Why the hell didn't Gloria tell me?'

'I suppose because she thought it was Moira who was stealing them, and it was her own business.'

'The stupid cow!' he howled, smashing his fist into the dashboard. 'It's her fault Moira's dead. The silly bitch!'

I took a deep breath, then said, 'I'm not convinced the two things are related. I've got an idea who was behind the heroin, and I don't think it was the murderer. It's a very different thing from being the passive supplier of the

213

means of death and actually killing someone with your own hands.'

'So who was giving her heroin?'

'I don't have any proof yet. And I'm not making wild accusations without proof.'

'You got to tell me. I'm hiring you. You got to tell me, Kate.' There was a note of desperation in his voice. Too late I realized he was desperate for a scapegoat, desperate to wreak his personal vengeance on Moira's killer. I'd have to learn to tread a lot more carefully with Jett than I had so far.

'When I find out for sure, you'll be the first to know,' I promised him. We were on the fringes of Moss-side, only a few minutes away from Moira's mother's house. I'd decided to leave for now any questions about other people's motives. The last thing I wanted right now was to put any ideas into Jett's head and have him flying off at half-cock. 'Can you give me some directions?'

In a dull monotone, he told me Ms Pollock's address and how to get there. I pulled up in front of a council maisonette. It was less than fifteen years old, but already the cement facings were streaked and crumbling. These buildings would be pulled down before we citizens of Manchester had even finished paying for them.

'Like I said, Jett, I've got a few leads I want to pursue.' I leaned across him and opened the passenger door. 'When you get back to Colcutt, make some music,' I advised him. 'Try not to brood on what you've lost. Concentrate on the positive things she brought you.' If someone had said that to me, I'd probably have hit them. But it seemed to appeal to Jett's New Age philosophy.

'You're right,' he sighed, his shoulders drooping. He left the car and bent down to give me a little wave as he closed the door. He didn't slam it either, not like most people do. I watched him till the door opened and a skinny woman

214

let him in. Then I got into gear and headed for friendly territory.

I hadn't been lying to Jett when I'd told him I had leads to pursue. Maybe I'd exaggerated their quantity and quality, but that was my business. Paki Paulie was high on my agenda, but there was no point in even thinking about that till later on.

There was a fax waiting for me from Josh, my financial broker friend. I'd rung him that morning to ask for a fully detailed breakdown of Moira's financial history, in the vague hope that there might be something of interest there. But right now, I was more concerned with the little matter Jett had just raised. I needed the answers to some questions. And I knew just where to go for them.

25

The smell of sweat was the first thing that hit me as I walked into the club. Not stale sweat, but the honest smell of hard-working bodies. Various voices greeted me as I walked over to the ringside where two teenage girls were engaged in kicking shit out of each other in as technically perfect a way as possible. For once, I hadn't come to fight myself, though just watching made my body yearn for release.

The man I'd come to see was standing in a line-backer's crouch, his face distorted by yells of encouragement. 'Go for it, Christine,' he was screaming. And we think we've come a long way from the primeval ooze, I thought, as I tapped my friend Dennis the burglar on the shoulder. He whipped round and I took a nervous step backwards.

When he saw me, he straightened up and grinned. 'Hiya, Kate. Just give me a minute. Our Christine'll be through to the semifinals in a couple of minutes.' Then he spun back to face the ring and resumed his passionate cheerleading. Nothing comes before Dennis's family.

The bell sounded for the end of the round, and after a moment's conferring with the judges, the referee held Christine's gloved hand up in victory. Let's face it, with Dennis's reputation, there wasn't a judge in the place who wouldn't have given any benefit of the doubt to Christine. Not that she ever needed that, I had to admit.

Christine emerged from the ring to a bear hug from her father. Even her body protector wasn't enough to stop her wincing at the force of his embrace. She gave me a wry grin and said, 'I'll soon be good enough to lick you, Kate.'

'On that showing, you could do it now,' I told her. I wasn't joking either. I turned to Dennis. 'She's really got it.'

'You're not wrong. She could go all the way, that kid. She's well sound. Now, what can I do for you, Kate?'

'I need your brains and your body, Dennis.'

He faked a wicked leer. 'I always said you'd never be able to resist my animal magnetism. Did you finally ditch the wimp, then?'

I didn't take offence. He affectionately calls Richard 'the wimp' to his face. Richard returns the compliment by calling Dennis Neanderthal Man, and Dennis pretends not to understand what it means. They're all big kids, men. And just like kids, they're ruled by their appetites. Like Jett with Tamar.

'Sorry to disappoint you, Dennis, but it's just your muscle I'm after.'

He pretended to be devastated by the news, clapping his hand to his forehead and saying, 'How can I face tomorrow, Kate?' Then he became serious. 'Is this going to take a while?'

'Couple of hours at the most.'

'Let me take Christine home, and I'll meet you in half an hour at your place. OK?'

Dennis was true to his word. Exactly half an hour later, my doorbell rang. I had the kettle boiled in readiness. He likes to stay in shape, does Dennis. He seldom drinks alcohol, never touches drugs, and runs six miles every morning, rain or shine. His only vice, apart from burglary and

GBH, is cigarettes. I greeted him with a cup of sweet milky coffee, placed an ashtray by his feet and settled down with my vodka and grapefruit.

'Schneids,' I announced.

'I told you all I could about the Smarts,' he said, wagging a finger at me. He was right. He'd given me a head start in my inquiries. He's a great source, is Dennis, as long as the people I'm after have no connection to his friends or family. Well, those of his extended family that he's on speaking terms with at any given time. And sometimes, he spontaneously brings me little gems if he owes someone a bad turn. His moral code is stricter than that of a Jesuit priest, and not a lot easier to figure out.

'It's not the Smarts I'm interested in right now, I don't think. It's a guy in Bradford called Fat Freddy. Mean anything to you?'

Dennis frowned. 'I think I've heard the name, but I can't put a face to it. He's not connected locally.'

'He's in the schneid merchandising area – t-shirts, pirate cassettes. Anyway, there's a tie-in to another case I'm working. What I'm trying to get at is why someone who's legitimately involved in the merchandising business would have anything to do with a schneid merchant.'

Dennis lit a cigarette and flicked a trace of ash off his shell suit bottoms. 'S'easy, Kate. Say I'm licensed to produce the straight gear for a top band like Dead Babies, and I'm a bit bent myself. I find out who's doing the schneids and I offer them a deal. I won't shop them if they cut me in on their scam. I mean, a couple of years ago, shopping someone was no big deal. They just got raided and their gear confiscated. But now they've changed the law, you can go down for these trademark jobs. So it's a real threat. Also, if I was double bent, I'd offer my schneid merchant advance copies of the designs I was going to put out next, so he'd have a head start against the competition.' He sat back and blew smoke rings, well pleased with himself. It made a lot of sense.

'I like it. Thanks, Dennis. That was the brain bit. Now the muscle bit. You know a dealer called Paki Paulie?'

Dennis scowled. He hates dealers more than he hates bent coppers. I think it's something to do with having two young kids. He once broke the legs of a pusher who was hanging round the local school gates, after the local police had failed to arrest the guy. There were a dozen mums who saw Dennis go berserk with a baseball bat, but not one of them ID'd Dennis when the cops arrived. They're used to rough justice round there. 'Yeah,' he growled. 'I know that scumbag.'

'I need to know if he sold any heroin to one of the people involved in this case I'm on. I've got a funny feeling he's not going to roll over for me. That's why I need a bit of muscle. You game?'

'When do we start?' Dennis asked. He drained his coffee mug and leaned forward expectantly.

We found Paki Paulie an hour later in a seedy bar in Cheetham Hill. The front bar looked like any other run down pub, its clientele mainly middle-aged, poor and defeated. But the back bar was like walking into another world. In the dim light, a handful of guys in expensive suits held court at the tables lining the walls, accompanied by their muscle. Scruffy kids meandered in and out, pausing by one table or another for muttered conversation. Sometimes cash was passed over fairly discreetly in exchange for dope. More often, the dealer got up and accompanied his punter out of the bar's back door into the car park.

On my own, I'd have been scared I'd be taken for a cop. But with Dennis by my side, there was no danger of that. He nodded towards one of the corner tables while we waited for our drinks.

'That him?' I asked, trying to keep my glance casual. Dennis nodded.

Paki Paulie wore a shimmering silver grey double-breasted suit over an open-necked cobalt blue shirt. The clothes were obviously expensive but he looked cheap as a bag of sherbet lemons. He was leaning back in his chair, gazing at a point on the ceiling as if his only worry in the world was what to drink next. Next to him, a hard-looking white youth stared gloomily into an almost-empty pint pot.

Dennis picked up his glass and strolled over to the table, with me in his wake. 'All right, Paulie?' he said.

'Dennis,' Paulie acknowledged with a regal nod.

'How's business?'

'Not good. It's the interest rates, you know?' Paulie replied, twitching his mouth into a smile. That was all I needed. A smack dealer with a smart mouth.

'A word, Paulie,' Dennis said softly.

'Dennis, you can have as many words as you want.' Paulie's urbanity was firing on all four cylinders now, but it wasn't polished enough to cover the quick flicker of concern in his eyes.

'You heard about Jack the Smack?' Dennis asked innocently. Paulie's eyebrows rose. He clearly knew all about Dennis's little vigilante action. 'Bad time for accidents in your line of business,' Dennis went on conversationally. 'State of the health service these days, nobody in their right mind'd want to end up in hospital.'

Paulie's protection seemed to gather himself together and shifted forward in his seat. 'You want to . . .' was all he got out before Paulie snapped, 'Shut it.' He turned back to Dennis and said, 'I hear what you're saying, Dennis.'

Dennis gestured towards me with his glass. 'This is a friend of mine. She's looking for some information. She's not the law, and if you're straight with her, there's no comeback.'

Paulie looked directly at me. 'How do I know I can trust you?'

'The company I keep,' I answered.

Dennis put his glass down and cracked his knuckles dramatically. Paulie's eyes flicked from me to Dennis and back again. I took a photograph of Tamar out of my bag. It was one I'd clipped from the papers that morning, with Jett cut out of it. 'Has this woman ever bought anything from you?'

He barely glanced at it and shrugged. 'Maybe. How do I know? I serve a lot of punters.'

'I can't believe you've got a lot of punters like this, Paulie. Natural blonde, doesn't dress out of a catalogue, accent like Princess Di? Come on, you can do better than that.'

Paulie picked up the picture and studied it. 'I seen her down the Hassy,' he finally conceded.

'How much did you sell her, then?' Dennis butted in, thrusting his face forwards till it was only inches from the dealer's.

'Who said I sold her anything? Shit, man, what is this? You joined the drugs squad?'

Dennis's head snapped back, like a cobra ready to strike. Before he could complete the manoeuvre that would spread Paulie's nose over his face, the dealer shouted, 'Wait!' Dennis paused. The sound level in the room had dropped to an ominous level. A sheen of sweat had appeared above Paulie's top lip. His hand fluttered at his bodyguard who was straining at an invisible leash. 'It's OK,' he said loudly.

Gradually, the noise picked up. Paulie wiped his face with a paisley silk handkerchief. 'OK,' he sighed. 'About a month ago, this tart came up to me in the Hassy saying

221

she wanted some smack. She didn't seem to know what she wanted or how much. She told me she wanted it for a coming home present for a friend, enough for a dozen hits. I thought she was full of shit, but what the hell? I don't give a monkey's what they do with it. So I sold her ten grammes. I never saw her again. And that's the truth.'

I believed him. It wasn't so much the threat of Dennis breaking his nose that had changed his mind. It was the thought of what would happen to him if the O'Brien brothers came looking for him. Even bodyguards have to sleep.

The thing that bothered me was that Dennis's methods hadn't bothered me. Maybe I'd been reading the wrong books. Perhaps tonight I should tuck myself up with an Agatha Christie and a few balls of pink wool.

26

I was thirty pages into *The Murder At The Vicarage* when Richard breezed in through the conservatory. 'Sorry to interrupt you while you're working,' he teased. I put the book down as he sat down beside me and pulled me into his arms. It was a long kiss, as if to make up for the little time we'd spent together in the previous few days.

'Fancy an early night?' Richard whispered.

'That's the nicest thing anybody's said to me today,' I replied, snuggling into him. 'How in God's name do you manage to put up with your job? If I had to spend my time with assholes like that lot, I'd slit my wrists.'

'You just tune it out. I always treat it like I'm watching *Dynasty* or the *South Bank Show*. You know, it's either glitz or pretension. I never let myself believe it's the real world. Sometimes I feel like David Attenborough, sitting in a hide watching the habits of a strange species,' he told me. 'It's fascinating. And I like most of the music, so I try to forgive them their worst excesses.'

'Like murder?'

'Maybe not murder,' he conceded. 'Though I'd have to say I think that someone like Jett is a bigger contributor to the quality of life than your average copper.'

'He's not contributing much to the quality of my life right now. This job is mission impossible. A house full of people and not a decent alibi among them. And everybody has some kind of a motive. Except for Neil, who seems to be the only person who had a vested interest in her staying alive.'

Richard snorted. 'Him? I wouldn't put it past him to have bumped her off just to stir up a bit of scandal for his book.'

'That's outrageous!' I protested. 'Besides, she was an important source for him on Jett's early days in the business.'

'Yeah, well maybe he milked her dry then bumped her off. From what I hear, he's been talking to the world since she died.' Richard sounded mean and spiteful, which isn't like him.

I tried to show him he was just talking out of blind prejudice, explaining that Kevin had asked Neil to handle all the press liaison. 'So of course he's had to talk to people.'

'It's not just all the copy he's been flogging,' Richard replied, still peeved. 'He's been doing the hard sell on this biography too, telling people that there's going to be stuff in there that no one else even guessed at before.'

I was puzzled. I remembered Neil telling me that his biggest problem with the book was that there were no new, exciting revelations. However, that had been before Moira had reappeared on the scene. 'Maybe he's just talking it up,' I suggested.

'I don't think so. I suppose he could just be trying to cash in on the interest in Moira's death by trying to stitch up a serialization deal sight unseen, but most feature desks won't play unless they've got a bloody good idea what they're getting for their money. Everybody's under the cosh financially these days. The golden age when you could talk a story up and still get paid when the end product didn't match up to expectations is long gone. The emperor's new clothes trick just doesn't work any more. Now they want to talk to the tailor.' Richard shifted away from me and got up. 'I need a beer,' he said, heading for the kitchen.

While he was off examining his collection of exotic beers of the world, I thought about what he'd said. I still couldn't believe he seriously thought Neil would have killed Moira for a few headlines. But I know from Richard that there is still big money to be made in the seedy world of newspaper exposés. I began to wonder just what Moira had told Neil. I'd have to ask him some more questions. The trouble with this investigation was that I just didn't know the right things to ask. It wasn't like insurance fraud or software piracy, where I knew who knew exactly what I needed to know. I was floundering, and I knew it.

Richard came back with a can of Budweiser and leaned against the door jamb. 'Am I drinking this on the couch, or are you still in the market for an early night?'

An hour later, I felt different again. It's amazing how good sex with someone you love puts everything back into proportion. If I didn't discover who had killed Moira, it wouldn't be the end of the world. I'd have given it my best shot, and that was all anyone could demand from me. Richard wouldn't think any the less of me, and I sure as hell wasn't going to beat myself up for not being clairvoyant.

I pulled my arm out from under Richard's shoulders as I felt the tingle of pins and needles. It disturbed his little post-coital reverie and he turned on his side to plant a soft kiss on my nipple. I felt warm and languorous, and kind of sorry for Miss Marple.

'What's happening about your schneids case, by the way?' Richard asked, with all his usual tact and sensitivity.

'You pick your moments, don't you?' I complained. 'The police and the Trading Standards guys are planning another raid some time in the next few days, I think. They probably won't tell us till it's all over, if they even bother then. They're a bit embarrassed about us doing their work for them.'

'So they should be. You'd think they'd be a bit more grateful that you're there to hand them the stuff on a plate.'

'It doesn't work like that. There's still a fair few of them who think that proper coppers shouldn't be spending their time on things like trade mark infringements,' I told him ruefully.

'Well, they can't catch burglars or car thieves. They should be glad somebody's doing something that gets a conviction or two.'

Sometimes I think Richard's spent so long in the cloud cuckoo land of rock that he's lost touch with the real world. But what he'd said about schneids had reminded me of something I wanted to ask him. 'Is there a lot of schneid merchandising around on the rock scene just now? You know, sweatshirts and all that?'

'You wouldn't believe the half of it,' he assured me. He was wrong. After the day I'd had, nothing would stretch my credulity. 'It's an epidemic. Top name acts are losing a fortune from it. Do you know, sometimes the schneid gear even ends up on sale at the official stall at gigs? God knows how they get away with it.'

My ears pricked up. 'You mean, it's an inside job?'

'Depends. It can be done one of two ways. Either they hire a couple of kids locally to run the stall and they're doing it as a bit of private enterprise, if the schneids are good enough. Or else somebody high up in the organization is slipping them in and not putting them through the books. I don't really know how it would work, but that's the word on the street.'

I needed the answer to one more question. 'Do you happen to know if Jett's been having any problems like that?'

'If he wasn't, he'd be unique. But I don't know for sure. Why don't you ask him?'

I did just that. I rolled over, picked up the phone and dialled Jett's private line. Tamar answered, and called to Jett that it was for him. A couple of moments later, he was on the line.

'Hi, Jett. Just a quick query. You know you told me Moira thought you were having problems with merchandising rip-offs? I mean copycat versions of your tour t-shirts and sweatshirts, that kind of thing? Did she give you anything specific?'

'Well, she didn't exactly, but there was a load of fake stuff around on the last tour. I got Kevin to call in the cops, but they apparently couldn't find anything. But what's that got to do with Moira?'

'It may have nothing to do with her murder at all, but I believe she had some information connecting the fake merchandise to someone who works for you,' I said cautiously.

There was a long silence from the other end of the phone. I almost thought we'd been cut off when Jett finally said, 'She should have come straight to me. She knows I wouldn't stand on for that. Do you know who it was?'

'Not yet,' I stalled.

'Well, find out, and when you do, you let me know. You hear?'

'Will do, Jett. Good night.'

He put the phone down. Before I untucked the receiver from my chin, I heard the sound of another phone clicking into place. Interesting. Someone had been listening in.

It all fitted. Moira had told Maggie that she'd seen someone from the manor talking to Fat Freddy. Fat Freddy was doing schneids of Jett's gear. Kevin had handed Fat Freddy an envelope on the steps of the bank. And the only person at the manor in a position to exploit that relationship was Kevin.

Then I remembered something that hadn't registered at the time. When Kevin had appeared on the landing after the police arrived, he'd been suited up. Not even his tie had been loosened. Now, I know people who fall into bed with their clothes on, but Kevin didn't strike me as one of them.

'Penny for them, Brannigan,' Richard said. The sound of his voice startled me. I'd almost forgotten he was there.

I lay down beside him and thought about sharing my ideas with him. By the time I'd decided it wouldn't be a bad idea, his soft, regular breathing told me that the only information I'd be getting into his head would be subliminal. Richard was out for the count.

I couldn't believe it when the phone woke me up yet again. Blearily, I disentangled myself from Richard and grabbed the phone, checking the clock. Five past seven. This was getting silly.

'Kate Brannigan,' I barked.

'All right, kid? Sorry to wake you. It's Alexis here.'

She didn't need to announce herself. I'd recognize Alexis Lee's voice anywhere. The combination of Scotch, cigarettes and Liverpool have produced a unique Scouse growl. Alexis is the crime reporter on the *Manchester Evening Chronicle*, and we've done each other a few favours in the past. I didn't count waking me up as one of them.

'What the hell is so urgent you need to call me at this time in the morning?' I moaned as I dragged myself into a sitting position. Richard mumbled in his sleep and turned over. Lucky bastard.

'Jack, known as Billy, and Gary Smart,' Alexis said. 'A little bird told me you could give me the SP on their little operation.'

'You woke me up for that? Listen, Alexis, I can't tell you a damn thing about the Smarts. If it's not already *sub judice* it soon will be.'

'I thought you were half a lawyer, Kate. You should know you can't charge dead men.'

'You what?'

'The cops raided their warehouse in the early hours. Billy and Gary did a runner in a hired Porsche. They got as far as Mancunian Way, then Gary lost it and they went off the elevated section. Car ended up the thickness of a club sandwich on Upper Brook Street. I'm surprised you didn't hear the bang round your place. Anyway . . .'

'Hang on a minute,' I protested. 'I need to take this in. So they're both dead? You're sure?'

'Believe me, Kate, I saw the wreckage. A gerbil would have struggled to make it out alive. So that's why I'm picking your brains. I thought it would make a nice little plug for Mortensen and Brannigan. Efficiency in contrast to the boys in blue.'

'Look, Alexis, I'd love to help, but I've not even had a cup of coffee yet.'

'No problem. Get some clothes on and meet me in the office canteen in quarter of an hour. Breakfast on me.'

People think private eyes are hardnosed. They sure as hell don't know any journalists. I sighed and bowed to the inevitable. Better than having Alexis round here discussing my latest case with Richard. 'Make it half an hour.'

Now I knew I was never going to have to visit another disgusting greasy spoon on the tail of Billy and Gary Smart, bacon, eggs and fried bread held a strange appeal, even in the subterranean gloom of the *Chronicle* canteen. I tucked into breakfast while Alexis filled in the gaps in our telephone conversation. I couldn't believe how bright and bouncy she was at that time in the morning. And she'd been up a couple of hours before me, after a tip-off from a contact in the police control room.

I first met Alexis a week after I started working for Bill. One of her contacts had told her there was a new woman PI in town, and she'd come along to try to persuade me into a profile in the paper. I'd refused, not wanting to run the risk of being recognized on the job. But we'd hit it off, and over the years she'd become the kind of friend I could go shopping with and count on to tell me when an outfit made me look like a candidate for Crufts. And her girlfriend Chris is the best architect in town. I know – I've got the conservatory to prove it.

But this morning, she wasn't interested in my latest discoveries in skin care. She was being professional. Her untamable mop of thick black hair was growing more unruly by the minute as she ran one hand through it while taking notes with the other. After half an hour, she knew almost as much about the Smarts as I did.

The surprise of her news had worn off, and I'd begun to feel sorry for Billy and Gary. OK, they'd been villains, but they hadn't been the kind of villains who cause individuals pain. They hadn't been burglars, or armed robbers or killers. They hadn't deserved to die like that just for ripping off a few big companies who would barely notice the hole in their balance sheets. I said as much to Alexis, albeit off the record.

'Yeah, I know. We're going to run a reaction piece about the number of people who die as a result of police chases. It's well out of order. Mind you, I think I'm going to have to give Richard a warning,' Alexis added, her blue eyes giving a twinkle as she smiled. I swear she practises that twinkle in front of the mirror to charm cops and victims of crime alike.

'A warning? What about?'

'Well, there seems to be a lot of death and destruction

hanging around you these days.' Alexis lit a Silk Cut and blew a plume of smoke over her shoulder. She's always had interesting manners.

'I don't know what you're talking about,' I lied. I drained my polystyrene cup of coffee-flavoured dishwater and tried to look innocent.

'Come on, supersleuth. It's me you're talking to. Everybody knows you're working on Moira Pollock's murder. I'll admit, I was surprised to find you off your usual white-collar beat, but then I heard on the grapevine that it was you that found the body. Care to go on the record about it?' Alexis's voice was offhand, but her eyes were hard.

I shook my head. 'No way. Sorry. I can't even confirm what you've just suggested, on or off the record.'

Alexis shrugged. 'Oh well, it was worth a try. We'll just have to make do with Neil Webster's copy. Not that I've any complaints on that score. It's been remarkably detailed for supposedly official stuff. Would you believe, he's even pitched us into paying him for it? He actually managed to persuade the newsdesk that he wasn't just issuing press releases, but operating as a freelance inside Jett's camp.'

'Really?' I was interested, in spite of my desire to keep Alexis's nose out of my business for once.

'You can come upstairs and have a read through it if you want. That'll keep you quiet while I write my copy, because I know you'll want to check it. After all this time, I'd have thought you'd trust me to spell Brannigan,' she grumbled good-naturedly.

I jumped at the chance. Neil was more accustomed to interrogating people than I was. Maybe there was something in his reports that I'd missed. Either way, as Alexis said, it would pass the time.

231

27

Alexis hadn't exaggerated, for once. Neil's copy was all she'd claimed for it. Dramatic, detailed and accurate. That was what puzzled me. 'Alexis?' I interrupted the rush of her fingers over the keyboard at the next terminal.

'Mmm?' she paused, keeping her eyes on the screen.

'Are these stories arranged in the order they came in?'

'Probably. They arrive in a special directory for electronically transmitted copy, and then whoever is on the newsdesk sends a copy of anything crime related into my electronic desk. The dates on the files refer to the last time I entered it, but the order they're listed in is the order in which they were put there,' she explained, pointing out what she meant with her pen.

'This first batch of copy from Neil. When did it arrive?' I asked.

'Not sure. It was waiting in the transmission desk when the day staff came on duty, that's all I know.'

'What time would that be?'

'The early newsdesk guy comes in at half-past six. I was in around half-past seven myself that morning. He told me the copy had come in overnight. I helped myself to a print-out and went over to Colcutt. Got bloody nowhere, of course. I'm busy telling my desk that nobody's talking, nobody's even reachable, and he seems to think that I can fly over the gates and pick up all the stuff Neil isn't telling.'

'Poor you,' I sympathized absently. 'Is there any way of telling exactly when Neil's copy arrived in your transmission desk?'

Alexis ran a hand through her hair. The effect would have frightened small children. 'Not that I know of. Not at this end. Maybe he date-stamps his files, but we don't keep any copy trail that gives that kind of info. That all you wanted to know?'

I nodded, and she returned to her story. I wondered how exactly I could get the information I needed. It seemed to me that a lot of the details in Neil's copy were only generally known at the manor much later than he'd transmitted them. I needed to know who'd given him that information, for as far as I was aware, it was known only to me, Jett and the killer. If Jett had told him, there was no problem. If it had come from anyone else, then I'd have my killer. Unless, of course, Jett was the killer. God, this was all so complicated. I yearned for a nice, clear set of fraudulent accounts.

Alexis hit a key with a flourish and swivelled her chair to face me. 'All done. Want a look?'

I read the copy. It was good. It made Mortensen and Brannigan look efficient and subtle, as opposed to the police, who came out smelling of the stuff you put on roses. I pointed out a couple of minor corrections, to keep Alexis on her toes. Muttering about 'nit pickers anonymous', she made the changes.

As I got to my feet, she said, 'When you've got anything to report on Moira's murder, give us a tip-off, eh? And if you're going to point the finger and get the cops to make an arrest, my edition time's ten a.m.'

I was still smiling when I parked outside the office ten minutes later. I was first in, by five minutes. Shelley looked shocked to find me at my desk when she walked in at five to nine. I winked and said, 'We never sleep.'

233

'I can tell,' she replied. 'Next time you kindly grant me a holiday, remind me to borrow those bags under your eyes.'

I was desperate to get back to the manor and ask more questions, but I knew it would be too early for the night owls. Instead, I decided to ring DI Tony Redfern to ask what they'd found in the Smarts' lock-up.

Tony sounded almost relieved that someone wanted to talk to him about anything other than the fatal car chase, so he gave me all the details I needed to write my report. I'd only just put the phone down on him when Shelley buzzed me. 'I've got Inspector Jackson on the line for you,' she said. 'He sounds like he's just been stung by a wasp.'

'Thanks for the warning. Put him through, would you?' My heart sank. The events of the morning had put my appointment with Jackson right out of my mind. Besides, I couldn't imagine what more he thought he could get out of me than he'd done the previous afternoon.

'Good morning, Inspector,' I greeted him.

'Why am I speaking to you over the phone instead of face to face?' he demanded.

'I thought we covered the ground yesterday afternoon, Inspector. Besides, I've been a little busy this morning with your colleagues in the Greater Manchester force. If you'd like to check with Detective Inspector Redfern . . .'

'I'm a busy man, Miss Brannigan, and I'm in the middle of a murder inquiry. When I make appointments, I expect them to be kept.'

His dignity had obviously taken more of a bruising than I'd realized after Kevin's entry yesterday. Time to smarm. 'I appreciate that, Inspector. Perhaps we could make it another time?'

'How soon can you get round here?'

'I'm really sorry, Inspector. But I'm tied up for the rest of the day. Perhaps tomorrow?'

'Tomorrow morning, same time,' he snapped. Obviously he didn't feel he could push it. I suppose I should have felt relieved I wasn't actually a suspect.

'That's a date,' I promised. 'Sorry about today, it went clean out of my mind with the other business. By the way, have you charged Maggie Rossiter yet?'

There was a silence. Then he said stiffly, 'Miss Rossiter was released at eight-thirty this morning.' The line went dead.

Surprise, surprise. They'd had their hands on Maggie for thirty-six hours and they hadn't been able to manufacture enough of a case to hang on to her. I flicked open my notebook and called her number. She answered on the third ring. 'Maggie? Kate Brannigan here. I've just heard that you'd been released, and I wanted to tell you how pleased I was.'

She cut in, her voice remote and cool. 'Yes, well, I owe that to Moira.'

'I'm sorry?'

'My next-door neighbour, Gavin, picked up the post this morning. He noticed a letter to me in Moira's handwriting. It was posted second class the night she was killed. She must have dropped it in the box on her way to meet me. She was like that, you know. Thoughtful, romantic, even. Take it from me, it's not the letter of someone who's splitting up with her lover.'

'So Gavin got it to your solicitor, did he?'

'That's right. He's got a friend with a fax machine, so he opened it and sent it straight over to my solicitor. She brought it round to the police station right away.'

And of course, with no motive, the police case collapsed. They had nothing at all to base a charge on. No wonder Jackson was looking for someone to kick.

'Thank God that's over,' I said.

'Don't be too sure,' she replied glumly. 'I got the distinct

235

impression that they haven't given up on the idea of pinning it on me. Let's face it, if they can't stick it on the dyke or the black, they'll be less than happy. I'd make sure you're covering your client's back, if I was you, Kate.'

The phone went dead, before I even had the chance to tell her about Fat Freddy. I decided I'd try her again in the evening, once she'd had a bit of time to get used to being home alone again. I used the rest of the morning to type up a report for Bill and our clients about the morning's events. It was a sorry ending to a successful investigation.

I was putting a new pack of microcassettes in my handbag when I caught sight of the detailed info Josh had faxed me about Moira's financial problems. In the recent chaos, I'd completely forgotten to look at it. I smoothed it out and started to read.

The very first debt, for £175, caught my eye immediately. The County Court judgement on it dated from a few months after she'd left Jett. The creditors were an outfit called Cullen Holdings in Bradford. The name rang a vague bell. I went through to Shelley's office for the Bradford phone directory and looked it up. There was no listing for Cullen Holdings, but there was a listing for The Cullen Clinic. That was what had rung the bell. Before I'd joined Bill full-time, I'd done a company search on The Cullen Clinic for a client in the same line of business who was looking for traces of financial shenanigans. Or any other kind of dirt.

Shelley found the relevant records disc and I loaded it into my computer. The Cullen Clinic was owned by Dr Theodore Donn. In spite of the title, he was no medical man. His degree was a Ph.D. in electrical engineering from Strathclyde University. He'd set up The Cullen Clinic for one reason only. To make money out of abortion. He'd been running the clinic at a substantial profit for nearly ten years. He'd even survived a Department of Health inquiry into the connection between his business and a pregnancy advisory service owned by his sister, which referred their unhappily pregnant clients to The Cullen Clinic for terminations. Very cosy. And they'd sued Moira Pollock for the non-payment of a bill incurred just a week after she'd left Jett.

I closed my eyes and breathed deeply. I couldn't believe that Jett had known about that when he hired me to find her. If he'd found out after she'd come back, it gave him one hell of a motive. I knew his rigidly hostile views on abortion. I'd seen how mercurial he could be. I'd seen his rages. And above all, this crime was spontaneous, panicky and angry.

I changed discs, just to confirm what Josh's printout had told me, and called up Moira's medical records from the Seagull Project. Halfway down the page, there it was. VAT. Voluntary Assisted Termination. She must have been going through hell. Hooked on smack, pregnant, alone. It was a miracle she'd survived as well as she had. And all the more of a crime that someone had killed her when she'd finally got her life back together.

I leaned back in my chair and thought. If I'd been able to find out about Moira's abortion, the chances were that Neil could have too. Good journalists use exactly the same kinds of sources that investigators do. The only question for me was if Neil's sources in the financial sector were as efficient as mine. And if he'd told Jett about his discovery. That could be just the kind of scandal he'd been looking for to sell his book. Whether he'd still be getting any co-operation from Kevin and Jett if he'd told them he planned to use material like that was another matter entirely. It was time to ask Neil Webster a few more questions.

It was lunchtime for the world, breakfast time at the manor when I arrived. The atmosphere in the kitchen was less

237

than welcoming. Jett looked up from the toast he was buttering to say hello, but no one else paid me a blind bit of notice. Kevin and Micky were sitting opposite Jett, both leaning forward earnestly over their cups of coffee. Tamar was shovelling down Weetabix, spluttering between mouthfuls that Jett ought to listen to Kevin and Micky, that they were right.

'Right about what?' Jett was paying me to poke my nose in, after all.

Micky's brow corrugated in a simian frown. Kevin delivered one of his ingratiating smiles and said, 'We've just been telling Jett, the best thing for him is to get back to making music. Take his mind off things, let him work through his grief.'

'How near is the album to completion?' I asked.

'It'll never be finished now,' Jett replied morosely. 'How can I even think about it?'

A look of irritation was chased off Kevin's features by a spuriously sympathetic expression. 'Hey, I know you feel like that now, but you should think of this as a tribute to Moira. A way of making her spirit live on.' I had to hand it to Kevin. He was shrewd when it came to manipulating Jett.

Jett looked doubtful. 'I dunno, seems like bad taste, and her not even in her grave yet.'

'That's just her body, Jett, you know that. Her spirit's free now. No fear, no hate, no pain, nothing to worry about. She came back because she wanted you to make music together. You owe it to her to finish that work.' I cast my eyes heavenwards at Kevin's words. God, I'd be glad when this job was over.

Gloria swept into the room and headed straight for the kettle. 'The police have released the rehearsal room,' she announced. 'We can use it whenever we want.'

Jett shuddered. 'No way. Kevin, I want my instruments moved out of there and up to my sitting room.'

238

'But what about the piano? And the synths?'

'Them too. If I'm going to work, I can't do it in that room, with all the negative energies from her death.'

Kevin nodded in resignation. 'There's a couple of road crew live locally. I'll get them over to sort it out.' He got to his feet and left, followed at a trot by Micky. Gloria finished making her herbal tea and turned to glare at Tamar, who was helping herself to a slice of Jett's toast. If I had my breakfast in an atmosphere like that, I'd be sucking Rennies for the rest of the day.

'While you're all here, can I ask when it was that you knew how Moira had been killed?' Time to get to work.

Gloria looked uncertainly at Jett. Tamar covered her toast with strawberry jam and said, 'The first I knew was after I got up that morning. Jett was the only one who knew, and he wasn't in the mood for talking. Besides, PC Plod was standing over us in the drawing room till well after four o'clock. It really wasn't the atmosphere for cosy chats about murder methods.'

'Gloria?' I asked.

'I knew before I went to bed,' she admitted reluctantly. 'I went to my office after they told us we could go to bed, and I overheard one of the policemen saying he'd never seen anyone battered to death with a saxophone before.'

I couldn't disprove it, and she couldn't prove it. 'Did you discuss it with anyone else?'

'Of course not,' she retorted, back on her dignity.

'And was there anyone else in your office with you?'

'No. I just wanted to make sure everything was locked up securely before I went to bed.'

'Jett, did you discuss the method of Moira's death with anyone at all apart from me?'

He shook his head. 'Kate, I was too fucked up for con-versation. No way did I want to talk about it. Also, you

239

told me to keep my mouth shut, so I knew there had to be a good reason for it.'

I thanked them all, and went off in search of Neil. He was in his office, battering the keyboard of his computer as if it were an old manual typewriter. I winced as I perched on the edge of his desk. 'I can see you're not exactly familiar with the leading edge of modern technology,' I said sarcastically.

He paused and grinned. 'I know exactly as much as I need to do the job,' he said.

'And if all else fails, read the manual?'

'You got it in one,' he replied, still smiling.

'It's a shame,' I said. 'I always feel sorry for people who don't use their machines to their full potential.'

'How do you mean?' he asked, finally intrigued enough to give me his full attention.

'Well, for example, you must have a comms setup here to send your copy, am I right?'

'You mean the modem and the Hermes Link?' he asked.

That answered one question. Now I knew which electronic mail service he was hooked into. 'That's right,' I said. 'But have you ever used bulletin boards and public domain software?'

He looked at me as if I had lapsed into Mandarin. 'Sorry, Kate, I haven't a clue what you're on about.'

I explained at mind-numbing length about communicating with other users through bulletin boards, about capturing free software programs over the phone lines, and about game-playing via modems. He looked just as dazed and confused as I'd intended. 'I bet you don't even do the things that make it easy on yourself, like date-stamping your files.'

That earned me a blank look. 'Pardon?'

'You date-stamp your files, that way you can check

when they were sent and what mailbox they were sent to. A great come-back when people haven't paid you and claim they never had the copy.'

'Oh, right,' he said blankly.

'You want me to show you?' I asked, sidling over beside him. 'Just connect yourself to Hermes and I'll show you how.'

Right according to plan, he connected his computer to the telephone system. He had an autologon program, which only revealed his mailbox number, not his ID and passwords. But that was probably enough for what I had in mind. I memorized the eight digit number, ran a routine quickly by him, then exited from the link. 'If you're interested, I'll come over one afternoon after all this is finished and show you how to do it for yourself,' I offered.

He gave me a sly grin. 'Be my guest. Maybe I can do you a trade. I'm sure there's one or two things I could teach you.'

How to slide under a stone without disturbing it, perhaps, I thought. Time for a bit of hardball, I decided. 'Neil? How did you hear about the way Moira was killed?'

He shifted in his seat. 'Why do you want to know?' he asked.

'I'm just checking with everyone. Routine. I'm not very accustomed to investigating murder, and there were one or two things I forgot to ask last time around.'

'Obviously, I was dying to find out exactly what had happened, but the cops told us not to talk about it while they had us cooped up in that bloody blue drawing room. Besides, the only person who seemed to know what was going on was Jett. Anyway, after the police told us we could go to bed, I collared Kevin. I told him the best way to control any bad publicity was for me to handle all the stories. I know, I know, it's earned me a few bob, but why not? Anyway, I asked him for the details, and he told me

241

she'd been battered to death in the rehearsal room with a tenor sax.' He smiled disarmingly. I wondered if he knew he'd just given me the last brick in my case.

28

Cracking a case is a unique feeling, a mixture of relief, self-congratulation and a curious sense of deflation. I felt all that and more at Neil's words, and I struggled not to show him any of it. Until the net was ready to close round Kevin, I didn't want anyone to know how much I had on him. I searched my mind for another question to ask Neil, so his last reply wouldn't stick in his mind as the thing that had sent me haring off. 'Have you told Jett about the abortion yet?' I hazarded.

He froze, and a mottled flush spread up from his neck. 'A-abortion,' he stuttered.

I'd got him. Time for the major league bluff. 'I know all about it, Neil. And I know you know. I just wondered if you'd told Jett yet.'

He shook his head. 'I don't know what you're on about, Kate, I swear.'

'You can't bullshit me, Neil. Either you co-operate with me, or I go straight to Jett and tell him you're planning to drop that little bombshell in the public domain just to make yourself a shilling.'

'You're a hard-faced bitch,' he complained, his face the picture of petulance.

'Yeah, but I'm good at it. Now talk. When did you find out about the abortion?'

'A few days before Moira died,' he admitted sulkily.

'Just as a matter of interest, how did you find out?'

'I ran a financial check on her, then I rang the clinic pretending to be Moira's accountant, saying she was now in a position to settle the outstanding amount, and could they send the account to me. I confirmed it was for a termination, and gave them a fake address to send it on to.' He couldn't help himself. He looked smug as a Cheshire Conservative.

'So how did you plan to use the information?' I asked.

He shrugged. 'I thought about telling Jett, but it didn't seem like a good idea when he and Moira were working so closely together. He's not exactly what you'd call a New Man when it comes to abortion and working wives, is he? It would have caused an almighty row, and God knows what would have happened. I decided to hang on and see what happened after the album was finished.'

'You mean you were going to wait till the book came out, then sell it separately, and to hell with the damage it caused?'

His angry look told me I'd hit the nail right on the head. But he wasn't going to admit it. 'Of course not,' he said hotly. 'What do you take me for?'

If I were American, I'd have pleaded the fifth. As it was, I just gave him my most contemptuous look and walked out.

Two doors down the hall from Neil's office, I found the dining room. It looked as if it got about as much use as Richard's vacuum cleaner. I sat down on an antique balloon-backed chair and inserted a fresh tape in my recorder. I dictated a report of the case to date, explaining the reasons for my conclusion that Kevin was the killer. The problem was that I still lacked any substantial proof. I had no doubt that would be easy enough for the police to find once he was arrested. A serious probe into his finances would be one place to start. But I had to produce enough evidence to convince the police to take that first step.

It seemed to me there were two ways to approach it. One was to 'persuade' Fat Freddy to co-operate. The other was to try to flush Kevin out into the open. That was risky, but the results would be much more damning than anything a Bradford villain might have to say.

I found Jett in his sitting room, talking music with Kevin and Micky, who both looked less than thrilled to see me again. 'Sorry to interrupt, but I've got something important to say,' I announced.

Jett jumped to his feet and crossed the room in a rush. He gripped my upper arms so tightly I knew I'd have to forget sleeveless dresses for a few days. 'You know who killed Moira? I sense it, Kate. You know!' he said intensely.

'I've got a pretty good idea,' I said.

'Tell me,' he shouted, shaking me.

I tried to wriggle out of his grasp, but he held on. 'Jett, you're hurting! Let me go!' I demanded.

His hands fell to his sides and he slumped into the nearest chair, drained. 'I'm sorry, Kate. I didn't mean to hurt you. You gotta tell me, though.'

Micky lit a cigarette and inhaled deeply. 'He's right. If you know, he's got a right to be told.'

'I haven't got enough proof to start throwing accusations around yet,' I said. 'But I know where to go to find it. By this time tomorrow, I should know for sure. When I do, Jett, you'll know. What I want you to do is to get everyone together tomorrow at five. The blue drawing room's as good a place as any. I'll tell you everything I've learned then.'

'For God's sake,' Kevin exploded. 'This is ridiculous. I never heard of anything so bloody silly. What do you think this is? Some crappy detective novel? Showdown in the drawing room? Why the hell can't you just tell Jett like you're paid to do?'

'Shut up, Kevin,' Jett said forcefully. 'I gave Kate a free hand. She'll handle it. She knows what she's doing.'

'Thanks,' I replied. 'The reason I want you all together is that I have things to say that affect each and every one of you. And there are people who know more than they've told, for whatever reason. Once they know they're no longer suspects, they'll be more willing to give me the full picture.'

'Can't you give us some idea now? I don't fancy spending another night under the same roof as a killer,' Kevin protested.

I had to hand it to him. He had bottle. Either that or the arrogance of the criminal who thinks he's cleverer than the investigators. 'No. All I will say is that Moira was killed because she knew too much. Someone in this house got greedy. They were trying to make a fast buck. And purely by chance, Moira found out. And once I've made a little trip across the Pennines tomorrow to talk to a certain businessman, I'll know everything Moira knew. And more. Now, if you'll excuse me, gentlemen, I've got work to do.'

I didn't hang around waiting for a response. Within five minutes, I was heading back to town. I'd done my best to flush Kevin out. Now I was going to have to cover my back.

I double-tracked the busy line between Essen and Utrecht and monitored the effect on my station boxes. Railroad Tycoon, the ultimate computer strategy program, was doing the trick of taking my mind off the waiting game. It's not just little boys who like playing trains.

I'd been building my trans-European railroad for about an hour when the doorbell rang. I froze the game and went through to the hall. The security lights blazed down on a uncomfortable-looking Kevin. Surprise, surprise. I was a little taken aback by the full frontal approach, but if he'd been planning to take me by surprise, he would have been foiled by the lights as soon as he got within twenty yards of any of the windows. I must remember to tell clients that they're a great deterrent against potential murderers.

'Can we talk, Kate?' he said as soon as I opened the door.

'I was actually having an evening off, Kevin. Can't it wait till tomorrow?'

'We've got some things to clear up that won't wait.'

'We do? You'd better come in then,' I said grudgingly, leading the way back through to the living room. I gestured to one of the sofas, and he perched on the edge.

I sat down opposite him, deliberately not offering him a drink. I wanted to keep him edgy. 'What did you want to talk to me about?' I inquired.

'You're setting me up,' he said abruptly, lacing his fingers together tightly. 'I didn't kill Moira, and you're trying to make it look like I did.'

'I am? What makes you say that?' I asked coolly.

He cleared his throat and swallowed hard. 'I overheard your conversation with Jett last night. I picked up the extension because I was waiting for a call.'

'On Jett's private line? You'll have to try harder than that, Kevin.'

He sighed. 'All right, all right. I picked it up because I was nosy, OK? That suit you better?'

'Much better. I prefer it when people tell me the truth. You overheard our conversation. So?'

Kevin unlocked his fingers and massaged the back of his neck with one hand. 'I'll come clean. I admit I've been doing one or two side deals that might not be strictly kosher.'

'You mean you've been ripping Jett off with fake merchandise. Let's stick to plain English, Kevin.'

He flinched. 'OK, but that doesn't mean I killed Moira. I don't even think she knew anything about it.'

'She didn't tell you she'd seen you and Fat Freddy together?' I was intrigued by the line he was taking. I had to admit what he was saying wasn't impossible. After all, at the time of Moira's death, Maggie still hadn't found out exactly what line of work Fat Freddy was currently in. For all Moira knew, it could have been nothing to do with Jett.

'No, she didn't. And if she'd known about it, do you really think she'd have kept her mouth shut? She was quick enough to badmouth me to Jett and to anyone else who'd listen about her bloody royalties money. She couldn't have resisted telling him anything she found to blacken my name with,' Kevin protested.

The psychology sounded credible, I had to admit. But my belief in his guilt didn't just depend on one thing. I was torn between letting him stew till the following evening, and fronting him up with what I suspected, to see if I could nail him once and for all. Arrogance won, for a change. 'You must have wanted rid pretty badly,' I observed.

Kevin gave me an admiring smile, all expensive dentistry and insincerity. 'Nice try, Kate. I'll admit that if she'd said she was leaving, I'd have carried her bags to the station. But murder? That's not my style.'

'You had plenty of motive, though.'

'Me?' Kevin threw his arms out in a gesture of supplication. 'Kate, if I bumped off every musician who made my life difficult, I'd have been in Strangeways a long time ago.'

'I hear Moira thought that's where you should be.'

Kevin's eyelids fluttered as his body tensed. 'Look, you

keep making these innuendos, but I'd suggest you don't repeat them outside these four walls.'

'I'm talking about money, Kevin. Not just the business with Fat Freddy, or Moira's back royalties. She was convinced you were doing some fancy footwork with Jett's cash. Otherwise, why would he be on the constant treadmill of tours and albums? Most people of his stature who've been in the game as long as he has take it a lot easier than him. A few big stadium dates, an album every eighteen months or so. But according to Moira, Jett had to keep working to keep paying the bills. So where was all the money?' I pinned him with a hard stare, and I was gratified to see his hands grip his knees tightly.

'Look, I told you. If she'd had any proof of anything like that, do you think I'd still be around?' he exploded. 'She was full of shit! She loved to stir it. I told her a dozen times, her cash was all accounted for. It was tied up in a high interest investment account that I have to give three months' notice of withdrawal on. Out of that tiny, insignificant fact, she built a whole edifice of poisonous rumour. That shows you the kind of woman she was.'

'Frankly, I'm amazed. I'd have expected you all to fall on her neck weeping tears of joy and gratitude, given the way Jett's career's been going of late,' I retaliated.

Kevin's head seemed to shrink into his shoulders, like a tortoise in retreat. 'Listen, Kate, I said when you started looking for Moira that we were looking at trouble. She was always a manipulative bitch. She loved playing us all off against each other, always had. OK, Jett's been going through a difficult patch in creative terms, but he would have come good again, with or without Moira. He just got this crazy obsession that he needed her. So we all got lumbered with her. She was only through the door five minutes when she had us all at each other's throats. I've told you already. We're not killers. We're putting an album together, that's the number one priority. No one would jeopardize that by making us the focus of all these shitty stories in the press,' he added.

'I thought Neil was controlling the press for you.'

Kevin snorted. 'Might as well try to knit a bed jacket out of a mountain stream as try to control those toe-rags. Neil's done his best, but he's got an uphill struggle on his hands. God knows where they've got some of this stuff from. I mean, one of them's even got some tale about Moira and Tamar being at each other's throats. I've a good mind to sue, except that it would only cause more bad publicity.'

'You'd have a job suing.' I couldn't resist it.

'What d'you mean?' he asked indignantly.

'I don't think you'd have any grounds,' I said sweetly. 'But let's leave that aside for a minute,' I continued. 'Cast your mind back to the evening of Moira's death.'

He butted in eagerly. 'I suppose you want to know what I was doing when Moira bought it?'

I nodded. He nodded. We were like a pair of toy dogs on a car's parcel shelf. 'No problem,' he said. 'I'd been over to Liverpool for a business meeting and I got back around nine. I stuck my head round the TV room door and said hi to Jett and Tamar. Then I nipped up to my office to make a few phone calls. Around ten, I went downstairs and made myself a steak sandwich, then I popped down to the studio for a word with Micky. That must have been getting on for eleven. He was up to his eyes in it, so I left him to it and went back up to the TV room. Gloria was watching Dead Babies on *The Late Show*, and I sat in for a while. I went back down to the studio about quarter to twelve, and listened to a couple of tracks with Micky, then I hit the sack. Next thing I knew, all hell was breaking loose.'

It was just detailed enough to be credible, if a bit glib.

'You don't have any problem with your memory, do you? Not like Micky?'

Kevin pulled a face. 'Nose like mine, Kate, you don't mess about with it, if you catch my drift. Anything other than music goes out of Micky's head like water down a drain. Besides, I've already been through it once for the boys in blue. I was there twice, and he can't deny it.'

'Did you see anyone near the rehearsal room?' I asked.

'Afraid not. The whole thing's a mystery to me. I can't accept it was one of us, you know. It must have been someone on the outside,' Kevin told me confidently.

I ignored the pathetic attempt at a red herring. 'You say you went up to bed after you'd spoken to Micky?'

'That's right. You saw me come downstairs yourself,' he pointed out, his tone grievance incarnate.

'Precisely. And do you normally go to bed in a suit and tie?'

His eyes widened, and the fingers of one hand started to beat a nervous tattoo on his knee. 'Just because I hadn't actually gone to bed yet doesn't mean a thing.'

'You'd been upstairs nearly two hours. And you hadn't even loosened your tie, Kevin. That's not normal behaviour. And in a murder investigation, anything that's not normal behaviour is automatically suspicious. So what was going on?'

Kevin took a deep breath, leaned his elbows on his knees and rubbed his face. 'If you must know,' he said, his words curiously muffled, 'I was going out. I haven't always shacked up in a grace and favour corner of Jett's house, you know. I've got a home of my own, Kate, a beautiful place down the road in Prestbury. Queen Anne style house, five bedrooms, gym, jacuzzi, swimming pool, the works. The wife lives there. When we split up, I moved in at Colcutt temporarily while I sorted things out. Only, my wife, she's screwing me for every penny she can get her hands on. And she's fucked off on a skiing holiday with her new boyfriend. I was going round to burgle the house.' He raised his head and stared defiantly at me.

'In a suit and tie?' I blurted out incredulously.

'I thought it would be the least suspicious thing to be wearing if anyone saw me or if I got stopped by the police,' he said lamely. 'I know it sounds stupid, but she'd got me so wound up, I just wanted to get back at her.'

'And make a few bob at the same time? That's some excuse, Kevin. God, you're pathetic.'

'I might be pathetic in your eyes, but I'm not a bloody killer,' he flared up.

This wasn't working out at all as I'd imagined. In my scenario, he was going to probe to find out what I knew then mount a murderous attack when he discovered I had him. Right now, he didn't look as if he could crush a daddy-long-legs.

I took a long swig of my drink and settled back to deliver the clincher. 'Can you explain something to me, Kevin? If you didn't kill Moira, how is it that you knew exactly how she'd been murdered before the police told everyone?'

He looked completely nonplussed. Gotcha, I thought. Prematurely, as it turned out. 'I don't know what you mean,' he said with an air of bewilderment. 'I knew the same time as everyone else. When the police interviewed me.'

I shook my head. 'Not what I've been told. According to my witness, you knew how Moira had died by the time the police released you from the blue drawing room, a couple of hours after the murder.'

'That's not true,' he cried, desperation in his voice. His eyes flicked from side to side, as if checking the escape routes. 'Who told you that? They're lying! They're all lying. They're trying to discredit me.' For the first time, his smart-alec composure had cracked wide open. He clearly hadn't been expecting this at all.

'You're the one who's lying, Kevin. You had means, motive and opportunity. You killed Moira, didn't you?'

'No,' he shouted, jumping to his feet. 'I didn't. You bitch, you're trying to set me up! Somebody's trying to push me out. First Moira, now someone else. Tell me who told you those lies!'

He lunged at me. I pushed myself sideways on the sofa. He crashed into the arm of the sofa, letting out an 'oogh' of pain. But he kept coming at me, yelling, 'Tell me, tell me.'

I couldn't find enough space to use any of my boxing moves on him. He threw himself on me, gripping me by the throat. His paranoia seemed to lend him extra strength. I'd miscalculated. This was something I couldn't handle myself. Red spots danced in front of my eyes, and I could feel myself retching and fainting.

29

I opened my eyes to a huge, out-of-focus face inches from my own, like a sinister Hallowe'en mask. I blinked and shook my head, and realized it was Richard, his face a mixture of fear and concern. 'You all right, Brannigan?' he demanded.

'Mmm,' I groaned, carefully probing my tender, bruised neck. Richard sat down heavily beside me and hugged me. Looking over his shoulder, I could see Kevin's legs. The rest of him was hidden under Bill's bulk. My boss was sitting astride Kevin, looking triumphant.

'Would someone pass me the phone?' he said calmly. 'I need to call the garbage disposal people.' A muffled grunt escaped from the body under him. He obligingly shifted his position slightly.

'On the table, Richard,' I told him, and he went to fetch it. Bill punched in a number and asked for Cliff Jackson.

'Inspector? This is Bill Mortensen of Mortensen and Brannigan. I'd like to report an attempted murder,' he began when he was finally connected. 'Yes, that's right, an attempted murder. Kevin Kleinman has just tried to strangle my partner, Miss Brannigan.'

I wished I could have been a fly on the wall in Jackson's office. The news that someone had actually done what he'd been longing to do since the beginning of the case must have provoked a serious conflict of interest. 'Well, of course it's connected,' I heard Bill protest. 'They were discussing the murder at the time of the attack . . . How do I know? Because I was listening at the door, man! Look, why don't you just get over here and we can sort it all out then?'

Richard, ignoring Bill's conversation, was fussing over me. 'Thank God we were there,' he kept repeating.

Losing patience, I said, 'It had nothing to do with God and everything to do with the fact that I told you to be there.' They had been my insurance policy; Richard crouching in the conservatory, Bill lurking in the hall. Arrogant I may be, stupid I'm not.

Richard grinned. 'I thought that came to the same thing? You and God?'

'They're on their way,' Bill interrupted, saving me the bother of having to think up a witty reply. 'Inspector Jackson doesn't sound like a happy man.' A muffled shout from under him indicated that Jackson wasn't the only one.

It took a couple of hours to sort everything out. They'd made Bill stop sitting on Kevin, and he'd immediately burst into a loud tirade of complaint. Jackson had shut him up briskly and removed him in a police car to Bootle Street nick. By the time he'd taken statements from all three of us, he grudgingly admitted that the assault on me gave him enough to hold Kevin while he made further inquiries into his financial background. I could see the whole episode hadn't improved his attitude to the private sector.

After he left, Richard found a couple of carefully hoarded bottles of Rolling Rock, his all-time favourite American beer. He and Bill toasted each other, boasting cheerfully about their rescue as small boys the world over will do. I poured myself a stiff vodka and said sweetly,

'Don't you think we should save the celebrations for when we've nailed the murderer?'

They stopped in mid-swig and stared blankly at me. 'I thought that was what we'd just done?' Richard said. 'You said Kevin had done it.'

'That's what I said. But now I'm not so sure.'

Richard gave one of those sighs that seem to come from his socks. 'I don't get it,' he complained. 'Two hours ago, you were accusing the guy of murder. Now you're not so sure?'

Bill shook his head, a wry smile lurking in his beard. 'OK, Kate, let's have it.'

I explained my theory, and he got to his feet, muttering about no rest for the wicked. 'Let's go, then, Kate,' he said resignedly. 'I'll see what I can do.'

'Can I come too?' Richard asked plaintively.

'You'll be bored out of your tree,' Bill told him. 'But you're welcome to come along if you want.'

'You can always make the coffee,' I added wickedly. I knew how to turn him off. And much as I love Richard, I didn't want him kicking his heels in boredom while we worked. I mean, would you take a four-year-old to the office with you?

My strategy worked. Richard shrugged and said, 'I think I'll just stay home. I suppose I could earn myself a few bob putting out the story of Kevin's arrest. I mean, even if you think he didn't do it, he's still down the nick, isn't he?'

'Good thinking. Why should Neil Webster be the only one making a shilling out of Moira's murder?' I teased.

He poked his tongue out at me and gave me a farewell hug before he disappeared into the gloom of the conservatory.

'You think you can do it?' I asked Bill.

He shrugged. 'Don't know till I try, do I? It won't be easy, but it shouldn't be impossible.'

'Well, what are we hanging round here for?'

Bill's attempts at hacking still hadn't borne fruit by midnight, when the phone rang. From force of habit, I picked it up. 'Mortensen and Brannigan,' I announced automatically.

'Is that Kate Brannigan?' an unfamiliar voice asked.

'That's right. And you are?'

'My name is David Berman. I'm Kevin Kleinman's solicitor. I'm sorry to disturb you so late in the day, but my client was most insistent that I speak with you. Would it be possible for me to come round to your office? I'm only a couple of minutes away.' His voice was soft and persuasive.

'Can you hold a second?' I asked him. I pressed the mute button and said, 'Kevin's solicitor wants to come round. I don't think he's just after a decent cup of coffee.'

Bill's eyebrows rose like a pair of blond caterpillars. 'Let's see what the man has to say,' he said. Sometimes I think I'd kill to be that laid back.

I reopened the channels of communication and said, 'That would be fine, Mr Berman, I'll meet you downstairs in five minutes.' I hung up and said, 'Curiouser and curiouser.'

'The time has come, the walrus said,' Bill muttered in cryptic response as he tried out another password. I left him to it and put on a fresh pot of coffee before I went downstairs to meet David Berman.

When I got downstairs, a prosperous-looking yuppie was waiting on our doorstep. Dark grey self-stripe suit, pale-blue shirt and a subdued paisley pattern silk tie. Not a crease anywhere, except in his trousers, and that could have sliced salami. His dark hair was fashionably slicked back and a pair of horn-rimmed glasses perched on the bridge of his nose. He smiled confidently at me as I struggled with the four locks on the plate glass doors.

As soon as I opened them, his hand was thrust towards me. The handshake was cool, with the carefully measured amount of pressure that gives the message, 'I could crush your hand if I wanted to, but who needs to be macho among friends?'

'Miss Brannigan? Pleased to meet you. David Berman,' he said cheerfully. 'I really appreciate you making time for me at this hour of the night.'

He followed me up the stairs, avoiding small talk in a way that I found slightly unsettling. I suspected it was deliberate. I showed him into the main office, and offered him coffee. Bill didn't even look up from his screen, though I caught Berman peering nosily through the door of his office.

I sat down at Shelley's desk and said, 'What makes you think we can help, Mr Berman?'

'It's a little difficult,' he admitted. 'I am well aware of the alleged attack earlier this evening, and I can appreciate that you might not be inclined to listen to what I have to propose.'

'That's one way of putting it. Your client tried to strangle me tonight. He's right off my Christmas card list. But I'm always happy to listen. You'd be amazed the things you can pick up that way.'

He smiled. He was meant to. 'I take your point, Miss Brannigan,' he acknowledged. 'It's my understanding that you have been retained by one of my client's artistes to uncover the identity of the murderer of Moira Pollock. Is that correct?'

Why do lawyers always ask questions they know the answers to? It was one of the things that made me decide I preferred being a private investigator. Maybe you don't always come across as omniscient, but at least you get the occasional stimulating surprise. 'Quite right,' I reassured him.

He gave a curt nod. 'And I understand that you made certain allegations against my client in this matter?'

'Right again.' Had it really been worth trekking downstairs for this?

'My client has instructed me to pass certain information on to you, without prejudice,' he said solemnly, as if he were handing me a gift of immense value and corresponding responsibilities. His glasses had slipped down, and he peered at me through them like a judge thirty years his senior.

'Indeed,' I replied. All this legalese was causing serious linguistic regression.

'You alleged that my client had knowledge of the crime at a time when only the murderer could have known it. My client denies this strenuously, and has asked me to ascertain the source of this false information so that he can refute it,' he said earnestly.

I should know better than to be surprised by the deviousness of lawyers. 'It sounds like you're looking for information rather than handing it out,' I told him. 'If your client is a murderer, would it not be rather irresponsible of me to identify a witness against him?' More linguistic contagion.

'My client is going to be charged with attempted murder,' Berman replied tartly, pushing his glasses up his nose. 'I don't think he'll be in a position to pose a risk to anyone. The point is that my client strongly denies possessing the aforementioned information at the time you allege. He denies vigorously passing that information on to anyone, and believes he can produce witnesses to all his conversations up to the time when he returned to his room.'

I felt a prickle of interest. Berman's words suggested there might be some corroboration of my fresh suspicions.

Before I could reply, Bill's voice rang through the office like a demented *Sun* journalist. 'Gotcha!' he cried.

'Excuse me,' I mumbled as I jumped to my feet and shot through the door. 'Have you cracked it?' I asked eagerly.

'Just a matter of time now. I've hacked into the accounts section, and it's just a case of working out how the files are organized and searching them,' Bill said triumphantly.

I hugged him. People need hugs, especially when they've just saved your life then made your day. Then, aware of David Berman's gaze, I returned to the outer office, this time closing the door behind me. 'Sorry about that,' I said. 'Bill's just cracked something we've been working on for a while now. If I can just go back to what you were saying. Has Kevin given you any account of what he said to whom?'

Berman compressed his lips, then said, 'I'm not at liberty to say.'

'Then it seems to me we're at an impasse. You can't tell me what he said, and I can't tell you who's making the claim.'

'It'll all come out eventually,' he said persuasively. 'You must be aware that if my client is charged, we will have to be told the names of the witnesses against him. It would surely be in everyone's interest to clear the name of an innocent man so that the search for the guilty party can go on. If my client is charged, this thing will drag on for months, and people's memories will start to fade. When he is eventually cleared, it may be too late to trap the real killer.'

It was a good argument. As I picked up my bag and told Bill I was going to Bootle Street with Berman, I tried to convince myself that it was the strength of his case that had persuaded me. After all, I thought sanctimoniously, even though Kevin was Mr Sleaze in my eyes, if I had wrongly accused him, I owed it to him to sort it out. Deep down, I knew otherwise. I had a theory, and I wanted to prove it to my own satisfaction.

It was nearly three when I got back to the office. After a lot of verbal ping-pong, with David Berman as the ball, I had obtained some very interesting material. As a result, I'd spent half an hour persuading Cliff Jackson that what I had to say to him was worth listening to. Credit where it's due, once he'd explained to me in graphic detail just why I was lower than a Salford sewer, he consented to pay attention. And instead of clambering on his high horse and ignoring what I had to say, he'd not only listened but had reluctantly agreed to give my suggestion a try. 'You get one shot,' he'd warned me. 'If you screw up, I'll bang you up as well as your chum in the cells. No messing.' I was so sure of myself I didn't feel I'd be risking that.

I found Bill leaning back in his chair, a look of deep satisfaction on his face as he puffed away on a Sherlock Holmes pipe filled with some noxious continental tobacco. 'Any news?' he asked me.

I told him where we were up to, and he smiled. He looked just like the Big Bad Wolf, his lips pulled back over teeth that gripped the pipe stem. Then he showed me what he'd dug up.

We were making plans until four. This time, everything was going to go like clockwork. This time, I wasn't going to end up with a necklace of bruises. Meanwhile, I had things to do. Unfortunately, sleep wasn't one of them.

30

Jett was waiting for me on the steps when I arrived at half-past four. His shoulders were hunched and his face had a tight, pinched look around the mouth and nose. 'You still going ahead with this showdown?' he greeted me.

'It has to be done, Jett,' I told him as we walked into the empty hall together.

'Why? They arrested Kevin. The word is he tried to kill you because you found out he killed Moira.' His tone was aggressive.

'I'm sorry, Jett. He did attack me.'

'No need for *you* to be sorry. You were just doing the job, like I asked you to. I'm the one should be sorry. I trusted that man with my life. And now I find out he killed the woman I cared for more than anything in the world. So why d'you have to put us through more?'

Jett hurried ahead of me into the blue drawing room. I followed more slowly, wondering how to placate Jett without giving too much away. He was pouring himself a hefty drink when I entered. 'Help yourself,' he told me. With a moody scowl on his face, he moved over to the spindly-legged chair and threw himself into it again. If I'd been the man from the Pru, there's no way I'd have insured it.

I poured myself a weak vodka and topped it up with

262

orange juice, in the absence of my usual. I didn't think this was a good time to demand a grapefruit juice. I positioned myself in front of the grate, where some logs were smouldering half-heartedly.

Jett took a gulp of his drink and started to say something. He was interrupted by a knock at the door, which opened before either of us could say 'Come in'. Cliff Jackson barged in with a face like a man with a bad case of piles. Gloria followed him, saying petulantly, 'Sorry, Jett, he wouldn't wait till you'd finished with Kate.'

'Never mind that,' Jackson grunted. 'Just what is going on here, Brannigan? You tell me last night that Kleinman was the killer, you set him up to assault you so we've got something to stick on him, then you leave messages all over town telling me to get up here if I want to find out the truth about Moira Pollock's murder. What the hell are you playing at?'

Jett got to his feet and shot me an angry look. 'You didn't tell me he was coming,' he protested. 'This was supposed to be between us.' Out of the corner of my eye, I spotted a complacent smile spreading across Gloria's face.

'What exactly was supposed to be between you?' Jackson demanded, rounding on Jett.

'Mind your own fucking business, pig,' Jett yelled back at him. Jackson flushed dark scarlet and opened his mouth to retaliate.

'If we could all stop shouting at each other, I'll happily explain,' I interjected forcefully.

'I'm all ears,' Jackson snarled. 'It better be good. I can feel an overwhelming desire to charge someone with wasting police time.' I was impressed, I have to admit it. It made me wonder just how much of his routine bloody-mindedness was an act too.

'I know that you've charged Kevin with attempted

murder after what he did last night, but there are still a few loose ends to be tied up. I asked you to come because I didn't want you to turn round and say things were being done behind your back.' I turned to Jett. 'I know you didn't want him here, but things have gone too far to be kept in the family. I'm sure you don't want Moira's killer to get away with it just because you left it all to me and couldn't deliver.'

Jackson was shaking his head in disbelief. 'You are unreal, Brannigan. I should nick you right now for this grandstanding.'

'Give me half an hour, Inspector. Then you can throw the book at me if you're still so minded.'

Jackson muttered something under his breath that I didn't catch. I don't think I was supposed to. He moved across the room to stare at an undistinguished oil landscape on the far wall.

Jett drained his glass and handed it to the hovering Gloria, who bustled over to the drinks. She threw a quick glance back at Jett as if to gauge what strength he needed, then poured. I noticed it was almost as large a measure as he'd poured for himself. Maybe I'd been underestimating Gloria.

The awkward silence was broken by Tamar and Micky who entered together just on ten to five. Tamar ignored me and headed straight for Jett, who gave her a perfunctory kiss and steered her towards the sofa.

Micky moved to my side and touched my elbow. Through the cloud of cigarette smoke, I could see the worried look on his face. 'When are they going to let Kevin out on bail?' he murmured.

'I doubt if they will. He's already facing one serious charge, and there's a possibility he'll be on a murder charge by morning,' I explained softly.

He shook his head. 'This couldn't have come at a worse

ime. We're at a crucial stage with the album. I don't know vhat we're going to do.'

I was spared having to answer by Neil's entrance. He vas positively bouncing with bonhomie as he crossed the oom and greeted me with a kiss on the cheek. I was so urprised I couldn't move out of the line of fire fast enough. Micky moved away, disgust written all over his face.

'I know it's tasteless to say so,' Neil whispered in my ar, 'but Kevin's arrest is going to make my book a best-eller. I've been on to my publisher this afternoon, and ve're going to have the book ready to roll as soon as the rial finishes.'

'Why don't you get yourself a drink,' I said through lenched teeth. The guy gave a whole new meaning to leaze.

He winked at me and made his way over to the bar. he distant sound of the gate intercom buzzer caught veryone's attention and Gloria moved automatically owards the door to the hall.

'It's all right, Gloria, I'll get it,' I said, moving swiftly across the room to head her off at the pass. I went out nto the hall, closing the door behind me, and opened the ,ates for the final arrival.

I stood in the doorway and watched as the car slowly nade its way up the drive. It pulled up at the foot of the teps, in a kind of defiance. Maggie Rossiter climbed out f the driver's seat and made her way up the steps towards ne.

cleared my throat and said, 'People, if I could have your ttention for a moment?' The murmur of conversation riggered off by Maggie's arrival ended as abruptly as if I'd ushed the mute button on their remote control. Jackson urned towards me and leaned against a marble topped ier table.

'You all know about Kevin's arrest, and I expect that most of you think that it's only a matter of time till he' charged with Moira's murder. But then, you already thought that about Maggie when she was arrested. However, I was hired to find a killer, and I suspect that most of you think that's exactly what I've done. But until I've cleared up some loose ends that are still remaining, I'm afraid I can't regard the case as being closed. That's why I've asked you all together. There are some inconsistencies in the stories I've been told, and I thought the best way to deal with them was to have you all together. It's a shame Kevin can't be here, but we'll just have to work around that.' I looked around at their expressions, some hostile, some fascinated.

I took a deep breath and continued. 'I hadn't been working the case for very long when I discovered that someone in this house had already been trying to get rid of Moira.

'Gloria, who is a diabetic, had noticed syringes going missing from her room. It was only a matter of time before she got round to telling Jett, who at the very least would have confronted Moira and accused her of returning to her old habits. But not content with that, the person who stole the syringes also purchased some heroin. According to Maggie, every few days some heroin and a syringe would appear in Moira's room, facing her with a temptation that most people in her shoes would have found impossible to resist.

'But she did resist, and so the first thing I had to ask myself was if the killer was the same person who'd been trying to get rid of her earlier. But you weren't the killer, were you, Tamar?'

Tamar was on her feet. 'You poisonous *bitch*,' she screeched at me. 'You poisonous, lying *bitch*!' Then she whirled round to face Jett, whose face was as cold

266

as a marble statue. 'She's lying, Jett, I swear she's lying.'

'I can prove what I'm saying,' I replied coldly. 'The pusher who sold you the heroin identified your picture. You might have tried to get rid of Moira, but I'm satisfied you didn't kill her. There's a big difference between offering someone the option of death and actually facing up to your victim and caving her head in.'

Tamar clutched Jett's arm and fell to her knees in a histrionic show of supplication. He shrugged her arm off roughly and hissed, 'Get away from me, slag.'

She collapsed on the floor and began to sob noisily. Micky moved across to her and jerked her to her feet. 'For fuck's sake, get a grip,' he shouted angrily, dragging her away and thrusting her into an armchair.

'Get on with it,' Jett snapped.

'Gloria wasn't telling me the whole truth either,' I reported. She looked startled and gazed at me with a terrified fascination.

'I don't know what you mean,' she stammered. 'I haven't lied to you.'

'You came downstairs on the night of the murder and saw someone leaving the rehearsal room. You denied it, but there's only one person you'd lie to protect, and that's Jett. It was Jett you saw leaving the room, and you lied about it.'

'I never,' she shouted, like a small child who's been caught out lying about a broken piece of crockery. 'I never did.'

'What you didn't realize was that Jett had admitted to having been in the rehearsal room earlier. But that was before Moira arrived there. So there was no point in your lie.'

Gloria collapsed into the nearest chair and buried her face in her hands. 'Is there anything else you've lied to me about?' I asked gently.

She looked up, tears streaking her cheeks and shook her head mutely. I was inclined to believe her.

'Micky.' As I said his name, he moved a couple of steps nearer to me, his long arms dangling at his sides like a caricature of a Western gunslinger. 'I want to ask you about events in this room immediately after Moira died.'

'I've already told you all I know,' he said mutinously.

'All I want is some more detail,' I said persuasively.

'Tell her what she wants to know,' Jett growled.

Micky looked as if he wanted to argue, but he quickly remembered which side his bread was buttered. 'OK, fire away,' he complained.

'Can you tell me where you were sitting and who you were talking to?'

'I sat down on that chair over there,' he said, pointing to the one where Tamar was currently leaving salt stains on the silk upholstery. 'Kevin was stood next to me, by the bar. He poured me a drink, and we talked about Moira being killed. You know, what a shock it was, that kind of thing. He was worried about the effect it would have on Jett. Whether he'd be able to finish the album, whether the bad publicity would affect sales, the usual kind of Kevin shit.'

'Did he say anything at all about how she'd been killed?'

'Only that nobody seemed to be telling exactly what had happened. He said it must have been a burglar, or somebody she'd brought back with her from the village.'

I hoped to hell Jackson was keeping an eye on everyone. I was concentrating too hard on what I was doing to check the reactions around me. 'Did Kevin talk to anyone else apart from you?'

Micky's forehead concertinaed as he thought for a moment. 'Yeah,' he eventually sighed. 'Neil came over and asked what he wanted doing about the press. Kevin told him to deal with it, and to put out a story on it, just giving the bare bones of what had happened. He said he wanted it all handled in-house, and that Neil should make it clear that any other journalist who tried to get an interview would be wasting their time and his.'

I felt that warm feeling in my gut that tells me I've cracked it. 'And that's all he said?'

Micky nodded. 'Yeah. Neil fixed himself a drink and kind of drifted off to the corner. He was sitting scribbling in a notebook. I suppose he was getting a story together.'

'When did you and Kevin separate?' The crucial question.

Micky looked exasperated. 'I don't know what this has got to do with anything,' he stalled while he visibly cast his mind back. 'Let me see ... We came out of here together and walked up the stairs after the cops said we should all go to bed. I said good night to him outside his bedroom door. He looked as sick as a parrot. No wonder, after what he'd been up to.'

I turned my head towards Neil. His eyes were calm and clear as they met mine, as if he were offering me some kind of challenge.

31

The temptation to go for the high melodrama was almost overwhelming till I looked at Jett. It didn't take much perception to see that the guy was near the end of his rope. So I didn't point dramatically and say, 'Inspector, there is your murderer.'

Instead, I took a swig of my drink and said casually, 'Neil, why did you lie to me about what Kevin said to you?'

He smiled disarmingly and spread his hands out in a gesture of innocence. 'But I didn't, Kate. You're surely not going to take Micky's word against mine? A cokehead who relies on Kevin for the pennies in his bank account? He's got every reason to lie to protect Kevin. But me? Why should I lie to you?'

'There's only one reason why, Neil. You killed Moira.' A strange stillness seemed to have descended on the room. I'd certainly captured their attention now.

If I'd expected Neil to cave in, I was swiftly disappointed. He grinned and said, 'I hope Mortensen and Brannigan have made a good profit this year. When I sue you for slander, I want it to be worth my while.'

I returned his grin. 'I know I only managed to complete two years of law school, but it's always been my understanding that truth is an absolute defence in slander actions.'

'But you have to prove truth,' Neil parried swiftly. 'And I fail to see how you're going to provide proof of something I didn't do.' His smile had a triumphant edge that almost made me doubt what I knew to be true.

'But there is proof, Neil. Right under this roof is all the proof I need.'

He shook his head at me incredulously. 'She's out to lunch and not coming back in a hurry,' he said to the room at large.

Just then, Jackson moved forward into the room. 'I'd be interested in seeing your idea of proof, even if no one else is,' he said. I had an idea how much it cost him to utter those words, and I had to grant him a reluctant respect.

'If you'll follow me, Inspector, we need to make a little visit to Mr Webster's office,' I said formally.

'Wait a minute,' Neil said, showing traces of apprehension for the first time. 'What the hell do you think you're going to find there?'

'My proof,' I said, stalking out of the room. I didn't need to look back to know that I could easily have passed for the Pied Piper.

Neil overtook me on the threshold and snapped loudly enough for Jackson and everyone else to hear, 'Just what the hell do you think you're playing at? All this because your precious boyfriend wasn't good enough to write Jett's biography?'

'This has got nothing to do with Richard,' I informed him and everyone else within earshot. The tension was beginning to eat into me, and I didn't know how long I could maintain my cool façade.

'Oh no?' he sneered.

Ignoring him, I went straight to his computer, sat down in front of it and switched it on. Jackson leaned over my shoulder, while the others crowded round behind him. Neil hung back slightly, but his eyes were glued to the

271

screen. I briefly looked through the text files in the directory where he stored his stories, then I moved over to his communications program and keyed into it. 'For those of you who aren't familiar with computers,' I said as I hit the keys, 'this is a program that sends material over the telephone lines to another computer. Journalists use it to file copy electronically to newsdesks.'

I chose the 'text edit' option and called up the first story he'd sent out about Moira's killing. I slowly scrolled through the story till only the last line remained off screen. 'As you'll see, Neil had all the details of how Moira was killed. No problem with that if the story was filed after the police gave you all the details of how Moira was killed. Details which none of you who were shut up in the blue drawing room knew except Jett.'

'Which it was,' Neil blustered. 'And you can't prove otherwise.'

In silence, I brought the last line up on the screen. It gave the date-stamp on the story. 2.35 a.m.

'It's a set-up,' Neil shouted wildly. 'She's set this up, can't you see? She's the only one who knows enough about computers. She's framed me.' His face was glossy with sweat and his eyes flicked nervously round the room.

'You can confirm that evidence with the company who transmit the electronic mail, I should imagine, Inspector,' I said coldly.

'Neil Webster,' Jackson intoned, pushing through the press of bodies. 'I must warn you . . .'

The rest of his official caution was drowned by the sound of breaking glass as Neil threw himself through the window in a sparkling shower of splinters.

A soft kiss tickling the back of my neck woke me up. 'I hear you nailed the bastard,' Richard murmured into my ear. 'Well done.'

I groaned softly and rolled over on to my back. I could feel the warmth of his naked flesh next to mine, and the prospect of snuggling into him was more tempting than I wanted to admit. So I complained, 'Couldn't it wait till morning?'

'I only just heard about it. I went in to the *Mirror* to drop off some copy, and they told me Neil had been arrested, thanks to some nifty footwork by Mortensen and Brannigan,' he said proudly.

'Mmm,' I said. 'That's about the size of it.'

'So tell me all about it,' he demanded enthusiastically. He moved away from me and I heard the soft pop and hiss of a champagne bottle being opened. There was no hope of catching up on sleep now. I sat up and switched on the bedside light.

Richard blinked in the unexpected glow, then gave me his cutest smile as he handed me a fizzing glass of pink champagne. 'Every cough and spit,' he demanded.

So I told him all about the showdown, and how Neil had been picked up within five minutes by the team Jackson had wisely stationed outside. He'd been taken to hospital where he'd been formally charged while the casualty staff sewed up his cuts.

'Great job,' Richard said with as much satisfaction as if he'd been the prime mover. 'But I still don't understand why he killed her. Surely it wasn't just to produce a scandal that would sell his book?'

'Not quite. I don't think he actually meant to kill her. There was nothing premeditated about it. He was just incredibly lucky that no one else had an alibi and everyone else had better motives.'

'But why?' Richard howled in frustration.

I smiled sweetly and took a long, slow mouthful of champagne. 'Can't tell you. It's all *sub judice*, and you journalists can never keep your mouths shut.'

'Kate!' he wailed, his face a mixture of injured innocence and pure frustration.

I had to relent. 'When Moira left Jett all those years ago, she was pregnant. She had nowhere to go, and not a lot of cash left, so she had an abortion. Jett never knew about it, and it's a pound to a gold clock that he would never have had her back if he had done. The guy's notoriously anti-abortion, and he'd never have forgiven her for killing his own kid. Anyway, Neil found out about the abortion, and he told Moira he knew. Maybe he was even trying a spot of blackmail. She didn't want a walking time-bomb like that around the place. I questioned Kevin about it last night, and it turns out that she was trying to do a deal with him where Neil would be kicked out. In exchange, Moira wouldn't tell Jett about Kevin's little games with the money. Once Neil was out the door, anything he said would be seen as sour grapes.

'She must have been crowing to him about it in the rehearsal room. The prospect of being deprived of what must have been his last chance of a meal ticket was too much for him. He snapped and picked up the nearest object and thumped her with it. Like I said, I don't think murder was part of his plans, but having done it, he did his damnedest to make sure he got away with it.'

'And he would have done, too, if you hadn't known about the date-stamp on the files,' Richard said. 'Bloody clever of you.'

'Mmm,' I said. 'I wouldn't have known what to look for if Bill hadn't been able to hack into the electronic mail company's records to check exactly when those files were sent.' I carefully put my glass down on the bedside table and rolled over into Richard's arms. I deserved some fun after the last few days.

As my body started to tingle under Richard's familiar caresses, I made a mental note to burn the cassette of that earlier interview with Neil. It wouldn't do for Inspector Jackson to find out that Neil not only hadn't date-stamped his files. He hadn't even known how to.

Kick Back

Val McDermid

Kate Brannigan, feisty Manchester-based PI, is back, investigating the bizarre case of the missing conservatories. Before long she's up to her neck in crooked land deals, mortgage scams, financial chicanery – and murder. But when a favour for a friend puts Kate's own life in danger, bizarre is not the first word she thinks of . . .

'A satisfying range of villains, Manchester and its environs turn deeply sinister and Brannigan toughs and wisecracks her way to a solution'   *The Times*

'Plot, characterization, pace are all first-rate, and Brannigan is one of the most likeable of all today's PIs'
Sunday Telegraph

ISBN: 0-00-714292-7

Crack Down

Val McDermid

There was only one reason Manchester-based private eye
Kate Brannigan was prepared to let her boyfriend help out
with an investigation into a car sales fraud – nothing bad
could happen. But by now Kate should know that with
Richard you have to expect the unexpected.

With the unexpected being Richard behind bars, Kate
seems to be the obvious choice to look after his eight-year-
old son – who proves even more troublesome than his
father. Kate finds herself dragged into a world of drug
traffickers, child pornographers, fraudsters and violent
gangland enforcers . . . bringing her face to face with death
in the tensest, toughest and most terrifying investigation
of her career.

'Touch, funny and intensely topical. McDermid stands
out as one of the few contemporary writers actually
nourished by the here and now'   *Literary Review*

ISBN: 0 00 649008 5

Clean Break

Val McDermid

Manchester-based private eye Kate Brannigan is not amused when thieves have the audacity to steal a Monet from a stately home where she'd arranged the security. She's even less thrilled when the hunt for the thieves drags her on a treacherous foray across Europe as she goes head to head with organized crime. And as if this isn't enough, a routine industrial case starts leaving a trail of bodies across the North West, leaving Kate with more problems than she can deal with.

Cleaning up the mess in *Clean Break* forces Kate to confront harsh truths in her own life as she battles with a testing array of villains in a case that stretches love and loyalty to the limits.

'Tough, funny and intensely topical, McDermid stands out as one of the few contemporary writers actually nourished by the here and now' *Literary Review*

ISBN 0 00 649772 1

Blue Genes

Val McDermid

Kate Brannigan's not just having a bad day. She's having a bad week. Her boyfriend's death notice is in the paper, a neo-punk band want her to find the saboteurs who are trashing their flyposters, *and* Kate's business partner wants her to buy him out. Fine, except private eyes with principles never have that kind of cash.

Kate can't even cry on her best friend's shoulder, for Alexis has worries of her own. Her girlfriend Chris is pregnant, and when the doctor responsible for the illegal fertility treatment is murdered, Alexis needs Kate like she's never done before.

So what's a girl to do? Delving into the alien world of medical experimentation and the underbelly of the rock-music business, Kate confronts betrayal and cold-blooded greed as she fights to save not only her livelihood but her life as well . . .

'This is crime writing of the very highest order' *The Times*

ISBN 0 00 649831 0

Star Struck

Val McDermid

Bodyguarding had never made it to Manchester PI Kate Brannigan's wish list. But somebody's got to pay the bills at Brannigan & Co, and if the only earner on offer is playing nursemaid to a paranoid soap star, the fast-talking, computer-loving white-collar-crime expert has to swallow her pride and slip into something more glam than her Thai-boxing kit.

Soon, however, offstage dramas overshadow the fictional storylines, culminating in the unscripted murder of the self-styled 'Seer to the Stars', and Kate finds herself with more questions than answers. What's more, her tame hacker has found virtual love, her process server keeps getting arrested, and the ever-reliable Dennis has had the temerity to get himself charged with murder.

Nobody told her there'd be days like these . . .

'*Star Struck* is Val McDermid at the top of the ratings'

IAN RANKIN

ISBN 0 00 649832 9